# BEACHCOMBING IN THE BAHAMAS

## JENNIFER SKULLY

Redwood
Valley
Publishing

# GET A FREE STORY!

Join our newsletter and receive **Somebody's Lover** for free!

You'll also receive for free both Jasmine's **Beauty or the Bitch** and Jennifer's **Twisted by Love**!

Plus you'll get the scoop about new releases and sales, exclusive excerpts, as well as subscriber-only contests. Sign up at **http://bit.ly/SkullyNews**

# BEACHCOMBING IN THE BAHAMAS

## A ONCE AGAIN NOVEL

## Book 11

Turquoise waters, sultry nights, and holiday romance await in a Caribbean island paradise...

When Yvette Donnelly lost her husband, she was grateful to his elder brother Brock for being there for her and her two children. She never meant to fall in love with him...

Brock Donnelly, the family's eldest son and CEO of their thriving shipping empire, must stand against the force of his own tempestuous emotions. Divorced and a doting father of three college-age children, he never anticipated the storm his heart would unleash when he gave in to his attraction for his stunning sister-in-law, Yvette.

Their desire is a forbidden fire, burning hot and unquenchable. And while Brock yearns to declare his love to the world and make Yvette his forever, the consequences of revealing their secret affair will bring chaos to the family dynasty.

As the Christmas season beckons, a family vacation on the sun-soaked shores of the Bahamas seems like the perfect way to end the year. And Yvette and Brock's craving for each other has never been stronger.

Can the star-crossed lovers summon the courage to defy the family's expectations and celebrate their love? Or will the revelation crush their hopes of happiness forever?

Dip your toes in warm aquamarine water in this later in life, second chance, Christmas romance.

# ACKNOWLEDGMENTS

A special thanks to Bella Andre for this fabulous idea and to both Bella and Nancy Warren for all the brainstorming on our 10-mile walks. Thank you also to my special network of friends who support and encourage me: Laurel Jacobson, Kathy Coatney, Shelley Adina, Jenny Andersen, Jackie Yau, and Linda McGinnis. As always, a huge hug of appreciation for my husband, who helps my writing career flourish. And to Wriggles, that funny little cat. She's out in the atrium crying to come in. But when I open the door, she just sits there looking at me with pleading eyes that say, "Please come out to play with me!" How can I resist? Even if I'm supposed to be writing.

"I want her out of the gatehouse now." Brock's mother tapped her fingers on the big oak desk.

It had once been his father's desk, and this darkly paneled room had been his study.

But Harris Donnelly had been gone over fifteen years. And Brock's mother Adeline had taken over. Not the shipping business—that was Brock's—but everything else at the manor house was her domain. Including the gatehouse at the bottom of the quarter-mile drive.

Nestled in the Fremont Hills on the east side of San Francisco's Bay Bridge, the family estate was like a kingdom unto itself. And Adeline Donnelly reigned as its queen.

Seated on the other side of the desk as if he were a minion, Brock said, "I'm not kicking Yvette out of her home," with as many clipped words as his mother had used.

Adeline didn't like saying Yvette's name. And now she winced at his use of it. Weak November sunshine leaked through the sheers over the latticed windows, turning her skin sallow, and her pursed lips melted her too-red lipstick into the tiny lines around her mouth. At eighty years old, she prided herself on being an elegant older woman, with snowy hair she had permed regularly and styled every day. She probably didn't know about the lipstick or she'd have stopped making that expression years ago.

"Your brother and his wife are about to have a child," she declared, as if Brock didn't know. "They need the space." Narrowing her eyes at him accentuated Adeline's crow's feet, something else she probably didn't know, because his mother would never practice those looks in front of a mirror. "Since her children are now in college, Yvette doesn't need that big house anymore. And your brother does."

Brock resisted the urge to drum his fingers on the armrest. They'd had this argument the first time last year, when his youngest niece had finally gone off to university, turning Yvette into an empty nester. "The gatehouse has been Yvette's home—and the girls' home," he said, "since she married Pierce." Over twenty years ago. Though to be correct, his brother hadn't moved the family down to the gatehouse until Yvette's oldest daughter was almost five.

"Your brother has been dead for five years," Adeline snapped.

He found it hard to believe that his mother could say the word so easily. Pierce had been the golden boy, five years younger than Brock, and only forty-eight when he crashed his car into a tree a hundred yards from the manor house driveway. The autopsy had found his blood alcohol level way over the limit. Adeline had fought vehemently against that autopsy, but she'd lost the battle, one of the very few she ever had, mainly because Pierce had clipped another car ten miles away and sent it off the road. Thank God the driver and his wife had suffered only minor injuries. Brock wouldn't call it an accident, because an accident implied no one was at fault.

Pierce was an alcoholic, something Adeline had never wanted to admit. He'd been driving drunk, as usual, on his

2

way back from the casino. That was another of Pierce's addictions, gambling, and another thing Adeline didn't want to admit.

Unless she was blaming Yvette for what happened to him. According to Adeline, he only drank and gambled because he wanted to get away from his harridan of a wife.

Yvette was the furthest thing from a harridan. In fact, she'd stood by Pierce their entire marriage. But Adeline blamed her, because she'd gotten pregnant and Pierce had to marry her. Although Brock didn't think there was any "had to" about it. Pierce had wanted out of his engagement to an actual harridan, the one Adeline had chosen for him because the woman came from good stock. Whereas Yvette was nothing more than a gold-digging secretary, a chauffeur's granddaughter. That had been his mother's refrain ever since.

Adeline's first words upon hearing of their elopement were, "How can a thirty-year-old woman allow herself to get pregnant unless she's trying to trap a Donnelly?" And she'd never wavered from that notion in the past twenty years.

"Just get her an apartment in the city," Adeline insisted. "She can even walk to work from there."

Yvette was now Brock's executive assistant. And she did an amazing job keeping his work life in order. She knew all his appointments, got him to wherever he needed to be on time and equipped with everything he required.

"Tell her we'll pay for the apartment, even at the exorbitant cost of San Francisco real estate."

That was Adeline. Out of sight, out of mind, exactly where she wanted Yvette.

He said mildly, in contrast to Adeline's irritated tone, "She wants to stay in the gatehouse until both the girls have graduated from university and have their own apartments. It's important to her they can come back to their own home on holidays, school breaks, and summer vacation." He tried guiding the conversation back to an even keel. "Just like they're home now for Thanksgiving."

But his mother said, "They can each have a suite here in the big house when they're home. They'd love that."

Yvette wouldn't. And for reasons of his own, Brock wouldn't either.

His great-great-grandfather, shipbuilding magnate Liam Donnelly, had built the mansion in the Fremont Hills right after the 1906 earthquake. Although there was damage all over the Bay Area, he'd felt the East Bay would be safer. The gatehouse had four bedrooms and had been used by an actual gatekeeper before the automatic gates went in.

Liam Donnelly had laid out sod on the scrubby earth, planted trees and flowering shrubs, hydrangeas and rhodo- dendrons and azaleas. Which were now massive after more than a hundred years of growth. The mansion had eighteen suites, because the Donnelly patriarch had loved to entertain and wanted to provide for any guests who stayed overnight. In later years, he'd rivaled Randolph Hearst, inviting movie stars, and even the kings and queens of small principalities, to his home.

And Liam Donnelly had built this study. The thick carpets had been shipped from some far-off country, the lamps special-ordered from Tiffany's, and the furniture hand- crafted by the best manufacturers in England and New York. The massive fireplace could turn the room into an oven on winter days, the perfect spot for a young boy to curl up on a window seat and read the latest adventure book. Built-in bookcases housed first editions from the likes of F. Scott Fitzgerald, Ernest Hemingway, and John Steinbeck, the books purchased and signed even before the authors had made names for themselves. Liam Donnelly had prided himself on picking the next Dickens or Poe.

Though a family-held corporation, Donnelly Shipping still

had a board of directors and shares owned by far-flung family members. Brock held the largest share block, and being this generation's eldest son, he was in charge. The board had never overruled him. Trevor, his younger brother, was Chief Financial Officer, and his salary matched Brock's. Donnelly Shipping had been in business for two hundred years. In the early days, their primary market had been shipbuilding, but when Brock took over after his father's death fifteen years ago, he'd expanded into cruising and cargo shipping. The cruise subsidiary had taken a huge hit during the pandemic, when everyone stayed home, and it had taken over two years to recover. But there'd been enough cash in the company to float them. Shipbuilding had taken a hit, too, but nowhere near what happened to the cruise industry. But Donnelly Shipping had recovered well, and was now even bigger than before.

His mother was looking at him, her eyes gleaming with plans. "That's a perfect solution. The two girls can each take a suite in the big house when they're home from school. It'll be good for them. They won't want to stay in the city in a cramped flat with their mother. They'll be much better off here."

Right, exactly what Yvette feared, Adeline having the girls under her thumb where she could fill their heads with all their mother's misdeeds according to Adeline.

"You can stop all the scheming," he said sternly. "The gatehouse is Yvette's home, and she can stay as long as she likes."

Adeline flashed him a dark look. "But it wasn't Pierce's home. They only moved down there because of her." The tone in which she said *her* could have flayed flesh from bone. "His place was up here at the big house."

"Pierce liked the gatehouse too." Where he wasn't under their mother's thumb. But Adeline would never see that.

5

"That's what he told you," she said snidely. "But moving down there was when all the trouble began."

The trouble had existed for as long as Brock could remember. Pierce always drank too much, always gambled away his allowance. He'd had a job at the company, one where he could do little harm. Their father had chosen it for him, and he'd hand-picked Yvette as Pierce's assistant. If anything, Yvette had kept Pierce more on the straight and narrow than he would otherwise have been. But Adeline was right, things had deteriorated with Pierce after the girls were born. Brock had bailed him out of his gambling debts more than once.

But Adeline had rewritten history, turning Pierce into the golden boy with just a few minor problems. She raised an imperious eyebrow. "The big house seemed just fine for you and your wife and the boys."

"That's because Corrine was different. And we had our own suite of rooms with a separate entrance. It was like having our own apartment. We *were* separate."

She sniffed. "If that were true, then why did Corrine always want to come down for dinner with me and the rest of the family?"

His wife had treated the house as if she were its lady of the manor. And his mother had let her. Maybe it was because she liked Yvette far less. And she liked Corrine far more. Corrine had the proper breeding.

His three sons had all left the house now. Garth, his oldest at twenty-four, was employed by the company and lived in his own apartment in the city. Malcolm, the youngest, was a college freshman, and Ethan would graduate from UC Berkeley in June, when, if he chose, he'd also take his place at the company. Not that Brock wanted to force any of his sons into a slot they didn't fit. They were free to make their own choices.

As kids, they'd loved racing through the house or playing

hide and seek in all its nooks and crannies. In a house this size, there were many.

Living here had never been a problem for his family. The problem had been between him and Corrine. Maybe he'd never loved her. He was no longer sure. How did you remember what you'd felt in your twenties? He'd wanted her, that was true. But over the years, he'd realized she was too much like his mother, all about appearances. And maybe that was why the two of them had gotten on so well.

At fifty-eight years old, he'd now been divorced three years. Right after Ethan went to university and Malcolm had his school sports and was rarely home, Brock and Corrine found they had nothing tying them together except this big mausoleum of a house. Corrine brought up divorce first, but he'd quickly gotten on board.

His mother had fought the divorce as vehemently as she'd fought against Pierce's autopsy results. But Adeline hadn't won that battle either, both he and Corrine wanting the divorce, each for their own reasons.

So his wife was gone. Their sons were gone, too, coming home only for holidays and breaks.

"If you think your sons and grandchildren belong in the big house," he asked, "why do you want to send Trevor down to the gatehouse so badly?"

She paused a moment, obviously not expecting the question. His mother didn't like to be questioned, but she always had an answer. "Because he and Lorna deserve a space of their own."

"Then why don't we get *them* an apartment in the city?" he countered.

Both her eyebrows went up this time. "Don't be ridiculous," she snapped. "That wasn't what I was saying at all."

What she meant was that she wanted Yvette out in any

way she could throw her out. And if she had to use her youngest son to do it, she would.

"They have a baby coming," she said imperiously. "And I can't abide hearing a baby cry all over again. It's been years since I've had to endure that."

It was another of her excuses. She would love taking over or constantly telling Lorna what she was doing wrong with the baby. Just as she had with Yvette. Between his mother and his wife, they'd made Yvette's life miserable.

Wanting all the attention, Corrine had hated that Yvette stole the spotlight from her second pregnancy. After all, Yvette was carrying Pierce's child. And Pierce was the golden boy, even if his wife wasn't his perfect match.

Brock hadn't truly seen what was happening all those years ago, at least not then. Corrine was always moody when she was pregnant, and he'd tried to be understanding. Although really what it meant was that his office hours grew longer.

In the end, Pierce's family had moved into the gatehouse.

The memories churned in Brock's gut. He hadn't stood up for Yvette. He hadn't been able to help his brother overcome his addictions. And now he was harsher with his mother than he meant to be. "This discussion is over. Yvette stays where she is until she chooses to leave. Her daughters can come home from university to stay in their childhood bedrooms for as long as they wish. And that's final."

He stood then, towering over his mother behind the desk. Of course, that never cowed her. Nothing ever had. He forced his voice to a milder tone. "They'll all be waiting for us downstairs." The aroma of roasting Thanksgiving turkey wafted through the house. "We should go down now."

He turned on his heel, leaving his mother behind, her harrumph carrying out the door after him.

The massive dining room paneled in deep mahogany housed a long sideboard, a cabinet holding all the family porcelain and silver, and a dining table that could easily seat twenty-four. And it often had in the past. But for the family's Thanksgiving dinner, three of the leaves had been removed to accommodate the ten family members: Brock, his sons, his brother and wife, his mother. And Yvette and her girls.

The light of two crystal chandeliers shone down on them.

Yvette hated these holiday dinners. She came only for the girls' sake. She'd done her best never to color their emotions about the family with her own. They would have to make up their own minds about their grandmother.

But of course, around them, Adeline was on her best behavior.

The only good thing about the holiday was that the girls were home from San Luis Obispo, where they attended Cal Poly State University. They sat on either side of her, Kacey, twenty-one, and Jodi, nineteen. They both had the Donnelly dark hair and blue eyes like their father, and nothing much of her, other than her lithe figure. She was light where they were dark, even her eyes a paler shade of blue than theirs. She could only thank God that neither of them had their father's temperament. If they took after any Donnelly, it was Brock. Both studious, they made the honor roll every quarter. Smart as a whip, Harris, their grandfather, had often said. And they were beautiful, like all the Donnellys.

It was only because of them she'd remained part of the family. She could never have abided Adeline's viciousness toward her if not for them. To them, Adeline was just a sweet old lady, the grandmother they loved. She never showed them the other side of herself, the nitpicking, even nasty side Yvette had seen all too often.

Mrs. French, their robust cook with a head of silvery curls, pushed open the wood-paneled swing door to the kitchen. She signaled Brock, who was seated at the head of the table, the place his father had always taken until the day he died.

Rising, Brock said, "I believe our turkey is ready."

They'd started with butternut squash soup, and while the staff had already set out the side dishes on the sideboard, tradition dictated that the head of the family should carry in the turkey and do the carving.

Brock headed to the kitchen. He was a handsome man, like all the Donnelly men, like her husband Pierce had been, at least until his bad habits had gouged deep furrows along the sides of his mouth and across his forehead. But Brock, five years older than her age of fifty-three, was tall, toned, and distinguished, his dark hair shot through with silver. Age had only added to his handsome features.

Yvette didn't watch him disappear through the door, leaving it swinging behind him, as Brock's son Malcolm said, "Grandmother, have you ever thought of doing something different at Thanksgiving? Like baked ham? Turkey isn't one of my favorites."

Eighteen and several months younger than Jodi, he was the youngest of Adeline's grandchildren. A Donnelly through and through, just like his father Brock, he was well over six feet, dark hair, blue eyes, handsome face. Like all the Donnelly sons, he attended Berkeley. And like all the Donnelly sons, after university, he would work for Donnelly Shipping. None of them had broken tradition. Yvette didn't think any of them ever would.

Adeline didn't snap at him the way she would have snapped at Yvette. "My dear boy, turkey is tradition on Thanksgiving in this family. Turkey and stuffing on Thanksgiving." She smiled. "Roast beef and Yorkshire pudding at Christmas."

Tradition also had the entire family gathering for holiday meals. Though Brock had been divorced for three years, and his ex-wife Corrine remarried, the boys still attended holiday dinners with the family, going to their mother's the day after, no matter what holiday it was. That was Adeline's power.

Mrs. French once again pushed through the swing door, holding it open as Brock carried in the turkey on its silver platter. He walked the length of the dining table, the scent of perfectly roasted bird following him. Yvette's mouth watered. Unlike Malcolm, she wasn't tired of turkey since she ate it only once a year.

Easing the turkey down on his place setting, Brock pushed his chair back, giving himself room to carve. Mrs. French followed with the carving knife, a large fork, and another silver platter for the meat. But before he set to the task, he looked at his brother Trevor. "Why don't you do the honors this year?" He held out the utensils.

Trevor, thirteen years younger than his brother, looked at Adeline as if he needed her permission. Yvette expected her to say it wasn't tradition. Harris, the patriarch and her husband, had always carved the turkey. He'd never offered the honor to any of his sons. But then, more likely, it was Adeline who hadn't offered it.

Seemingly in a rare mood, Adeline gave a slight nod. And Trevor rose from his seat next to Lorna. His wife put her hand on her belly, almost protectively. A pretty, smiling brunette, she was almost seven months along, the baby due around the beginning of March.

The family sat silent as Trevor took the knife and fork, and Brock stepped aside.

When Yvette was young, holiday dinners, any dinners in fact, were filled with laughter and chatter. Her father had died before she could even form memories of him, and she and her mother had lived with her grandparents. They lacked for money but not love. Whereas the Donnellys had more than enough money, but lacked the laughter, and yes, much of the love too. Though she didn't doubt that Trevor adored his wife or that Brock loved his boys.

With the bird carved and the stuffing spooned out, Adeline clapped her hands. "Good job, Trevor," she said, as if the man was barely out of prep school instead of the CFO of Donnelly Shipping.

Mrs. French, who'd been standing in the corner, whisked the platter of turkey and stuffing over to the sideboard, while one of her staff returned the carcass to the kitchen.

Brock, still standing, flourished a hand toward the row of chafing dishes. "Don't let the turkey get cold."

As Adeline started to rise, Garth, who'd been sitting next to her, jumped up to help her out of her chair. Not that Adeline Donnelly, even at eighty years old, was frail. Despite her arthritis, which seemed to affect only her fingers, she stood tall, and Yvette was sure she hadn't lost more than a quarter inch of her five feet six inches. Though Yvette was still taller by an inch—three inches when she wore high heels as she did now. That Adeline was shorter had never stopped her from lording it over Yvette.

But as the woman headed to the sideboard, Yvette noticed for the first time how she put a hand to each chair-back as she walked, as if she needed that small bit of help to keep her balance. Maybe the arthritis was moving to her knees. Not that Adeline would ever admit it.

Trevor guided Lorna to her feet, who was pregnant enough to feel awkward. Yvette remembered the changes in her body as each of her babies had grown inside her. It was a beautiful time, even more special when your husband doted on you the way Trevor doted on Lorna. Yvette joined the line behind them, then Kacey and Jodi, and finally Brock's boys. Brock went last.

Mrs. French had prepared all the traditional Thanksgiving fare, candied yams, mashed potatoes, an assortment of roasted vegetables from beans to carrots to broccoli and cauliflower, along with homemade gravy for the turkey and potatoes, and a creamy cheese sauce for the vegetables.

Adeline didn't wait to eat until Brock was once again seated. She didn't like her food to go cold. Yvette's former mother-in-law—goodness how she loved that word, *former*—was a dainty eater, setting her knife and fork down every third bite.

In one of those breaks, she smiled, looked from Kacey to Jodi and said, "Now that you're both at university, it will be perfect if you each had a suite up here in the big house. There's no need for you to stay in the gatehouse anymore." She made it sound as if Yvette's home at the bottom of the long drive, the girls' home where they'd lived since they were toddlers, was no longer appropriate for two college-age Donnelly women.

Yvette's heart pumped faster, and heat rushed to her

cheeks. Trust Adeline to bring this up in front of everyone at the holiday dinner.

With a sickly sweet smile on her lips, Adeline added, "Then your mother can feel free to find a lovely apartment anywhere she wants." As if a lovely apartment was a bone she threw for Yvette to chew on. "And Trevor and Lorna can take over the gatehouse where they can have privacy to start their new family." She beamed a smile at Lorna.

Yvette wanted to smack it right off her face.

When the girls were young, Adeline had fought like a mother bear to keep Pierce installed in the big house. Yvette had wanted her own home. She'd wanted to get away from Adeline.

Life in the big house had been tolerable, though barely, when Harris was alive. But after he was gone, Adeline no longer felt the necessity to curb herself. Even Corrine, Brock's wife, had gotten in on the act. She'd been the perfect daughter-in-law who'd loved raising her three boys in the big manor house. She'd adored their massive suite of rooms, like they were all one big happy family. And, since the suite had its own entrance, Adeline couldn't see Corrine's comings and goings. Especially when the boys were in their teens.

Finally, Yvette had compromised by moving into the gatehouse. Though Adeline—and this still made Yvette want to either laugh or scream—had suggested that Pierce could stay in the big house and visit the girls and Yvette whenever he liked.

How sweet of her.

Yet now, Adeline was eager to send Trevor and Lorna down there.

Of course, the real reason was so she could finally rid herself of Yvette.

While Yvette truly wanted to keep the home for her daughters to have their old rooms to come to on holidays and breaks, she had to admit she also didn't want Adeline to win. She would go when she chose. Not when Adeline wanted to throw her out. When the girls had graduated and gotten jobs, whether or not they chose to work at the family company, then she would leave.

And Adeline could stick it where the sun didn't shine until then.

The thought brought a smile to her lips.

Until Adeline wiped it off with her next declaration. "Brock has even offered to subsidize an apartment in the city for your mother. What do you think of that, girls?"

Yvette flashed Brock a glare. That traitor. How could he?

Adeline turned her phony smile on Yvette. "And you'd be so much closer to work, dear. Wouldn't that be nice?"

Where once Yvette had been Pierce's administrative aide, she'd gone back to work after the girls were both in school, and she was now Brock's executive assistant. Every morning she, Brock, and Trevor were driven to work across the Bay Bridge in the family limousine.

Brock set down his knife and fork. "Adeline, you know I said no such thing. You made the suggestion. I never ratified it." Then he turned to the girls. "You and your mother are welcome to stay in the gatehouse as long as you'd like."

She could tell by the flare of his nostrils that he was angry with his mother. She knew very well that Adeline had been griping at him incessantly since the girls had started university. Probably even since Pierce had died.

But that made Yvette even more solid in her resolve, and she said, "What a lovely offer, Adeline." Her clipped tones meant exactly the opposite. "But as I've always said, the girls and I plan to stay until they've graduated."

Adeline pursed her lips, the only sign of her annoyance. She thought she'd get the better of Yvette by broaching the subject in front of the girls, but the moment Yvette had spoken, her daughters shut up. They knew their mother was adamant about staying, even if they didn't know her true reasons.

Before Adeline could say anything else, Trevor spoke up. "Lorna and I are perfectly fine staying in the big house. Since Brock gave us his suite, we've got more than enough room."

After he and Corrine divorced and the boys were out of the house, Brock had switched suites with Trevor and Lorna. Though he'd had his own entrance installed in the smaller suite he took over.

"Well, since Yvette has made up her mind," Adeline said with a snap in her words, "I suppose that's that." And she dusted off her hands.

Yvette knew that wasn't the end of it. Adeline wouldn't give up. She'd find another way.

Adeline clapped lightly. "There's plenty of seconds left. Let's not let all this food go to waste." She stood, carrying her plate to the sideboard.

As everyone else got up, Yvette debated. While she wasn't hungry anymore—after Adeline's attempted power play—it would at least give her something to concentrate on. And perhaps keep her out of Adeline's crosshairs, at least for the rest of the meal.

Everyone followed Adeline's edicts. Because that's what they all did. Yvette got in line after the kids, Brock taking up the last position as he had before.

With the brush of his hand against hers, a frisson of heat washed through her and her cheeks flushed.

She looked at him. He smiled. And an undeniable shiver ran through her.

As she picked through the seconds on her plate, she reflected on how her life was tied to this family. It wasn't just marrying Pierce. It wasn't bearing his children.

It started long before that. Her grandfather had once

worked as Harris's chauffeur. But even after he retired—or rather after Adeline put him out to pasture, Yvette was never sure which—Harris had come by to see him often, talking with Grandpa Remy as if he was the only man Harris felt he could be himself with.

Harris had grieved with her mother when Yvette's father died, and he'd helped with cash infusions. He'd even wanted to pay for her college education, but her mother had refused. Yvette hadn't gone to college. She'd began work in a department store right out of high school, intending to work her way into management. But her grandparents had both been sickly by then. She'd clocked out on time, often having to take days off to help Mother care for them, and her bosses claimed she didn't have the proper initiative. Then, soon after her grandparents passed, her mother was diagnosed with cancer. Yvette went to Harris, asking for a job, one with a better salary than the department store. When Harris offered to pay for a caregiver to come in while she was at work, Yvette gratefully accepted.

Harris put her to work as Pierce's administrative aide. He claimed Pierce was still sowing his wild oats, even though Pierce was twenty-seven at the time, a year younger than Yvette. "You'll be a good influence on him," Harris had told her.

And Yvette thought she had been. Pierce was charming— he charmed his mother, his father—but Yvette prided herself on resisting those charms, at least as long as she could.

Of course she had the inevitable fall. Just like everyone else, except Brock, who'd never found his brother's antics charming.

Still, back then, Yvette believed she'd been a good influence on Pierce. She'd wanted to believe he was a changed man, a better man. It was only after she'd married him, after she'd moved into this house, after Kacey was born, that she realized he'd never changed at all. He was still a drinker, a gambler, a skirt chaser.

And he always would be, until the day he died.

After clearing the plates away, Mrs. French and her staff carried in freshly baked pumpkin pies topped with hand-whipped cream. Brock tapped his spoon against his wineglass, the sound tinkling in the air. "I have an announcement."

Yvette's heart raced.

But then he said, "I've booked a trip for all of us to the Caribbean over Christmas."

Jodi clapped her hands, Kacey put a hand over her mouth, and Malcolm punched the air.

"We'll leave on the Sunday after Berkeley lets out for the break and come back a couple of days before Cal Poly starts the winter quarter." The two universities had different holiday schedules, and Brock had accommodated both. "That means we'll have almost two weeks over the winter break to bask in the sun. I've booked a private cove with several cottages on it. We won't all have to crowd into one house. The compound comes with a cook and a maid, so we don't have to do anything except enjoy ourselves. The island is fairly small, but that means there won't be a lot of tourists. There's nightlife in the town and plenty of activities, swimming, snorkeling, horseback riding, zip-lining."

When Kacey raised her hand, Brock answered before she could even ask the question. "And yes, you can each bring a friend." He winked at Kacey. "Or boyfriend." Then looked at his sons. "Or girlfriend."

While Kacey still maintained an immaculate grade point average, she'd recently fallen for a senior, and could talk of nothing else but the wonderful Darryl.

Adeline rapped her knuckles on the table. "But we will have a girls' dormitory and a boys' dormitory." She stretched her mouth in a smile or a grimace. "I'm still old-fashioned."

Yvette had a feeling there would be a lot of sneaking back and forth.

But she had to trust her daughter to take care of herself. She didn't want either of the girls to end up like her, knocked up by her boss and having to get married.

---

ADELINE

I pour myself a stiff whiskey.

  I always keep Harris's whiskey decanter primed. He loved it. And now I like a little tipple after dinner. And sometimes before bed. It helps me sleep.

  The study might look like his, but it hasn't been since Death took him. Then I made it mine. Without changing a thing, not the Persian carpets, not the dark wood paneling, not this massive desk that should dwarf me, but only makes me feel bigger. Because now I am head of this family. Even if Brock wants to think he is. I run the show.

  Except this time. Why isn't he falling in line the way he should?

  I turn to Harris's portrait over the fireplace. He was a handsome man. His dark hair had been so thick and silky when he was young. I loved running my fingers through it. I loved his powerful body. I loved the way he could make mine sing when he touched me.

  Until he no longer did.

  But that portrait of a younger Harris hangs in the living room downstairs. He'd posed for this one when he was older, his dark hair turning silver, his aquiline nose even more prominent.

But he'd still been in his prime.

My hand shakes, the whiskey in the glass sloshing over the top. "This is all your fault," I snarl at him. "You had to bring that girl into the company. You ruined everything."

He doesn't smile down from the portrait, though he'd smiled frequently when he was young. But his face is tougher here, his features less amiable. Life had hardened him. Doesn't it harden everyone? It has certainly hardened me. But then I had to be hard.

I detect a sneer on his lips. Had it been there before? Or am I imagining it now? Maybe because of that woman. Because Brock isn't doing what I want him to do. He should have gotten rid of her years ago. Right after Pierce died.

Harris sneers at me, I'm sure.

"You never forgave me for a firing Remy, did you? For sending him and his whole damn family packing. But he was just a chauffeur. The hired help. He was just..."

But Remy had been so much more than that. Because it all started with that rotten family. And getting rid of them changed nothing.

"But you're not claiming you're blameless for what happened, are you, Harris?" I sneer right back at him. "I loved you with all my heart. I gave you everything. Everything I did was for you. And you left me to clean up your mess."

And now, finally, I hear him laughing at me as he says, "You don't have a heart, Adeline. You never did."

My hands shake. My entire body shakes. And I throw my glass at the painting, whiskey dripping down his face as the glass shatters on the hearth.

## ❧ 4 ☙

The girls left Sunday morning, and the gatehouse felt empty again. Yvette had a great time while they were home, taking them to Golden Gate Park and then a show in the city. And now she missed them. San Francisco and San Luis Obispo weren't that far apart, only a three-hour drive. They could have stayed longer and headed back in the afternoon, but Kacey wanted to see Darryl.

So Yvette spent her Sunday puttering around the house, doing laundry, some cleaning, some reading. Loving domestic thrillers, especially the British ones, she'd just snapped up the latest Ruth Ware. Mrs. French had parted with some leftover turkey, and she'd made herself a sandwich. She didn't go up to the big house for dinner, hadn't done so in fifteen years. Except for those obligatory holiday celebrations.

It wasn't Trevor or Lorna, not even Brock. It was all Adeline.

But she didn't need to think about that woman, and in the evening, she ran herself a bath, pouring in lavender bath salts, the scent and the steam filling the bathroom. She'd kept the old-fashioned pink and gray tile, the painted wainscoting, and the massive clawfoot tub. With hardwood floors and flocked wallpaper that hadn't lost its flock, she'd always loved the house and never felt the need to remodel.

She lay in the hot, scented water, shaved her legs, rubbed sugar scrub all over, then read for a while. When the water grew lukewarm—after running hot into it several times—she finally climbed out, dried off, and smoothed her favorite lotion all over.

Another work week started tomorrow, and she crawled beneath the covers, naked. She always slept naked, which reduced the chances of a night sweat. Besides, she liked to feel the smooth sheets against her skin.

She dreamed of strong male hands caressing her, warm lips kissing her neck, and a hard body nestled against her back. She woke to pleasure rippling through her breasts, woke to the man who wasn't a dream, the man whose lips and kisses were the fantasy.

"Christ, you smell good." His breath whispered over her ear and sent a delicious shiver through her. "You taste even better."

His voice filled her up as he pulled her leg over his, spreading her for his touch. Then he found her center, and she moaned. Even as his body throbbed along her spine, he murmured sweet dirty nothings in her ear as he brought her over the edge.

She couldn't help the words spilling from her lips. "Oh God, Brock, please, I need you inside me. Don't stop. Please don't stop."

And he was already there, plunging deep inside her. But instead of taking her hard the way she needed him, he rocked slowly, caressing that spot inside her until she thought she'd go mad with need.

"I had to wait all week for this." He licked her earlobe. "I don't want to rush it."

"But you're making me crazy."

Brock Donnelly had been making her crazy for nine months. Maybe that was another reason she didn't want to leave the gatehouse. And oh how she loved the way he made her crazy. She trembled around him, squirmed against him, trying to take him deeper. He stroked her nipple, shooting sparks down to the spot where their bodies joined.

"Oh God oh God oh God," she chanted.

"I love how you feel around me," he murmured. "Your body milking me. I thought about you all weekend. I almost paid you a visit last night."

She knew she should tell him he could never come when the girls were here. But she couldn't get the words out. Besides, he already knew. He was just teasing her, with his words, with his touch, with his body.

Then he trailed a hand down her stomach and put his fingers between her legs. His touch on the outside, his stroke on the inside, he swore in her ear. With his warm breath washing over her, her body clamped down on him. Then he gave her what she needed, pounding her hard, deep, and so high he touched the very heart of her.

Dirty words, her name, everything spilled from his lips. She loved how she could bring it out of him. Brock Donnelly, CEO, a man with an iron will and steely control, she loved when he lost it all for her.

He pulsed inside her, his heat filling her up, and she fell again, this time falling into the bliss with him.

HE WOULD NEVER GET ENOUGH OF HER, THE SILKY BLOND hair he could wrap around his fist, her soulful blue eyes he could stare into, her hot, sexy body he could make love to for hours. She was warm against him and scented with her favorite fruity lotion. He could never smell a mango or a peach without thinking of her, but then he never stopped thinking about her anyway. But more than anything, he loved the scent of their sex surrounding them. Sometimes, when he couldn't be with her, he lay on his bed, closed his eyes, and remembered their blended scents.

Cradling her against him, he banded one arm beneath her breasts, burying his face in the thickness of her blond hair as he pressed her against him. "What my mother said about an apartment." He let the words rest a moment against her warm skin.

"You know I want the girls to come back here on their breaks," she said into the pause.

"I know. But even if you moved, they could always stay at your flat with you. We could get something with at least three bedrooms."

"We?" she whispered.

He murmured against her ear, "I can stay with you on weeknights. We can go to work together in the morning."

"The girls wouldn't want to stay in the city."

"You might be surprised if you asked them." But he knew she would say no anyway.

"I told you, not until they've both graduated." There was no heat in her voice, no anger. It was simply what she'd decided.

He knew it was partly to tweak his mother's nose. The more Adeline wanted her out of the house, the more Yvette was determined to stay. But she couldn't stay here forever. Something had to change.

"Then marry me," he whispered the words.

She went stiff in his arms. It was not a new discussion. And he knew her answer would be the same as always. "It'll never work, Brock. I've been Adeline's daughter-in-law one too many times. I'm not doing it again."

"It doesn't have to be like the last time."

"You should already know how a family can tear a love apart. Your mother tore up Pierce and I."

Brock wasn't so sure about that. He wasn't sure how much Pierce had loved Yvette, but he sure as hell knew it wasn't more than he'd loved his addictions. Yet he couldn't say any of that to Yvette. "I'm not like my brother. I won't let that happen."

She didn't even turn to look at him over her shoulder as she denied him what he wanted most. "I can't do it, Brock. I won't be your mother's daughter-in-law ever again. What we have right now is perfect. I don't need any more than this."

And he thought, *But I do.*

He stroked his thumb across her abdomen. "All right. Then let's just get a flat in the city and live together."

A harsh laugh shot out of her. "Oh my God, that's ten times worse. I'll never hear the end of it from her."

"She doesn't even come into the city. You'll never see her. You don't even have to come home for the holidays."

She rolled over then, put her hand to his cheek, the moonlight through the window lighting her pastel blue eyes. "Why can't we just keep on doing it this way? You sneak out of the house, walk down the hill under cover of darkness, and make love to me for hours."

"I love this." Yet his heart ached on the nights he wasn't with her. "But I want to go to bed with you at night and wake up with you in the morning. I want to take you to a show, wine you and dine you. I don't want to pretend anymore."

She smiled, seduction on her lips. "But isn't it sexy as hell?"

He knew she was deflecting. But he took her face in his hands. "I love you. I want to be your husband. I want to get a freaking dog together."

That made her laugh. "You don't have time for a dog."

"We do. I want a dog who comes to work with us and sleeps under your desk and everybody stops by to bring it a biscuit."

"We'd have to be married to do that," she said softly.

He wanted to shake her. She was deliberately misunderstanding him. And he changed tack. "What will you do when the girls graduate?"

She shrugged against him. "I don't know. Jodi won't graduate for almost three years. She's only a sophomore."

He thought of the next three years. He was nothing more than a secret to her. Three years would drive him nuts. He'd already waited too long.

He'd never allowed himself to think about her when she was married to Pierce. But then Pierce died. And things between him and Corrine had gone sour long before that. Then, after Ethan went to university, Corrine asked for a divorce, saying she wanted a man who was present in her bed. And she'd already found one. He didn't blame her, because he hadn't been present, not for a long time. Their marriage had ceased to be a marriage. And not because of Yvette.

But then he was free. And he could finally admit to the feelings he had about Yvette. Yet even after the divorce, even after Pierce's death, there were complications. Too many of them. While he'd been like a teenage boy wondering how to tell the prettiest girl in his class how he felt about her, he couldn't tell Yvette. Because he was CEO and she worked for him. Because she was his brother's widow. And perhaps most of all, because she was the daughter-in-law Adeline hated, and he knew Yvette was never going there again.

But then there'd been that night. The night neither of them could take back. The night he hadn't wanted to take back.

That had been nine months ago. And he'd been sneaking into her bed ever since.

He had no idea how to change Yvette's mind, but he couldn't bulldoze her. Even Adeline couldn't bulldoze her now, not the way she had when Yvette was young and a new mother. He could issue an ultimatum, tell her she had to marry him or they were done. But you never issued an ultimatum unless you were willing to lose. And he wasn't willing to risk her leaving him. He couldn't live without her. But he wasn't so sure she'd say the same about him.

Because of Adeline. Adeline, who'd driven that wedge into Pierce and Yvette's marriage. Adeline, who'd made Pierce the man he was. Adeline, who'd blamed his drinking, his gambling, and his adultery on Yvette, as if Pierce hadn't made his own choices. She'd even blamed the accident on Yvette, when Pierce had clearly been on his way home from carousing, drunk as a skunk, and wrapped his car around a tree only a mile from the gatehouse.

Brock was stuck between the proverbial rock and a hard place, the rock being his mother and, as soft as she was against him, Yvette being the hard place.

He didn't know how much longer they could go on this way.

Something had to break.

ON MONDAY MORNING, YVETTE SAT IN THE BACK SEAT OF the car facing her two bosses. She drove to work every weekday in the big car with Brock and Trevor. It was her job to go over the day's schedule with each of them. "You've both got the meeting at ten with the executive staff. Then there's all the prep for the presentation for Avanti Cruise Lines next week."

Although Donnelly Shipping had its own cruise line, their principal business was still shipbuilding, something they'd been doing for the last two hundred years. They built the biggest, fastest, safest, and most beautiful cruise liners sailing the oceans today. And Brock had no problem selling ships to his cruising competitors. Avanti Cruise Lines was looking to commission sister ships, something that would rival the Disney Wish in size and the Queen Mary in elegance. There would be massive profits if Avanti chose Donnelly Shipping.

"You've prepared all the slides?" Brock asked.

"They're done." Brock had given her manufacturing estimates, engineering schematics, marketing brochures, and Trevor's budgets, which she'd assembled into a neat package. "I've also typed up notes for you." Not that Brock needed notes. He carried everything in his head.

"I'll do the budget and cost projections for them," Trevor said. The numbers were his game as CFO. While Trevor was a handsome man with the Donnelly looks, Brock would always be a bit more, more handsome, more powerful, just *more*.

"Great," Brock said. He never tried to upstage his brother, though, since Brock was CEO, that meant Trevor worked for him. But they'd always worked well together.

Not like Pierce.

These days, she tried to think of Pierce as little as possible. When she was at the office, she concentrated on business. When the girls were home, she gave them all her attention. And when she made love to Brock, there was only the two of them.

She could close her eyes now and feel his touch on her skin, his taste on her tongue. But she didn't think about that. She didn't think about how handsome he was in his tailored suit, how perfectly toned his body was beneath the jacket, how beautiful and knowing his blue eyes were, how lush his hair felt when she ran her fingers through it. Or how his deep voice could send tingles racing through her body.

And she didn't think about last night's proposal. It hadn't

been the first proposal he'd made. It wasn't the first proposal she turned down.

As the two brothers discussed the strategy for the Avanti proposal, Yvette thought of Brock's mother. If Adeline knew about her affair with Brock, the woman would make her life miserable. Just as she had when Yvette was married to Pierce. If she married Brock, it would be the same thing all over again. She couldn't do it.

It wasn't a question of love. Because she loved Brock, and she felt no guilt about the fact that he was her dead husband's brother. He was a good man, a formidable man. And therefore, he thought he could protect her from Adeline. But someone as relentless as her former mother-in-law eventually wore down all the soft, beautiful edges of love and turned it into sharp angles that sliced you in two.

She wouldn't let that happen with Brock. She loved what they had. The illicit nature of it was sexy. That she couldn't have him all the time made her hunger for him grow that much greater.

And she did hunger for him, even now, as he sat across from her.

It hadn't started when she was married to Pierce. It hadn't started while he was married to Corrine. And the man Pierce had become wasn't his brother's fault. At times, she thought it was Adeline's fault. At other times, she thought Pierce had been born that way, lost from the very beginning.

But she'd never thought of Brock as anything more than a brother. Or her boss.

At least that was what she'd always told herself. It was what she believed.

But then Pierce was gone. And after that, Corrine gone. Then somehow, something had changed. She couldn't say exactly when or why or even how. But something was there that hadn't been there before. Or if it had been, she'd buried it so deep it hadn't even been real. She never would have done anything about it, would never even have admitted it. If it hadn't been for that night.

God. That night in Chicago.

They'd just closed a big deal Brock had worked on for two years. He'd been wired. They both were. Too wired to sleep even though was eleven o'clock at night.

"Let's walk along the waterfront for a bit," he'd said.

They'd strolled the lovely promenade. Though the evening was cool, she'd thought the walk would warm her up. Brock enumerated all the things they needed to do now they'd secured the project. As his executive assistant, she often went on trips with him. She arranged venues, set up the AV, arranged the dinners or lunches. She did whatever Brock needed. That was her job. And that night, he needed to walk.

He'd laughed. "Here we are supposed to be taking a relaxing walk, and I'm reeling off orders at you."

She smiled back. "That's fine, just as long as you don't expect me to remember it all tomorrow morning."

He looked down at her then, just as she shivered. "I'm an idiot. It's freezing out here."

She laughed that off. "Not exactly freezing."

But shrugging out of his jacket, he draped it over her shoulders. Holding the lapels together across her throat, his body already warming her, he stood like that for a long moment. A moment that stretched and changed. And heated. Had she looked into his eyes? Had her gaze dropped to his mouth? Had he read her thoughts and seen how badly she wanted his lips on hers?

Then he kissed her, a gentle kiss at first. The voice in her head, whispering what a bad idea this was, never made it past her throat. She parted her lips, letting him in, taking the kiss from gentle to all-consuming in little more than a breath. He didn't touch her, didn't wrap her up in his arms. And yet she lost herself in the scent of him, the taste of him, the heat of him.

When he set her back on her feet, his forehead against hers, his breath whispered across her lips, lips that still tasted of him. "Christ, you can't know how badly I've wanted to do that for so long."

Maybe if he hadn't spoken, she could have gone on in a daze, let him do anything he wanted and everything she wanted.

But she knew what was good for her. And this wasn't.

Soft but sure, she said, "We can't do this."

"Why not?" His voice held no harshness, but a flame burned in his eyes.

"I'm your brother's wife."

"You're my brother's widow."

"You're my boss."

"You're part of the family. Not my employee."

She didn't say the one thing that meant the most. She didn't say Adeline's name.

He would have found a reason for that not to matter either. So she stepped back, once, twice, and said, "We can't do this. We *aren't* doing this."

He didn't reach for her, yet she felt his touch on her. And she made her voice a force in the night. "We're going to forget that ever happened. And I'm going back to the hotel now."

Of course he wouldn't let her go alone. He wasn't the kind of man who could let a woman walk alone in a city they didn't know well. She heard his footsteps a few paces behind her, matching hers.

Back at the hotel, he stepped into the elevator with her, she on one side, he on the other. She felt his eyes drilling into her as she removed his jacket and handed it to him. They didn't have connecting rooms, but they were next to each other. And he followed her down the interior hallway, the carpet plush beneath her feet. Her door was first, and she used her keycard.

She was about to say good night, when he said, "I can't forget." She looked at him, her heart beating hard. Then he whispered, "I don't want to forget."

And when he reached for her, she was lost forever.

Now, nine months later, she'd never stop. She loved him. She wondered if she'd ever loved Pierce at all because it had never been the way she felt about Brock.

If only they weren't who they were. If only he wasn't Brock Donnelly running Donnelly Shipping. If only Adeline wasn't his mother. If only they could run away together.

As she sat across from him now, she knew Brock for the fighter he was. She knew he thought he could turn her around to his way of thinking.

But he was wrong.

## ❧  5  ❧

---

### ADELINE

I sit with Lorna in the conservatory a few days after Thanksgiving. "My dear girl, you should stick up for what you want. I'm sure you'd like to live in your own home by the time you have the baby. The gatehouse is perfect. You shouldn't let Trevor speak for you."

"I love the big house, Adeline. Especially now that Brock has given us his suite."

I pour the silly twit another cup of tea. She's such a vapid little thing, ten years younger than Trevor, with mousy brown hair and brown eyes like a sad puppy. And always smiling no matter what anyone says, as if she doesn't truly understand what's going on around her. I can't imagine why Trevor married the girl. Just like I couldn't imagine why Pierce had married that woman.

I let my thoughts take over as I add sugar and cream to the cup and slide the tea across to her. The girl likes it far too sweet, but then I'm trying to be sweet to her.

But oh, how the thoughts come. Why do the men in my family champion that woman at every turn? First, Harris just had to bring Yvette into the company. Then Pierce fell for her. Now Brock is suddenly standing up for her. And Trevor isn't even bothering to push her out when it's in his best interests to do so.

So I have to deal with this daughter-in-law, who is having a girl, for God's sake.

Doesn't she understand that I'm creating a dynasty? Both Yvette and Lorna are spoiling my plans by having girls. I want to be like the Habsburg Queen Maria Theresa, who'd had sixteen children and married them off to the kings and queens of Europe so she had dominion over all.

At least I have Brock's boys. Garth is working for the company, and I'm already steering him to the right girl, one who will be advantageous to the family and, more importantly, to the company.

I'll just have to make advantageous marriages for those two girls. If only I can get them to stay in the house the way I want. And get rid of their mother.

I look at Lorna, who sips her tea.

Good God, I'll be dead before I can do anything with Lorna's child. That's Trevor's fault for not marrying years ago.

"We can remodel the gatehouse in any way you like," I tell her. I'll hate to remodel the old house, but if I can displace Yvette, which is the most important thing, I'll be happy. "We can make it more of an open plan. We can tear down a wall between two bedrooms so you'll have a larger nursery for the baby." I smile. I don't like myself when I smile. For some reason, I can never make it appear genuine.

Lorna, thank God, appears to fall for it. "That's so kind of you, Adeline. But there's no need to go to that kind of expense. Trevor and I are happy up here at the big house." She smiles. It's a disgustingly sweet smile.

I want to slap it right off her face. But then I'm being friendly today.

Because I have only one goal and that's to get rid of that

woman, who's been the bane of my existence since Harris took a liking to her. Actually, since he'd taken a liking to that damned chauffeur and worse, his family.

Even firing the man didn't stop Harris from running down to their house as if he preferred it to his own.

But it was Yvette's fault that Pierce was dead. She drove him to all the drinking and gambling. Before she came on the scene, he'd been sewing a few wild oats, yes, but nothing more. He'd have gotten over it. But then she trapped him into marriage by getting pregnant.

I'd had such a wonderful future mapped out for him, with a woman worthy of the family. But Yvette ruined everything. That's why he took to the drink, because of her.

And I hate the woman for it.

I'm not ashamed of saying that Pierce was always my favorite. Every mother has a favorite. They just won't admit it.

And she was responsible for his death. She'd wanted to send him to rehab, for God's sake. No Donnelly has ever gone to rehab, because they've never been the problem. It's always the people who surround them. I gave Pierce everything he wanted, everything he needed. And what was a little carousing? That's what young men did back then. But now it's a sin, for God's sake, when really it was just boys being boys. And there was more than enough money to bail him out of any scrape he got himself into. I always took care of everything for him.

But there'd been no way to buy off that girl. And that was Harris's doing. He was the one who insisted Pierce break off his engagement and marry Yvette. What on earth had Harris been thinking?

That woman, she had all the men in this family fooled.

And here I am now, saddled with another of her ilk. This

one is greedy, too, I know full well. She wants to make sure that Trevor becomes the favorite.

"Honestly, Adeline, please don't put yourself out. Trevor and I would love to raise our children here. Look at the garden." Lorna sweeps her arm out, encompassing the massive floor-to-ceiling windows of the conservatory. The lush gardens are manicured to perfection, the azaleas and camellias and rhododendrons all deadheaded after their season. The new buds are already forming and will be magnificent in the spring.

Did this girl think her baby would be allowed to run around my yard? The child will ruin it. Just as Brock's boys had ruined it.

I didn't mind, though. After all, they were boys. And boys will be boys.

But the silly twit won't budge.

As Lorna leans forward for a biscuit, I say, ever so sweetly, "Should you have another cookie, dear?" I smile. It feels as if it could be a genuine smile. But then it takes the beholder to judge. When Lorna stills her hand, I go on. "You don't want to gain even *more* weight." I give that heavy emphasis. "Baby weight is so hard to get rid of. And you need to maintain your figure to keep your husband's interest."

Poor Lorna looks stricken. I was always scrupulous about losing my baby weight. After three strapping boys, it would have been hard if I'd allowed myself to gain as much as Lorna has. Although admittedly, she's probably on target for her pregnancy month. "I have a regimen of isometric exercises that I can give you. They worked wonders for me."

"Yes, yes," Lorna stammers, her face crestfallen the way I intended.

If I can't get Lorna to agree to push Yvette out, I'll just have to make her life so miserable that she'll beg Trevor to move down to the gatehouse.

I won't mind at all if Trevor goes. Brock can take over his suite again. And he'll never leave. Besides, Trevor was always my least favorite. Every mother plays favorites, if she's honest enough to admit it. And I am scrupulously honest. At least with myself. I'm honest enough to say that Trevor has the worst taste in spouses. And sadly, so did Pierce.

Corrine was the only one who was worth anything at all. She'd known the score. She'd known what was best for her. And she had the boys. I've always suspected she somehow assured that every one of her babies carried to full-term was a boy. Yes, Corrine was a woman after my own heart. Until she made the colossal error of falling for another man. What on earth was wrong with her? I suspect she was perimenopausal at the time and needed to affirm her beauty through a male's eyes. But to divorce Brock? What had the woman been thinking?

No, my sons are a lost cause. But my grandsons, they'll be different. With the proper training, of course.

I will have my dynasty before I shuffle off this mortal coil, as Shakespeare would say.

## 6

The family was safely aboard the charter plane, and they were three hours into the approximately seven-hour flight to the Caribbean. While Yvette's girls had been home for a week, the UC Berkeley final exams ended on Friday, and Brock chose the Sunday before Christmas for their departure. Since their destination was a relatively small island, it had no commercial airfield—and thus fewer tourists—they'd have to land on one of the bigger islands. He'd booked a helicopter to take them to their destination.

Brock usually traveled business class so he could work and still be fresh when he arrived, but for this trip, his mother had refused to fly anything less than the highest class. With the number of them, thirteen between family and friends, chartering was about the same as paying for first class.

He'd never bought a company plane. It was a waste of money, in his opinion. And even aside from the purchase price, the cost to keep it was prohibitive. But he'd never needed to charter a plane before. This was the first family vacation they'd all taken together.

He just prayed it would be good.

He'd invited all the girlfriends and boyfriends for the kids. Malcolm, his youngest, brought along Iris, a sweet girl with long blond hair that reminded him of Yvette the first time he'd seen her. Yvette wore hers shoulder length now, and he loved to curl the locks around his fingers when they made love. Ethan had invited Francine, a girl he met his first year at Berkeley, and they'd been together for three years. Brock liked Francine well enough. With her dark hair and green eyes, she was a perfect match for Ethan, the green a pleasant contrast to his blue eyes. Garth had come alone. He'd broken up with his girlfriend after graduation when he came to work for the company and she was accepted to Harvard Law School. Garth had claimed long-distance relationships never worked.

Brock wondered about secret relationships, whether the secrecy would eventually kill the passion. Or heighten it.

Jodi had no boyfriend, but Kacey brought Darryl. Brock didn't like the kid. There was something off about him, though Brock couldn't put his finger on exactly what that was. Maybe it was the way he'd walked through the big house, picking up Adeline's objet d'art as if he were cataloguing and pricing them. Maybe it was the way Darryl acted around Francine, Iris, and Jodi, as if he'd love to feast on each of them. Or all three at once.

But you could never tell a young woman that her boyfriend was bad news. That would only make her cling all the harder. Not that he had daughters of his own. But he'd been around Kacey and Jodi long enough to know how it would go. So kept his mouth shut. He never even talked with Yvette about it. Because what could either of them do?

His mother was napping in the front row, and Brock moved down the aisle to risk sitting next to Yvette. Though he was sure no one would care, he planned to keep the conversation light, even as he steeped himself in her scent and the heat of her body next to him.

"I wanted to let you know about the lodging arrangements."

He and Yvette had already discussed it, but it was an excuse to be close. "We'll put Adeline in the largest house, along with Trevor and Lorna. That's where we'll all meet up for meals. The cook and maid stay there, and the dining room is big enough to handle all of us. That would be the best place for her."

"What about the kids?" Yvette asked, playing along perfectly.

"There are two houses in the middle, with several bedrooms each. The boys can sleep in one and the girls in the other. Per my mother's instructions."

She took a chance and leaned close, saying, "You think they'll stay there?"

He laughed, looking at Ethan and Malcolm, who'd turned in his direction as if they knew he was discussing the sleeping arrangements. "They're adults. There's nothing we can do to stop them." Then he added, "There are two cottages at the end. Since we're both alone, I thought those would work out for each of us. Does that sound okay to you? Even though they're only studio size? You won't have anywhere to cook other than a coffee maker and a small refrigerator."

With a sweet yet sexy smile, she said, "That'll be perfect for me. As long as I have a bathtub."

"Definitely. Your own bathroom with a big tub."

Without words, only a smile and a look, they transmitted how easy it would be to sneak back and forth between the two cottages, no one being the wiser. Oh yeah, it would be perfect. He could stay with her until the dawn since the kids would never be up that early.

With a glance at his sons, he said, "I'm sure the kids will

want to go into town for some nightclubbing. Anything special you'd like to do?"

She shrugged. "Just relaxing, taking long walks on the beach, and naps in the afternoon."

That was another secret message between them. An afternoon nap, when he could join her. Then she asked, "What activities have you investigated?"

She knew very well, because she was the one who'd looked everything up. But it was an excuse for a few more minutes together. "Since it's a small island, and they want to attract more tourism, they've got a ton of things to do. There's a zip line and horseback riding in the ocean." He raised his voice so the family could hear. "We can rent a catamaran for some snorkeling."

She eyed him. "And you know how to pilot the catamaran?"

He shook his head, smiling. "I don't."

With a soft laugh, she added, "You're in shipping, but you don't know how to sail a catamaran?"

Sailing had never been one of his dreams, and he'd been too busy to learn anyway. Not like Ethan, who'd taken sailing lessons and loved it. "You know what I know how to do even better?" He waited for her to shake her head. "I know how to pay somebody to pilot it for us, and who also knows all the best snorkeling spots around the island."

She clapped her hands lightly, thankfully not waking up his mother at the front of the plane.

"There are some bat caves we can wander through," he told her. She hadn't pointed that out, but he'd noticed.

She shuddered. "Bats?"

"They won't bother you. And nearby, there's a series of waterfalls that we can all slide down." Then he shrugged, just like she had. "We can do everything on separate days."

She pursed her lips, then said, "I like the idea of the waterfalls, but I'm not sure about the bats."

He wanted to take her hand, raise it to his lips and kiss her knuckles. What a shock that would give his family. Of course he didn't. She'd probably scream in horror. "We can also rent some ATVs," he added.

Darryl, Ethan, and Malcolm punched their fists in the air. "We vote for that one."

Brock nodded his agreement, then turned back to his lover. "So besides long walks on the beach and long naps in the afternoon, and maybe some waterfalls and snorkeling, what would you like to do?" He almost waggled his eyebrows. Since he'd turned slightly toward her, no one would see.

She bit her bottom lip, something she did when she wanted him. Or when she was close to her climax and didn't want to cry out.

But while they were here, he'd make her scream.

"I'd like the horseback riding in the ocean. And of course, the waterfalls. And the ATV. Everything but the bats." Then she laughed, the sweet sound drilling right down into him and breaking something loose inside him.

He laughed to hide the emotion. "You want to do it all."

She smiled, her light blue eyes suddenly as bright as the sky. "Oh yeah. I want to do it all."

And he would do everything to her, all the sweet and naughty things he dreamed about when he wasn't inside her.

their luggage. They still had another half hour to the compound.

Trevor drove Adeline in a comfortable Town Car, along

43

with Lorna, who didn't want to bounce around in the Jeep, since she was pregnant. Brock had rented three Jeeps to get around the island while they were here. He drove one, Garth and Ethan the other two. Darryl had tried to take the wheel, but Brock was having none of that.

Taking off in a convoy, Trevor driving in the lead, a van followed with all their luggage. Finally, their compound came into sight.

Ancient trees grew like a canopy over the circular gravel drive, lined with shrubs in bloom—azaleas, hydrangeas, rhododendrons. Flowering vines clung to the buildings, and an overhang shaded the massive front porch of the big house. Wide rattan chairs invited them for a cool afternoon drink, and a porch swing hung by the front window. Overhanging trees would reduce the burn of the tropical sun on the roofs.

Seated by Brock in the front seat of the Jeep, Yvette murmured, "This is beautiful." She looked at him, smiled. "You chose well."

He reached out, probably to squeeze her hand, but aware of the girls in the back seat, he only said, "We found this together."

They'd looked through what seemed like a hundred rentals to find it. But this was beyond her expectations.

Climbing out of the Jeep, she let the warm air caress her skin. She'd checked her phone when they arrived; eighty degrees, a perfect temperature, not too hot and not too humid.

Their group followed Adeline into the big house, and the van driver and his helper began unloading suitcases. Yvette headed along a path between the big house and the slightly smaller one next door. There, she kicked off her shoes to wedge her feet into the warm sand.

Then she smelled him beside her. Brock.

"This is so perfect." She couldn't keep the awe out of her

voice. Under the waning sun, turquoise water lapped against white sand. "Isn't there supposed to be a setup for volleyball?" she asked. "The kids would love that."

He nodded. "The compound has every amenity."

Yvette spied the amenity she wanted. Beneath a palm tree, a large round swing with a teal pillow topping it swayed in a gentle breeze. She pictured herself lying there, soaking up the dappled sun. And she pictured Brock next to her. It was big enough for two.

An irresistible urge made her blood race. She wanted him to make love to her on that swing.

If she said it aloud, he'd make it happen. But they absolutely couldn't risk it.

"We won't work while we're here," he said softly. "We'll just relax and enjoy ourselves."

She was sure he'd had the same thought, making love to her on that swing, its gentle rocking adding to their pleasure.

Smiling, she said, "I'll hold you to that, Mr. Donnelly."

His voice low, he echoed her desire. "If they weren't all in that house and able to see out the back porch, I'd kiss you until you couldn't breathe. Until you couldn't even think."

Just like that, with a look and a few words, he turned her inside out. She was wet. She was ready. And she wanted him so badly she could taste him.

"Wow, Grandmother, you have to see this view. It's freaking amazing." Jodi's voice drifted to them from the screened-in porch.

From her vantage, Yvette saw that all the houses had screened-in porches overlooking the ocean and the white sand. Dense foliage on either side turned their cove into an oasis.

"Mom," Kacey called. "Isn't this totally sweet?"

Yvette whispered to Brock. "Oh yeah, it's totally sweet."

While she would rather stay here beside him, the warm

breeze stroking her skin, she turned to the porch as Kacey said, "You have to see this house. I can't believe the size of Grandmother's bedroom. It's a suite."

"And Olive is already making dinner for us," Jodi added. "Can't you smell it?"

Crossing the sand and slipping back into her sandals, Yvette climbed the porch steps and opened the screen door. "Who's Olive?"

Kacey rolled her eyes. "Our cook, of course." Then she flung herself at Brock, hugged him hard. "You are the best, Uncle Brock. This place is ah-mazing."

Darryl stood in the open French doors behind her. "But there's only one maid. And there's five houses to take care of," he said with a disgusted edge to his voice.

Jodi shot him a look. "I'm sure one person can take care of all of us." She added in a drawl, "Unless someone is incredibly messy."

There was no love lost between Jodi and Kacey's boyfriend, and Yvette stepped between them before a fight broke out. "I'm sure it will all work out. If we pick up after ourselves, that'll make it easier for everyone."

Yvette had the feeling the person the maid would have to pick up after was Darryl. And because he'd been challenged, she was sure he'd make a point of being extra messy.

It was safe to say she didn't like Darryl. But right now, he was Kacey's choice. Yvette had no say in it. She just hoped her daughter was smart enough to see what kind of person Darryl was before things went too far.

Jodi, excited, dragged her inside.

The living area was massive, with a pool table on one end and a fireplace on the other, which Yvette was sure they'd never use. Sofas and chairs surrounded the hearth, and a huge u-shaped sofa sat before an oversized TV screen. Bookshelves along the walls held paperbacks and hardbacks. A games cabinet offered the likes of Rummikub and Battleship, check-ers, chess, and backgammon. Two card tables sat before it, with packs of cards and two round racks of poker chips.

Yvette knew it was a vain hope that they'd all play a few games rather than sitting in front of TV. But then it was whatever the kids wanted to do.

Windows surrounded the open floor plan. She'd noticed hurricane shutters, and thanked God it wasn't hurricane season. In a large area to the left of the living room sat a massive dining table, enough to seat them all.

"The kitchen's through there." Kacey pointed beyond the dining room. "Can't you just smell it?" She closed her eyes, breathing in.

Yvette caught the scent of something deliciously spicy.

Then Jodi grabbed her hand. "You have to see upstairs."

The bedrooms were ginormous, two suites on either end, both with a sitting room, bedroom, and an incredible bath-room, each with a tub and a shower. In one suite, the tub was big enough for two.

Adeline sniffed. "I've already claimed this room." Even though she had no need of a two-person tub.

But Trevor and Lorna had obviously agreed. Their room was still amazing, with a balcony opening onto an ocean view. Between the two suites was a smaller bedroom, no less luxu-rious and also with an en suite bathroom, though this room would go unused.

Until Adeline said, "Yvette, you don't need a cottage all to yourself. You can take this room here. It's perfect for you."

On the second floor, the balcony's ocean view of the aqua-marine water beckoned her. But she smiled at Adeline. "I'd rather have my own cottage, even if it's smaller than this room. I'd like my privacy."

Adeline's eyes narrowed and her nostrils flared, but she wouldn't win this one.

As the driver brought up bags, Adeline ordered him imperiously into her chosen room. And in that same haughty tone, she said to her family gathered round her, "Dinner will be ready at seven. Don't be late."

Lorna shuddered with delight. "It smells so good. And seven gives us time to unpack before dinner."

She really was sweet. Yvette vowed she'd make time during this trip to have a talk with her about how to handle Adeline. She should have done it long ago.

Jodi and Kacey raced down the stairs. "I want to see our house," Jodi called.

Brock and Yvette followed at a more sedate pace, the kids eager to see if their accommodations lived up to the main house. Both were identical and on a smaller scale, with a sitting room and small kitchen downstairs, four bedrooms upstairs with Jack and Jill bathrooms. Darryl's voice rang out, "Jesus Christ, we have to share a bathroom? Why didn't we get a house with four bathrooms?"

As Brock waited outside, Yvette gave him an eye roll. Darryl was complaining about a free trip when he wasn't even part of the family.

Coming up on the porch, Brock stood in the doorway, his arm brushing her shoulder as he leaned in. "This is the guys' house," he called loudly enough so the kids would hear upstairs. "Next door is for the girls."

Jodi, followed by Kacey and the two girlfriends, bounded down the stairs and pushed past Brock, Jodi saying, "Thank you, Uncle Brock," as they all rushed to the next house.

Yvette whispered, "You know they'll mix and match anyway."

"Like we plan to mix and match," he said in a low, husky tone that strummed her nerve endings.

Then he shouted again, "Hey, guys, the drivers have your bags. You better get down here and tell them what goes where." He turned to the two unhurried men and pointed to the bags belonging to him and Yvette. "These go down to the last two cottages." Then he peeled off a few bills, handing some to each man. "Thank you."

Only a few minutes later, Jodi barreled out of the house Brock had deemed the girls' dorm. Rushing to Yvette, Jodi leaned into her, giggling. "Guess what? We have four bathrooms, one for each of us." Then she punched Yvette's arm lightly. "Don't tell Darryl. He'll probably try to make us switch with them."

Yvette zipped her lips. "I won't say a word. Now I'm going to unpack too."

Her cottage was a studio, with a big alcove for the bed, a sofa and chairs in the middle, and another alcove for a mini kitchen. She could make a coffee in the morning, and a piece of toast if she wanted. But the best was the screened-in porch along the back. Every morning, she could sit out there and enjoy her coffee. And a cocktail in the evening. Maybe she'd never have to go to the big house and subject herself to Adeline.

The driver rolled in her suitcase and set it on the luggage rack. Thanking him as he left, she unzipped the bag and threw it open. Taking out her toiletries, she headed into the bathroom, sighing with pleasure at the sight of the soaking tub.

When she returned to the main room, Brock stood in the middle of it. "Did you bring any sexy lingerie? Maybe a hot negligee?"

She laughed, pushing him aside. "I prefer to sleep naked."

"Jesus, you make me crazy." Then he grabbed her, pressed his lips to hers in a kiss drenched with passion.

When he went for the buttons of her blouse, she shoved him away, laughing. "Go back to your own room," she whispered. "Jodi could come down here at any moment to see what my room is like. Now get out of here." She pushed him toward the door, still laughing, but before she let him go, she leaned close to whisper, "You can come back tonight. When everyone's asleep."

She couldn't wait.

## 7

Brock wasn't disappointed that Yvette hadn't let him do anything when he'd gone to her cottage. It made him even hotter for the night.

And yet it smacked of being back home, where he had to sneak over to her place a couple of times a week, because that was all she allowed. And sneak out again in the deepest dark of the night so no one saw him.

He wanted more. He wanted to wake up with her in his arms.

Later tonight, he would hold her, make love to her. But now, there was dinner with his family, with Yvette seated next to him so he could breathe in the scent of her citrusy lotion.

"The meal smells delicious," he told Olive as she set out the selections in warming trays on a long table beside the kitchen door.

Yet again, that reminded him of the big house, with Mrs. French placing everything in the chafing dishes, then silently exiting as if she'd never been there and the food had appeared by magic.

He guessed Olive to be in her fifties as she smiled, her

teeth white in her ebony face. "I hope you enjoy everything. Please do not hesitate if you need anything else from me." Then she pointed at the array of dishes. "I have made jerk chicken and plantains, sliced and fried the way we prefer them here." Her accent bore echoes of French, but he wasn't sure what language was spoken in the Bahamas. "And we have rice and peas, another of our staples. But our peas are not like yours. They are pigeon peas, and the rice is spiced with tomato, onion, and thyme. There are also steamed vegetables. Please, help yourself."

She left the room, disappearing into the fragrant kitchen.

Since it was the first night, his entire family was here, along with boyfriends and girlfriends. Brock flourished a hand toward his mother. "Please, you first, Adeline."

Adeline always served herself first anyway. Taking a plate, she opened a chafing dish. "What is all this?" Leaning close to sniff, she turned up her nose.

Coming to stand beside her, his voice mild, he said, "You've heard of jerk chicken, plantains, rice and peas, and steamed vegetables." He didn't help himself yet.

"Is it all spicy?" She wrinkled her nose distastefully.

"I don't know. I've never had jerk chicken before." Though he suspected it was spicy. And it looked appetizing.

She took a bit of chicken, one plantain, a small scoop of rice and peas, and a much heftier portion of the steamed vegetables.

He called Trevor and Lorna next, because letting the kids go first would mean hours before his brother and wife got something. Then he jutted his chin at Yvette. But she smiled, saying, "I'll wait."

They got in line together at the end, where he could feel the heat of her body and dream about the night to come. He let his arm brush hers as he leaned over to open a serving tray.

And that was all he allowed himself. Too much and his eagle-eyed mother would notice.

For himself, he didn't mind, but he knew how Yvette felt.

His first bite of chicken was sweet and fiery, its flavors imbued with smoke and fruit. Oh yes, it was spicy, and he glanced at Adeline.

Her eyes narrowed, a grimace on her lips. But that was not an unfamiliar look for her. Seated at the far end, she called down the table to him, "What's in this jerk chicken?"

He replied as mildly as before, "I have no idea, Adeline."

"Then look it up on your phone," she snapped.

He smiled, despite her tone. "I thought you didn't like us to use our phones at the table," he chided her.

She glared. His mother's glare was meant to intimidate, but now it only made his smile grow. "All right, I'll look it up." And then he read aloud. "Jerk chicken is seasoned with scotch bonnet peppers." His smile stretched ear to ear. "I believe they're intensely hot peppers."

Adeline slammed down her fork. "I absolutely cannot eat anything that is intensely spicy. It will give me indigestion. I won't sleep tonight."

Wiping away his smile but still feeling it on the inside, he said, "I can't ask Olive to prepare two meals, one for you and one for the rest of us. And all of us want to try something new and different. So buck up, Adeline." He enjoyed baiting her, probably because she stood between him and the life he wanted with Yvette.

Oh, if looks could kill. But before she could stalk from the table, Olive pushed through the swing door, striding efficiently to set a plate in front of Adeline. "I have made a special fish for you, madame." She said it in the French way, ma-dame instead of madam.

"Is it fried? I can't have anything fried. And the only spices I tolerate are salt and pepper, if used in moderation."

"I think you will approve of its preparation. Please, try it," Olive urged.

Adeline brought the fish to her mouth, sniffing first, then chewing. When she closed her eyes to savor it, he knew Olive had saved the day. "Thank you," he said.

Olive replied smoothly, "I have no problem preparing extra dishes which do not have as much spice in them. It will be my pleasure." Then she left for the kitchen once more, the door swinging behind her.

Adeline smiled smugly at him as she enjoyed her fish. And he leaned to his right, saying to Yvette, "Too spicy for you?" Yvette loved a lot of spice, especially the things he did to her in her bed.

She shook her head. "Oh my God, this is so delicious. I need the recipe. I'd love to make this at home. I wonder if Olive gives out recipes."

His family enjoyed the feast just as much.

"This is freaking good." Jodi said. And her grandmother glared at her as if she'd used the *F-bomb*. Ignoring her, Jodi added, "I've never had jerk chicken before, but I'll sure as heck have it again."

Yvette smiled that beautiful smile of hers. "I'll make it for you the next time you and Kacey are home." Which would be spring break in about three months.

Brock found the rice and peas to be delicious also, dark brown pigeon peas, with the onion, thyme, and tomato adding extra notes of flavor. The fried plantains were crispy on the outside and subtly sweet on the inside, the grill stripes adding extra flavor.

Conversation flowed around the table, and Yvette said, "I wonder if I can get pigeon peas at home and make this dish as well."

"We can go shopping in the city to see what we can find," he suggested. "It's San Francisco, after all, and I'm sure we could find a Caribbean grocery store somewhere. You could probably find the Scotch bonnet peppers too."

It sounded innocuous, just a kind offer. But it would allow him to spend more time with her outside the office, maybe a three-hour lunch. He wondered if she'd let him rent a hotel room. They'd done that a time or two, when his need for her ratcheted up, and he'd seduced her into saying yes.

When they'd all devoured seconds, Olive sent in the maid —whom she introduced as Samara—to clear the dishes. Then Olive arrived with dessert, explaining as she placed slices onto dessert plates. "This is a very special dish of ours called guava duff. It is a steamed pudding rolled with fresh guava in the middle." After placing all the slices, she ladled sauce over each piece. "And this is a rum butter sauce." She and Samara passed out each plate, but to Lorna, she said, "I have not put the rum sauce on yours. For the baby."

Lorna smiled her thanks.

"This doesn't look like pudding," Adeline groused. "It's some sort of rolled cake."

Olive smiled. "It is denser than cake, which is why we call it pudding. But you're right, madame, it is not like American pudding." With a little wave, she added, "Enjoy," and once again disappeared into her domain.

"Oh my God." Francine, Ethan's girlfriend, moaned over the first bite. She was a lovely girl, her long dark hair trailing to the middle of her back, though now she wore it in a high ponytail. She closed her eyes, tipped her head back, and murmured her appreciation. "This is so good."

It was the same sound Yvette made, and the same words, as he feasted on her beautiful body and made her come. With thoughts of Yvette, he realized he should have changed into his shorts after the flight, because now his slacks were a tad too tight.

"This is yummy," Jodi said, licking the sauce from her fork. "Do you think Olive will offer seconds?"

Iris, Malcom's girlfriend, held up her hand as if she were in class. "I'm willing to go into the kitchen and beg." A tall blond woman with bright blue eyes, she and Malcolm made a handsome couple.

Before she could jump out of her chair, Olive waltzed through the door again, another platter in her sturdy hands, as if she'd been listening at the door. "I've made a second guava duff. Just in case." She set the sliced duff on the side-board, accompanied by a fresh bowl of rum sauce. "I must tell you, it is just as delicious for breakfast."

Beside him, Yvette said to the entire table, "If I keep eating like this, I'm going to gain ten pounds while we're here."

He wanted to say that he'd more than enjoy her lush curves, but when he rose to retrieve a piece for her, she waved him away. "No, not for me."

Adeline signaled Brock. "Just a half slice for me, please."

But when Lorna began to rise, Adeline waved a hand at her. "Dear. Don't you think one slice is enough?" She pursed her lips. "You know how hard it is to get rid of baby weight."

Lorna sat. Even Trevor didn't jump up to get her another piece, while Adeline tucked into her half slice, giving a dainty moan of pleasure.

It was a mean thing for her to say, and Brock said, "Your figure looks perfect, Lorna. I'll get you a slice."

The young woman waved him away. "No, honestly, I'm full." She put her hand on her belly. "The baby makes me feel it if I have too much."

Christ. His mother. Brock met Yvette's gaze. She would remember the games his mother had played with her all those years ago.

They rounded off the evening with coffee in the living room. Then Adeline stood. "It's been a long day. I'll turn in."

When she'd floated up the stairs like a queen leaving her subjects, Garth said, "Why don't we all have a couple of beers out on the beach by the fire pit?"

Kacey added, "Just one, then I'll go to bed. I'm tired." She yawned. Fishing her phone out of her pocket, she looked at the time. "Back home, it's already eleven."

Next to her, Darryl sniped, "Since when do you go to bed at eleven?"

She smiled at him, ignoring his tone. "Since we got up so early and it's been a long day and I'm tired." She let that sit for a moment before adding, "Aren't you a little tired?"

Brock recognized the invitation for him to leave the group, but Darryl just laughed. "I'll be tired after a few beers."

The rest of the party broke up then, first with Trevor leading Lorna upstairs, then with Yvette saying she also was tired. He was already planning his route to her cottage while the kids were on the beach.

But first, he needed to have a talk with Adeline.

## ADELINE

A knock sounds on my bedroom door as I'm seated in a comfortable wing chair by the window.

It must be Olive with my hot chocolate. I've given her strict instructions. None of that packaged abomination, not even made with cocoa but with chocolate melted in the milk. I brought my own chocolate and gave it to her.

The door opens. Brock. Of course he doesn't wait for my permission to enter. "I've brought your hot chocolate." Elbowing the door, he doesn't bother to close it as he crosses the room.

Brock is a law unto himself. He never truly obeys me, only doing what I say if it aligns with his plans.

That isn't necessarily a bad thing. In fact, for the company, it's an excellent thing. I can't abide a man with a namby-pamby leadership style. When the workers threaten to strike, I want them beaten down. And Brock has steered the company admirably, avoiding any impending disasters. At least up to this point.

He sets the cup on the table beside me, then takes the

chair on the other side, a snifter of brandy cupped negligently in his hand.

So, he's here for a talk. What will it be this time?

"You need to lay off Lorna," he says with a demanding harshness I don't appreciate.

I put my hand to my chest, as if I'm the offended one. I should have known it would be about Lorna. Brock is always the knight in shining armor, rushing to a damsel's distress.

"I have no idea what you're talking about." I give him my most innocent expression. Of course that doesn't work on Brock.

"Stop hounding her about what she eats. She's pregnant. She's eating for two."

I purse my lips. It should be a signal, but Brock ignores it, forcing me to say, "I'm only looking out for her. She shouldn't get fat. It'll be so hard to lose the weight after the baby comes. And you know what happens when a woman loses her shape."

"Jesus Christ, Adeline."

He only swears when I've pricked a nerve. Which is good. He needs to have his nerves pricked sometimes. And I go on. "Men stray if a wife doesn't watch her looks. It's in their nature."

He shuts his eyes and wags his head. Then he looks at me. "I never strayed after Corrine had the boys."

I raise a superior eyebrow. "She never lost her shape."

No, Brock hadn't strayed. It was Corrine who'd done the damage. And it was Harris who'd done the damage after I had my baby. I never forgave him. Even in death, I still don't forgive him. But I had my revenge. Brock doesn't know any of that. It's a secret I'll take to my grave.

Unless I need to use it to my advantage.

"Isn't it interesting that you're the one up here telling me to lay off Lorna?" I say in such a pleasant tone, as if we're talking about the weather. "Where's your brother? He should be here defending his own wife."

"Good God, woman. Will you never stop?"

Of course I won't stop. Not until my dying breath. And hopefully not even after that. I plan to run this family even from the grave.

"I'm glad he'll never be at the helm of Donnelly Shipping," I continue. "He just doesn't have it in him."

The way he looks at me sometimes, as if he can't believe I'm his mother. But, I have only one goal in mind, and that is Donnelly Shipping, this family's legacy. I will let no one, not even a weak son, take it down.

I wouldn't have let that happen even if Pierce had been the one to try. He might have been my favorite, but I would never have allowed him to run Donnelly Shipping. I am, after all, a realist. And now I smile. "What about Garth? How's he doing? I envision you fast-tracking him to CFO."

Brock laughs. And truly, it is full of humor. "We've already got a CFO. Trevor does an excellent job."

I shrug. That isn't worth fighting about. At least not now. "But you will want to retire eventually. We need to groom Garth." Then a horrific thought catches my breath. "He hasn't had a girlfriend since he broke up with that girl right after graduation. Is he gay?"

Now that wipes all the humor off Brock's face. I truly don't like to be laughed at.

"You're out of line, Adeline. I don't know what his sexual orientation is. And I won't ask. Because it doesn't matter. It's none of our business. He is whatever he is. So lay off him too."

I don't have a prejudiced bone in my body. But I can't build a dynasty with a gay man. "I only ask because I have a perfect girl in mind for him. Judith Amesbury's granddaughter. She's a lovely girl. She'd be perfect for Garth."

"I'm warning you, Adeline, butt out of his life."

I just smile. Because what can he do about it?

The voices quieted, the fire on the beach petered out, and the huddled masses silhouetted against the skyline dispersed.

Yvette had taken a bath, smoothed lotion into her skin. She loved the ritual of getting ready for him. And she loved the fresh scent of his still damp hair when he came to her.

He would be here soon. Yvette crawled into bed, the sheets like silk against her naked skin. She'd left the door unlocked, knowing he would come when it was safe.

She didn't have long to wait, the snick of the opening door filling the room. Just thinking about him had made her wet and ready for whatever he wanted, for every delicious touch and kiss she craved.

"Christ, I've missed you," he whispered before his lips took hers.

The girls been home for a week. It felt like years rather than days since he'd been in her bed, and oh how she'd missed him.

He trailed kisses down her neck, across her chest, to the tight bead of her breast. Taking her nipple in his mouth, he sucked, and exquisite pleasure shot to her core. His fingers walked leisurely down to her center, and she parted her legs for him. When he slid a finger inside her, he lifted his head to say, "Christ, you're so damn wet."

She whispered, "I've been thinking about you all night."

When he made to work his way down her body, she pulled at his shoulders. "No. I want you inside me. Right now. Don't make me wait."

His voice came hoarse and needy. "You can't imagine how badly I want to feel you around me." And going up on his haunches, he pulled her legs over his thighs until he was poised at her entrance. "Touch yourself for me."

As she did, he eased inside her, sliding over her G-spot, and excruciating bliss coursed through her body. She didn't tell him to stop, didn't tell him to go faster. She let him take her just like that, slow, short strokes while she caressed herself.

Inside her, she felt him grow even harder. He loved to watch her, loved to taste her, loved everything they did.

She trembled with the slow friction, her legs quivering, her toes flexing. She tensed every muscle, her calves, her thighs, her buttocks. An exponential wave of delight shot through her. It was coming, she could feel it, that heat growing, building, as if everything was being drawn to her very center.

Then it all exploded, and she bit down on her lip to keep from crying out. But he knew. He felt the way her body clutched him. And he rammed hard inside her, just the way she needed. The way she craved. He took her like a ram, like she was the prize he'd won over all the others. Every thrust shot agonizing pleasure through her. It went on and on, until tears leaked from her eyes and her body surged up to meet his, riding him as much as he rode her. Reaching between them, she squeezed that sensitive part of him, felt his impending climax throb inside her.

He cried out, a deep, guttural sound at such a low decibel that no one would hear it outside this room. But it was music to her ears as he came inside her, as he made her come again. Maybe she'd never stopped coming.

Then there were only harsh breaths and the slap of their bodies, then one last mighty thrust, and he tensed, his head back, his throat stretched, as he filled her with everything in him.

And she took it all.

"CHRIST, THAT WAS SO FREAKING GOOD." HOLDING HER close, he nuzzled her hair, loving the silky feel of her body along the length of his.

She traced a finger in the whorl of hair on his chest. "That was perfect," she said on an exhale.

"Hell yes," he agreed. "The nice thing is that everyone will sleep in tomorrow. So I don't have to go back to my room until dawn. I can wake up with you in my arms."

She shifted slightly, and he knew she wanted to say it was dangerous. But even as she tipped her chin, he took her mouth in a luscious kiss. Then he whispered against her lips, "Besides, I haven't tasted you yet. There's so much more of the night to come."

He wanted that, needed it. His talk with Adeline had left a sour taste in his mouth. But here with Yvette, he could forget about Adeline and her bullying. And the words welled up into his throat. *Marry me.* Yet he couldn't say them. He'd said them so often, and she'd turned him down over and over. The time wasn't right. He wondered if the time would ever be right.

He said the only thing he could, "I love you."

She kissed his chest. "I love you."

"That won't change, no matter how long I hold you in my arms. No matter how many years it takes." Then he murmured, "Are you expecting to wait until Adeline is dead?"

She squeezed out a long breath as if she'd been holding it. "I'm waiting for the girls to be on their own. I'm waiting for the time when she can't turn them against me."

"She'll never turn them against you," he said, with a sharp shake of his head. "They love you. Nothing she says can change that." And yet he thought of Adeline's sly bullying of Lorna. He didn't think the woman even knew what her mother-in-law was doing. Would the girls? Before it was too late?

Yvette tipped her head back to look at him, her eyes bright, even though she'd closed the curtains. "She could tell them I've been having an affair with you since before Pierce died. She could make them believe it."

Brock couldn't say it wouldn't happen. Relationships soured so easily.

And she went on. "That's why I won't allow them to live at her house when they come home for vacations. They'll stay with me until the day they move into their own apartments. And that's how long I'll stay in the gatehouse. I won't allow her to move me out."

This was the real reason she refused to leave. His mother. Adeline and her poison.

They could get a flat, live together, even marry. But his boys and Yvette's girls would remain to hear the vitriol.

Maybe Yvette was right. They should wait until all the kids were out on their own, when they would come only for a day in the big house, only for a holiday, when Adeline couldn't work on them.

Had his mother always been this way? Had he just been blind?

Yes. He probably had been. He could remember now some of the things she'd said to bully Yvette. Pierce had never spoken up for his wife. But Brock remembered times Adeline had nagged about what Yvette fed the girls, about letting them watch too much TV, about letting them talk too much at the dinner table. He remembered telling his mother to lay off, just as he had tonight. He just hadn't realized the extent of it, and God only knew what Adeline had said when he wasn't around. Now she was playing her games with Lorna. He knew why. Because she wanted her daughter-in-law to beg to move down to the gatehouse until Trevor finally forced Yvette out.

As if she could follow his train of thought, he said, "I had a talk with Adeline tonight about leaving Lorna alone."

"I planned to find a moment to talk to Lorna while we're here. Tell her that Adeline is a viper."

"That sounds good." But he was the man who'd let the viper take over. He didn't know how to curb Adeline. In a previous century, he could have stuck her in an institution, saying she suffered from so-called female hysteria. But first, it wouldn't work, and second, he'd never do it, not even in a past life.

"Let's not ruin the night with talk of Adeline," she said.

He rolled off the bed and padded to the curtains, pushing them aside, leaving only the lace sheers.

As he headed back to her, she said, "Someone might see us."

He laughed softly, climbing back into bed. "They'd have to put their hands up to the window and peer through to see anything. I seriously doubt anyone will do that." Pulling her beneath him, he said, "I want to see the sunrise with you in my arms." He bent to kiss her throat, to lick her sweet skin.

"And before that, I want to make love to you at least two more times tonight."

She finally smiled. "Promises, promises."

And he kept his promises.

THE LIGHT OF THE PREDAWN LEECHED THROUGH THE curtains. The sun hadn't yet risen over the horizon, but it was close.

Yvette lay in his arms, luxuriously satisfied in a way she hadn't been in a long time.

Brock was right. Waking up in his arms was what she'd craved. His body nestled against hers, the sheets drenched in the scent of their loving, their bodies beautifully musky from a long night of pleasure. Parts of her body ached from the feast of sensations.

Could she have this every night? When he was kissing her, she thought maybe she could.

Holding her close, he murmured, "This is exactly what I wanted. To kiss you awake like Prince Charming."

She laughed. "I'm too old to be Cinderella."

He didn't laugh with her. "You're not too old for this." He kissed her again, rekindling the night's passion. "One more time," he whispered.

When they were holding each other, sated, catching their breath again, the sun was over the horizon. "I'm heading back to my room." He stroked tangled strands of hair back from her face. "Meet me on the beach in fifteen minutes for a walk." He cut her off when she opened her mouth to protest. "It's just a walk on the beach. No one will think a thing."

He leaned over, sucked her nipple into his mouth, swirled his tongue around it until she felt she might go mad all over again.

Then he rolled to his feet. "And I promise not to touch you while we're walking."

The door snicked close behind him, and she could still smell him in the bed, on her skin, still taste him.

Fifteen minutes later, she met him on the white sand of the beach, the grains cool beneath her bare feet. While she'd pulled on a sundress, he'd changed into board shorts and a T-shirt.

The air wasn't hot yet, the night having cooled everything down. Brock said politely, "Fancy meeting you out here. I guess we're both early risers." He gave her a cocky grin. Anyone overhearing them would have no idea they'd spent the entire night together.

True to his word, he didn't take her hand as they walked. Not even as they rounded the bend in their cove and wandered onto the next beach. The rising sun spread fingers of yellow and orange across the white clouds of the morning.

She thought about the miracle of it all. To be here with him in the early morning. The beauty of waking up in his arms. The looseness of her limbs after all that pleasure. Of course, they'd slept together on business trips. But this was different. With no meetings to rush to, they could enjoy each other like this, on a simple walk. It might be dangerous, but she could get used to it, even need it.

While they were here, she wouldn't let him leave her bed until sunrise. Maybe she'd even make him stay to make love to her with the sun streaming like a ball of fire through the curtains.

Such wonderful dreams.

"I can smell you on me." He closed his eyes, breathed in deeply, as if he were savoring her scent. "After we've been together, I don't shower in the morning."

"You don't shower before going to work?" She tried to sound aghast, but it thrilled her.

"I want to smell you on me all day long. I want to close my eyes and remember every touch in the night."

She felt her limbs weaken and her body turn molten. Despite the fresh morning air, she was suddenly hot, as if it were the middle of the day and the sun at its zenith. She almost took his hand as she said, "I stayed in bed a couple of minutes after you left. Because I could smell us there. Our lovemaking. The two of us together."

His voice came out a little shaky. "I told you I wouldn't touch you. Not even hold your hand. But you should know that right now I want to throw you over my shoulder like a caveman and carry you off into the jungle to make love to you until you scream everyone awake."

Sometimes, when he couldn't come to her, he called her, telling her things that made her crazy, that made her need to touch herself. He was doing it now, but the impact was so much greater with his eyes on her. And she whispered, "I'd let you."

She'd let him do anything he wanted. Even if she wouldn't marry him, everything else was his.

His gaze stripped her down. "You're so tempting." Then he straightened. "We better go back. Or someone will see me dragging you into the trees."

They walked back slowly, heat sparking between them as the sun rose higher in the sky. But it wasn't the sun's heat that shot out the sparks. It was them. It was what lived and breathed between them. Nothing Adeline could do would ever douse it.

Back at their beach, they saw Jodi sitting on the turquoise swing. Before they were close enough to be overheard, Brock said, "Don't take a shower. I want my scent on you all day long. Just like yours is on me."

As he headed into his cottage next to hers, closing the

sliding glass door he'd left unlocked, Yvette strolled to her daughter.

The swing rocked gently, Jodi pushing with her toe in the sand. And Yvette said, "Is there room enough for me?" She had a fleeting fear that Jodi might smell the sex on her, like heat rising off concrete.

But her daughter merely smiled, squirming over so Yvette could curl herself onto one side of the swing. Her foot dangling, her toe only just touched the sand, still cool from the night where the sun hadn't hit it yet. "You're up early."

Jodi shrugged. "Time change." Her long dark hair was like silk over her shoulders. She took after the dark-haired Donnelly side, with the Donnelly mannerisms, the way her mouth curved when she smiled, the way her blue eyes flashed when she was excited.

Yet something appeared off. "You seem a little morose this morning," Yvette ventured.

Jodi stared at the rising sun, licked her lips, kicked the sand again to keep them moving. "He's such an asshole." Her eyes closed slightly as she said the word.

Sadly, Yvette didn't need to ask who. "But we have to put up with him. He's your sister's choice. We can only hope it doesn't last long."

Jodi turned to her then, her eyes a little bloodshot from the long day, the time change, and perhaps the drinking out by the fire pit. "It's like he's mesmerized her. I don't get it."

"Maybe he's nice to her," Yvette offered.

Jodi snorted. "Oh yeah, sure he's nice to her when they're alone. But I think it's gotta be the size of his—"

Yvette's hands flew to her ears. "I can't even think about that."

Her youngest daughter laughed. "She's not exactly a virgin."

"I understand that."

Jodi went on torturing her. "I hear them sometimes at night." The girls shared a two-bedroom apartment down at the university.

And Yvette said again, almost whining, "Please, please, please, don't tell me. I don't want to know." Especially not with Darryl. Because Jodi was right, he wasn't good enough for Kacey. He wasn't good enough for anyone. But anything she might have said to Kacey could only backfire. "She's a smart girl. She'll see the truth eventually. We just have to wait. But you know what will happen if we say anything." Kacey was as stubborn as any Donnelly.

Jodi rolled her eyes. "I've already said something. She didn't speak to me for three weeks. But only after she told me I was jealous because I was all alone."

Yvette ached for both her daughters. "I'm so sorry."

"I'm not lonely. I've made a choice. I'm looking for a guy like—" She shrugged, smiling. "Like Uncle Brock. Or even like one of the cousins. They're good men. I don't want to settle for an ass like Darryl just because I don't want to be lonely. I want the right guy."

A man like her Uncle Brock. Yes. He was the best of men.

Yvette wondered for a moment if maybe, just maybe, there was nothing Adeline could say that would turn her daughter against her if she knew about the affair. But she wasn't at all sure about Kacey.

So she said nothing except, "They're all good men. I know you'll find somebody of their caliber. It might take time. But you'll find him. He's waiting out there for you."

Just like Brock had been waiting for her. Except that Yvette had made the mistake of marrying his younger brother.

She kissed her daughter's cheek. "Let's go see what's for breakfast."

$$\text{❧} \quad \text{10} \quad \text{❧}$$

nother hour passed before everyone came in for the meal. Jodi left Yvette to take a shower, but finally they all breakfasted together on delicious banana fritters, sausage, bacon, fruit, and grits. Yvette hadn't been sure she'd like the grits, but found the dish surprisingly creamy and even a little cheesy. The girls were chipper, even Jodi, and the guys bleary-eyed as if they'd stayed out later by the fire pit. Darryl sat in morose silence, a hangover probably pounding in his head.

Adeline tinkled a bell she'd found somewhere. Yvette knew the sound would grate on her nerves for the next two weeks.

When Olive answered the summons, Adeline said, "I can't eat any of this. I'd like some porridge. Just a little honey, nothing else."

Not breaking her perpetual smile, Olive said, "Of course, madame. I have some on the stove." She reappeared moments later with a bowl and a honeypot. "I think it best if you add your own honey."

Adeline actually said, "Thank you." Then she added after

Olive was gone, "There. That's much better," as if she were talking to herself.

Brock pulled out his phone. "What does everyone want to do today? I can book tickets."

Malcolm asked, "What are the choices?"

"Pretty much what we talked about on the flight. Horseback riding on the beach. The zip line, the bat caves—"

Francine shuddered. "No bats. They get in your hair."

Ethan jumped in. "That's an old wives' tale. But if we go there at sunset, we'll probably see them all flying out."

"Like the Carlsbad Caverns in New Mexico," Iris said, her blue eyes sparkling. "I've always wanted to go there." She looked at Malcolm, as if he could make the wish come true. Being a Donnelly, he probably could.

"There're also waterfalls you can slide down." Then he explained exactly what that meant. "You walk up the trail to the top of the gorge and slide down each waterfall into a pool below."

"Does it hurt?" Francine asked.

"Not if you hold your elbows in so they don't hit the sides." He wasn't at all exasperated with the girl's questions.

But she still said, "I don't know."

And Brock went on. "There's also kayaking and snorkeling. We can rent a catamaran with an outfit that will take us to the good snorkeling spots."

Practical Garth said, "If we want to do that, we should book in advance and get there early, so we have the whole day."

"Good idea," Brock agreed. "We can also rent ATVs, like we talked about."

"What about something a little less strenuous?" Adeline asked. "Like shopping?" Although anything Adeline shopped for here, she would consider beneath her standards. She shopped only at exclusive stores. Adeline was a snob.

Brock answered reasonably, "You can have our driver take you anywhere you'd like. But the rest of us will wait until after we've tired ourselves out with some of these other activities."

She harrumphed and dug back into her porridge.

Then Brock looked at Yvette. "What would you like to do?"

All eyes were on her as if she were the decision-maker. And why shouldn't she be? "I'd like the horseback riding on the beach. And especially in the ocean."

Brock smiled, and she felt it reach deep inside her, all his longing, his need, and even his humor in that smile. "Horseback riding sounds great. Does everyone agree?"

Their children nodded. Then he poked at his phone, obviously booking tickets for the horseback riding.

Adeline set her gaze on Lorna. "You're pregnant, so don't be a ninny, thinking you can go horseback riding." She smiled quickly, adding, "You can stay with me. Olive can make us treats. We'll have a marvelous time, I promise."

Trevor spoke up, as if he saw the danger there. "I'll stay behind with Lorna. I don't need to go riding."

But Adeline wagged a finger at him. "Lorna and I will be fine. You need to go. You can't let a pregnant woman hold you back from the things you want to do."

Beside him, Lorna said, "It's okay, you go. I'll be fine. But I want to hear all about it when you get back," she added, as if she had no idea of the danger.

Trevor said softly, "Are you sure?"

She patted his hand. "Absolutely. Go have fun and take a bunch of videos for me."

God, she was sweet. But Yvette feared Adeline wanted to undermine the two of them.

Then Lorna said, "In fact, I'll take Adeline shopping, the way she wants to." She smiled as she boxed Adeline into a corner if she didn't actually want to shop. "Won't that be fun, Mother?"

For the first time, Yvette wondered if perhaps Lorna could call hold her own with her mother-in-law.

AS RECOMMENDED BY THE GROUP RUNNING THE HORSEBACK riding outfit, Yvette chose the leggings she'd worn on the plane, as well as a long-sleeved swim shirt, tennis shoes, hat, and oodles of sunblock. The kids, ignoring the suggested attire, dressed in cutoff jeans, tank tops, and sneakers without socks. She was happy to see the girls at least lathered up with suntan lotion.

They headed to the stables on the other side of the island, needing all three Jeeps, Brock, Trevor, and Garth driving. On the dryer side of the island, which received less rain, the terrain was scrubbier, unlike their wetter side, where the jungle seemed to take over almost from the edge of the beach.

Yvette sat in the front seat with Brock. Over the noise of the engines and the tires thumping into potholes along the road, she called out, "I've never been on a horse before." And yet, she wanted this ride into the ocean.

His smile turned her heart over. It always did. "I'll make sure you get an easy mount."

She knew he'd take care of her. He was an accomplished rider, often using the stables at the big house. Though these days, busy with work, he hadn't been riding much.

Upon arriving, they watched a short safety demonstration, with helmets handed out to everyone. One of the owners, also a guide, said to her in lovely accented English, "I've been told that you have never ridden before." His teeth were white in his dark face as he smiled and led her to a horse. "She is not tall, and she is gentle. She will do whatever the other horses do, so you should not have to give her much direction. But if you have any problems, both Juan—" He jutted his chin at an older man with weatherbeaten skin and probably of Mayan descent. "—and I will be available to you." He gave her a slight bow and, a hand to his chest, he said, "I am Mateo, at your service."

He drew her horse to a mounting block and helped her climb on. Brock, already mounted, not even using a block, watched her. She felt his eyes on her as if they were his hands.

She laughed, saying, "You look good on that horse, like the hero out of an old Western." With a smile, he twitched the reins, effortlessly turning his horse. The man knew how to handle the stallion. Maybe she should take up riding as a way of spending more time with him outside of work. And outside of her bed.

Jodi trotted over to Yvette. "You look great on a horse, Mom. I don't know why you never wanted to ride before. I mean, we've got all the horses in the stables back home."

She'd never wanted to ride because the stables weren't hers. They were Adeline's. But she'd never stopped the girls from learning.

With such a large family unit, no other riders joined them as the horses walked in single file out to a wide expanse of beach. Juan rode in front, while Mateo took the sweep position at the end of the line.

Not long after they'd started, Juan turned off the beach onto a sloping trail that led up to a ridge overlooking the ocean. Brock rode behind her, and she heard his gentle clicks to his horse, while hers, as Mateo had said, followed the rest without her having to do much. The trail switchbacked through the scrub, palm trees and foliage growing denser as they climbed. Their brood talked, shouted, and laughed ahead of her. God, how glad she was they were all here. Until she heard Darryl's loud squawk, complaining about the slow pace. Okay, there was one member of the brood she could do without.

Turning in her seat, she said to Brock, "He doesn't know how to ride either. If we were to go any faster, I'm afraid he might fall off."

"Then I'm sure we should speed it up."

They grinned like kids. God, she loved this family unit. She loved any activities with the kids. They'd never done much in the past as a full family. Why not? She couldn't recall a reason. Perhaps she'd kept herself aloof. When the girls, as children, had gone up to the big house to play with the boys, she'd rarely gone along. She much preferred when Brock's boys came down to the gatehouse. She hadn't learned to ride with them either. The most she'd done was suffer through those holiday dinners. Maybe she should have done more.

Then she shook herself. That was in the past. She could do nothing about it. But there was now. More trips together as a family awaited them. This Christmas trip to the Bahamas had been Brock's idea. But now she wanted more. Summer holidays at the beach, skiing in the winter, even if she wasn't a skier. It didn't matter. She wanted this togetherness.

It was also a way to spend time with Brock with no one thinking anything of it.

Moving her body to match her horse's gait as they climbed, she was comfortable. Twenty minutes later, they crested the ridge, Juan pulling his mount to a stop and signaling them into a single line to face the ocean. Brock reined in beside her.

From their vantage, whitecaps rolled across the aqua ocean, and the sun glared off the white sand. It was hotter here, a little muggy, but she'd never seen anything so stunning. "It's the most beautiful view," she said, exhaling in awe.

"Yes. This view is gorgeous." And when she turned to Brock, he was watching her rather than the ocean.

She wanted to reach over and nudge him, but that would seem too familiar to the rest. Laughing, she said, "Look at the water."

She snapped pictures of the blue ocean, the clouds drifting across the sky, the kids on their horses. And Brock.

Then Mateo swung down off his horse. "If you will allow me to handle your phone, I will take some good pictures of all of you."

"Thank you." She handed him the phone, and he stepped close to the edge. They all shouted and waved and laughed, and she knew the photos would be amazing.

Then Juan whirled his hand in the air as if he were about to throw a lasso around them. "And now we head back to the beach for a swim."

He led them down another switchback trail on the opposite side of the ridge, until finally they burst from the trees onto the other end of the same wide expanse of beach.

"Cut loose," Juan called, leading them all into a mad gallop along the beach.

Brock stayed behind with her. "You can do it. Just hold on with your thighs."

Mateo, flanking her other side, said, "I will watch out for you. Have no fear."

And she told Brock, "Go on. I know you want to."

Leaning over, he brushed his fingertips over her cheek. Then he took off, while Mateo clucked at her horse, saying softly, "Hold on. We can do this." And her horse broke into a gallop to match the others. She clung to the saddle horn with one hand, and just as Brock had told her, gripped the horse with her thighs. For a moment, it was terrifying. Then she felt as if she were flying along the beach.

The wind blowing through her hair was exhilarating, even

as it snatched her hat off her head, the chinstrap tethering it to her. She laughed like a child. Or like a fifty-three-year-old woman who'd suddenly cut loose.

At the other end of the beach, the kids turned the horses around, and Jodi sidled close to her, their calves brushing. "Wasn't that fun, Mom? We've got to do it when we get home. I'll teach you to ride. You'll love it."

Yvette smiled. "Yes. I would love it."

They did two more mad gallops along the beach, finally ending back by the stables.

She with breathless, giddy. Laughing. And her joy made her want to throw herself at Brock.

Of course she didn't. And maybe she'd regret that later.

Juan mimicked throwing his lasso again and led them into the stables. "It is time for our ocean swim," he said. "We must take off our saddles and ride the horses bareback in the water." He waved a hand at the ocean. "The waves are not too big today. Perfect for swimming."

They stripped the saddles from their horses, then undressed down to their bathing suits. With everyone prepared, Yvette, feeling slightly unstable on the horse's bare back with only the reins to hold on to, followed the others into the water.

The warm aquamarine ocean lapped at her bare feet, then her calves, and finally, her hips. Beneath her, the horse began to swim. Holding its head high above the gentle roll of the waves, the horse seemed to paddle through the water, Yvette dipping down with its movements.

And suddenly it was glorious. She felt as if she were floating on air. With the shifting height of the sand and the water not as deep, the horse sometimes walked, but even that was amazing.

She didn't know how to make her horse do anything in

the water, but Jodi did, somehow leading her mount over to Yvette.

"This is so cool, Mom. It's too cold to do it in San Francisco Bay, but this is awesome." Her daughter's eyes shone, and her smile was the most beatific Yvette had ever seen.

Over Jodi's shoulder, she caught Brock's eye, and felt the warmth of his smile envelope her. And she thought to herself, *best day ever*, as the horses alternately pranced and swam through the waves.

Then Darryl, in a booming voice that grated on Yvette, called out, "Look at me. I can stand on the horse's back." Somehow, he'd made his way into a standing position on the bareback horse, as if he were riding a surfboard.

Mateo called, "Watch out for that wave!"

But it was too late, and the wave hit Darryl at knee height, throwing him forward.

Jodi shook her head. "He's such a show-off. And he blew it anyway."

The horse swam away from him, and Darryl couldn't catch it as another wave rolled over him. Mateo guided his mount through the water to the riderless horse and grabbed the bridle.

Garth was shaking his head as he joined her and Jodi. "Your sister's boyfriend is a dick."

It was true. Although, perhaps, in this instance, Yvette thought Darryl was just having a good time. And he was laughing, not even seeming to mind that he was the butt of everyone's joke as he scrambled back on the horse with Mateo's help.

They hit a sandbar, and Garth said to Jodi, "Race you."

And they were off, their smiles beautiful against the crystalline water, their horses half galloping, half swimming. They turned then, heading back just as Brock reined in beside Trevor, who watched the family having a fantastic time.

Yvette saw how much she'd been missing. She and Brock didn't have a normal relationship. They couldn't go for hikes or bike rides. He couldn't take her out to dinner or to a movie. They couldn't even lay on the sofa and binge a TV show. Even now, they limited the time they spent together in case anyone noticed. They worked side by side during the day, pretending they were nothing more than coworkers, and made love only in the night. Otherwise, their lives were completely separate.

It seemed so sad. All because of Adeline.

For the first time, Yvette could admit she wanted more. She loved his arms around her in the dark. But she wanted all the rest of it too.

But with Adeline, she'd never have it.

TREVOR'S HORSE SWAM BESIDE BROCK AS HE SNAPPED THE pictures he'd promised Lorna. He even made Brock lean in for a selfie, which was a pain in the butt when the horses didn't stay still.

And he knew there were pictures of him and Yvette on the phone's camera roll. He so badly wanted to ask his brother to send them to him so he could remember this day, remember her face lit with joy.

As if reading his thoughts, Trevor said, "Yvette looks so happy right now."

Brock could only say, "She loves having her daughters with her." Then he hastily added, "I'm glad I could do this for everyone."

They were silent a moment as Yvette's horse trotted over a sandbar, then began swimming again, and Trevor said, "She never looks terribly happy unless we're all working hard on a project. She doesn't have a life outside of work now the girls are at school. She should be dating. She's still a beautiful, vibrant woman, and Pierce has been gone five years."

Brock would die if she ever dated another man. But all he could say to his brother was, "I guess she's making her own choice."

And yet it struck him that he was holding her back from something she deserved. He needed time to show her he was the only one for her, so much more time. But how could he eke out that extra bit? They could stay later in the city, have dinner out. He could get a flat where they'd meet, where no one would see them together. Except his mother would probably notice that when he was gone for a night, Yvette was gone too.

But he had to figure out something. He couldn't convince her to come out in the open, yet he could never let her be with another man. It was past that for them. He loved her. And he'd never let her go.

It tore him up to think about it, and he changed the subject abruptly. "You know, Lorna could have come with us. We haven't done anything risky."

Still gazing at the family dashing through the water, Trevor shook his head. "She doesn't want to do anything that might harm the baby." He looked at Brock, his gaze deep. "If she lost the baby..." He shrugged without finishing, but tense lines rode his features for a moment.

"I know," Brock agreed. "But leaving her with Adeline." A shudder welled up in him. "Your mother is being way too hard on her about her weight."

Trevor laughed, almost a snort. "*My* mother? Isn't she yours too?"

Brock chuckled. "Not when she's bullying your wife."

Trevor closed his eyes, tipped his face to the sun, and sighed. "Lorna's okay. She loves the house. She's so happy about the baby. And Adeline can't say anything to destroy that."

Neither of them called her Mother. They hadn't for years. Brock couldn't remember exactly when that happened, except that it was long before Pierce died. "It reminds me of the way Adeline treated Yvette."

His brother didn't look at him. "Lorna isn't Yvette."

Brock wondered what that meant. That Lorna wasn't married to the favorite son for whom no woman would ever be good enough? Or that Yvette had let Adeline's bullying get to her too much?

Then Trevor turned to him. "You don't have to worry. Lorna is good. I promise."

He let it go then. He'd said his piece. If he added any more, it was tantamount to saying his brother wasn't taking care of his wife.

## 11

"Oh my God, Grandmother, swimming with the horses was out of this world," Jodi said. Seated next to Garth at the dinner table, she punched his shoulder lightly. "Didn't you think it was a blast?"

"Yeah, it was great," he said with only slightly less enthusiasm.

Eyes as bright as Jodi's, Kacey added, "We swam bareback through the waves, Grandmother."

None of the children called Adeline by anything but Grandmother. She was never Grandma or Nana, especially not Grams. Adeline didn't allow it. Just as she didn't allow a single silver hair out of place in her perfect coiffure.

She gazed along the length of the table. "I'm so glad you had a wonderful time. That's what we're here for." Then she turned to Lorna. "And Lorna here had such a marvelous time shopping with me." She smiled like a shark. "Isn't that right, dear?"

Yvette waited for Lorna to deflate. She looked for signs of trauma. But Lorna merely smiled. "I had an amazing time,

Adeline. We had brunch at a lovely little cafe overlooking the ocean."

Yvette thought she might choke, though the conch fritters were amazing, especially dunked in the spicy mayo dip Olive had prepared.

She leaned across Trevor to say to Lorna, "You have to look at Trevor's pictures. And next time, after the baby, you'll go with us." She gave the other woman a smile that said, *I get you, I know where you're coming from, I know all about Adeline.*

But Lorna simply smiled. She had a sweet, almost child-like smile.

Yvette wondered when Adeline would bully it out of her.

"This is the best mac-and-cheese I've ever had," Garth said. "I wonder if we can get Mrs. French to make it exactly this way."

Adeline looked down her nose at him. "Don't even mention to Mrs. French that somebody made something better than she does. Or she'll go on strike."

They all laughed, even with Adeline's dry tone. Mrs. French was a very proud cook.

The mac-and-cheese was delicious, accenting the conch fritters, especially accompanied by the grilled plantains again. Yvette would never tire of them.

Seated at the opposite end of the table from Adeline, Yvette was on Brock's right. He moved his leg, brushing her knee. Then he curled his foot, minus his deck shoe, around her calf, letting her feel the warmth of his toes in an intimate gesture.

She wanted to smile because it was so damn sexy playing footsy beneath the table. She loved the games he played where no one could see. And she could feel it all. Even deep inside.

For dessert, Olive served Caribbean Black Cake made of

raisins and cherries and other fruit marinated in rum. A mixture of rum and cherry brandy soaked the cake, making a deliciously heady combination. Without fanfare, Olive gave Lorna a special dessert which had no alcohol.

After the cake, which Yvette was sure had gone to her head, she took the bull by the horns, as the old saying went, and invited Lorna for a walk on the beach. "The men can settle by the fire pit and have a drink."

Lorna smiled. "That would be wonderful."

No one invited Adeline to do anything. She rose from her chair, saying, "I'm tired. It's been a long day. I'm going to bed."

Did Yvette imagine the sigh of relief that everyone let out as Adeline climbed the stairs?

Brock said nothing about her invitation to Lorna, but when she looked at him, there was a promise in his eyes. Then he rose and clapped his brother on the back. "Let's do as Yvette suggests and have a drink by the fire pit."

He grabbed a decanter along with two glasses off the sideboard. Before they departed, Ethan said, "Dad, is it okay if we all take the Jeep into town tonight to do a little barhopping and dancing?"

Brock smiled, a twinkle in his eye. "Of course."

Yvette wondered if he was thinking how much easier it would be to sneak into her room with the kids in town. She kissed the girls, then looped her arm through Lorna's and led her across the screened-in porch to the beach.

Stars studded the night sky like a carpet of jewels. The warm, slightly humid Bahamas air bathed Yvette's skin. The real humidity would come in a few months.

Her arm linked with Lorna's, the younger woman's baby bump led the way across the sand.

"I'm so glad we've all come on this vacation," Yvette said,

waiting for the right opening. It wouldn't do to rush into things.

"We should do this every year," Lorna agreed. "I want my baby—" She put a hand on her belly. "—to know all her aunts and uncles and cousins."

Was it meaningful that Lorna hadn't mentioned Adeline? "Maybe even half yearly," Yvette added, already warming to the idea. "Like a hiking trip in Tahoe." She would love to sneak off for a hike with Brock.

Lorna put her hand over Yvette's. "That's a fabulous idea. We could go camping. In Yosemite. Or even in Big Basin over the Santa Cruz Mountains. That would be so amazing." Her smile lit up her face even brighter than the stars. "We can toast marshmallows over a fire."

Adeline surely wouldn't go along. Maybe there was a devious method to Lorna's ideas. "I love it. You tell Trevor, and I'll tell—" she cut herself off. Of course, she'd been about to say she'd tell Brock, as if they were a couple.

Lorna didn't seem to notice as she went on. "I used to go camping with my parents when I was a kid. I loved it. I didn't have to take a bath for days."

They laughed together.

Lorna hadn't been raised in an exclusive, pampered environment. She was like Yvette, coming from a middle-class family. Lorna had been a paralegal at a law firm Donnelley Shipping used. The way Trevor told it, he'd fallen head over heels the moment he saw her. And Lorna was pretty without the showy elegance of the upper crust. She was just as pretty on the inside. Adeline had put up a fight, of course, but Trevor was old enough to know what he wanted. And nothing Adeline said swayed him. They'd been married for four years now.

Yvette decided this was her opening. "Camping is an

amazing idea." Then she added, as if the thought had only just occurred to her, "Adeline definitely won't come along."

"No, she won't go in for camping." Lorna's sweet laughter filled the night. "That's part of the appeal."

Oh yes, this was her opportunity. "You know, whatever Adeline says to you, you just need to take it with a grain of salt." She wondered what the old saying actually meant.

But Lorna knew what she was talking about. "You mean when she picks on me about my baby weight?"

Yvette gave her a friendly hip bump. "That's exactly what I mean. And whatever else she says when nobody's around."

Lorna patted her hand. "Trevor warned me what she was like before we even got married. He wanted to live somewhere in the city, or maybe down on the Peninsula, in our own house or apartment or condo."

"But you didn't?" Yvette was astounded.

Lorna was shaking her head. "I loved that old house from the moment we stepped inside it. I don't mind living there."

"But Adeline?" Yvette said with a trace of wonder in her voice.

"I know how to deal with her. I just ignore everything nasty." Lorna stopped herself there. "No, not nasty, because she's never truly nasty to me. But every subtle dig that she makes, I just ignore it."

Yvette stopped walking to turn and stare into Lorna's face. She'd never managed to ignore a single dig Adeline ever made. Perhaps the woman had been worse to her than to Lorna. It was hard to say. Maybe she had just been much more thin-skinned, especially when Pierce had never supported her.

"My doctor tells me my weight is perfect for the month of pregnancy I'm in." Lorna rubbed her belly. She was beautiful in the moonlight, her hand a sweet caress over her baby. "But I still don't want to gain too much. Adeline's right, it'll be harder to take it off. But Trevor is so supportive. He wants to have it out with Adeline and tell her to bug off." She laughed softly. "But I told him I'm handling it just fine."

"You're amazing. I never handled it."

"Maybe Adeline has mellowed with age," Lorna mused. "Or maybe..." Her voice trailed off.

"Or maybe it's just me she doesn't like."

Yvette knew that was on Lorna's mind, but the woman said, "I don't mean it in a bad way. She's focused. I've never seen anyone so focused in my entire life. And yes, I think she takes things out on you especially." Yvette was technically old enough to be this woman's mother. And yet Lorna had so much more confidence than Yvette had at her age. Maybe it was being pregnant and having to get married to Pierce amid Adeline's relentless opposition.

"You don't need to worry about me." Then Lorna hugged Yvette, holding her tight for a moment. "But thank you so much for thinking about my feelings." She stepped back, her hands still on Yvette's shoulders. "I hope we can be friends. I'd like a friend like you."

Because she was rarely at the house and also went to work with the men every day, Yvette hadn't spent much time with Lorna. And now she smiled. "I'd very much like a friend like you too."

THE FIRE PIT WAS BLAZING. BUT BEFORE EITHER TREVOR OR he had even poured the brandy from the decanter Brock had brought out, Olive appeared from the house. "I've made drinks for you. This is our specialty. A Bahama Mama." She set a tray on the small nearby table. "It has both dark and light rum, with a hint of Kahlúa, giving it a lovely coffee flavor. Then there is fresh squeezed orange and lemon juice, along with pineapple juice." A cherry bobbed in each glass. She pushed one drink away from the others. "And for the mother-to-be, I made a special concoction that will taste almost the same, but without the alcohol."

"Thank you, Olive," Brock said before she melted once again into the house.

They retrieved two glasses and held them up to toast, their bare feet propped on the stone edge of the fire pit. "Cheers. Here's to a fabulous vacation," Brock said.

He was having the time of his life, crawling into Yvette's bed, waking up with her in the morning.

"You should marry her."

Brock felt his heart pound almost right out of his chest. He turned on his brother. "What the hell do you mean?"

"It's so freaking obvious driving with you two every day into work. You're totally besotted with each other. Just get it over with and tell her how you feel. I'm sure she feels the same way."

So his brother didn't know they were lovers. But he knew they were hiding big feelings. And maybe this was why he'd brought up the subject of Yvette's dating while they were on horseback.

"Your mother," Brock said harshly, "would have a heart attack."

Trevor turned to him. "What Adeline thinks doesn't matter. It's what you and Yvette want."

Unable to bring himself to say that Yvette was the problem, he felt Trevor out. "But she was our brother's wife."

"Pierce has been gone for five years."

So Trevor didn't care about that. "But you know how families can screw with a relationship," he said, realizing he was parroting Yvette.

"Your family won't care one damn bit. Your sons love Yvette. And her daughters feel the same way about you. It wouldn't bother me one damn bit either. And when you think about Adeline, ask yourself if her opinion is as important as she seems to think it is."

Brock watched the two dark shapes out on the beach, one obviously pregnant, the other lithe and sexy even at this distance. His guts twisted because he wanted her so badly. He loved her so freaking much.

Then he said to Trevor, "Adeline poisoned what Pierce and Yvette had together. What makes you think she wouldn't do exactly the same thing now?" He was admitting something to his brother. Something huge.

But Trevor shrugged. "She can only ruin it if you let her. Just like she can only ruin what Lorna and I have if we let her. But we don't. When she pulls a stunt, we laugh about it. Maybe you need to think about doing the same thing."

He wondered if he could explain that to Yvette. He wondered if she could ever let go of the past. Probably not. Adeline had not only ruined her marriage, she'd poisoned Yvette's belief in true love.

If truth be told, he wasn't sure their love was big enough to overcome it. At least not for her.

Then he realized they were both watching Yvette as Trevor said, "You don't have to admit it to me, brother. You don't even have to say anything to Yvette right now. But you do need to think about it. Because one of these days, and probably sooner rather than later, she's going to need someone. And I'm just saying that you need to make sure that someone is you."

Oh yeah, this was why Trevor had talked about Yvette while they were riding. Maybe he already had this speech planned. And Brock's heart punched all the way into his throat, choking him.

Because if she ever left him, if she ever wanted to choose

a man she could have an out-in-the-open relationship with, it would be over his dead body.

BROCK WOKE BEFORE THE SUN ROSE, WITH ONLY THE slightest lightening of the sky. The warmth of her in his arms could have been his undoing. Maybe it *was* his undoing. Because he needed this to go on forever. After his talk with Trevor last night, he would never be satisfied with anything less.

And in his heart, he knew that eventually, she wouldn't be satisfied with what they had now.

He could accomplish it by breaking completely with his mother. He could move out of the house, get his own flat, refuse her calls until she was the one who relented. But he knew Adeline. She was the most stubborn person on the planet. She would never forgive him.

And despite how cool she could sometimes be, she was still his mother and part of him still loved her. The danger was that if he broke with her, he might lose his sons too. Although that danger was far less for him than for Yvette and her daughters. Perhaps her thinking was infecting him.

He wanted Yvette. He wanted his family. He wanted everything just the way it was now, except that they would be openly together. And that was the conundrum. How could he have everything? He snuggled her closer in his arms. As if that would keep her there forever. She sighed, nestling deeper into him, on the edge of sleep, but not quite waking yet. He enjoyed these long moments of closeness with the memories of last night in his mind. The touches, the kisses, the caresses, the feel of her body tight around him.

He was already hardening against her backside.

Choices. His other choice was to convince Yvette to

ignore all his mother's barbs. They didn't have to live in the house. Yvette never even had to go there. But he understood her fear that Adeline would somehow turn the girls against her. But did Adeline have that much sway?

*You should marry her.*

Trevor's words echoed in his mind. God, what he wouldn't give for that. But would he give up sons? He couldn't dwell on that. The answer was too heartbreaking. And he didn't want to choose. He didn't want Yvette to choose.

Maybe there was a third choice. He could try talking Adeline around. He could be the one to threaten to take the boys away from her. To take Yvette's girls away.

But none of those solutions would be satisfactory. He knew that in his gut.

The sun tipped over the horizon, spreading its wings of color across the sky.

Yvette stirred in his arms. "It's sunrise," she whispered. "You better go before anyone else gets up."

"Not just yet." His words wafted his warm breath across her ear. He felt her shiver. He knew her signals. And he scented her arousal. "What do you want to do today?"

"Whatever the kids want to do. I like spending time with them."

He trailed his fingers up her torso, cupped her breast. "We can talk about it at breakfast." He dropped his head to kiss the fragrant skin of her neck.

"We don't have time," she said, already arching against him.

He rubbed, twirled, pinched lightly, and brought her nipple to a tight peak. "We have time. And I love a little quickie."

He'd once made love to her in the backseat of an airport limo, all the curtains closed, on the way from Atlanta's Harts-field airport to the hotel.

She moaned. "Then you need to make it real quick."

And he did, fast, hard, and mind-blowing.

Then she pushed him out of the bed.

He laughed, though his heart was still pounding, his body still quaking, his mind still reeling.

And he vowed to himself right then that he would find a way to make Yvette his forever.

## 12

Yvette concentrated on her breakfast the following morning. God. The food. It was as delicious as making love with Brock. Closing her eyes, she savored the flavors bursting on her tongue. They dined on delicious banana fritters, as well as plantain tarts, which were like a crusted popover filled with smashed plantains, the fruit a bright red. Augmenting the meal, Olive offered them a sweet and creamy cornmeal porridge made with condensed milk and cinnamon, sort of like the Cream of Wheat Yvette sometimes had at home.

"Did you all have a wonderful evening in town?" Yvette asked, mainly for Jodi and Kacey, but her gaze flashed over all the young people.

"Hell yes," Darryl jumped in first. "We—"

With an elbow to Darryl's ribs, Ethan cut off whatever he'd been about to say.

A smile creased Brock's lips. "I take it you did things we adults wouldn't approve of."

Malcolm and Ethan both waved their hands. "Of course not." The slight blurriness in their eyes attested to a minimizing of what they'd done last night. But they were all adults. Neither she nor Brock, not even Adeline, had the right to say a thing.

Though Adeline tried anyway. "I hope you have all your faculties around you when you do whatever you've got planned today. Of course, count me out." She glanced at Lorna. "Perhaps Lorna and I will go for a drive."

Lorna didn't so much as groan, and Yvette wondered if that's exactly what her sister-in-law wanted. Maybe she thought the more time she spent with Adeline, the more she would ingratiate herself. And that was probably a good thing.

"Speaking of which," Brock raised his voice over the table's chatter. "What do you want to do today? It's Christmas Eve, so let's do something special. Even if it's a warm Christmas, not a white Christmas."

"Is anything even open today?" Yvette asked. They hadn't talked about that this morning. They'd been thinking about other things.

"I checked. Open today, closed tomorrow."

Malcolm jumped in. "Zip-lining. I looked it up, and you take a chairlift up through the jungle, then there's like seven platforms to get you back down through the canopy."

"But the waterfalls sound pretty awesome too," Garth said. He looked at Jodi seated next to him, and she nodded.

"All right, let's vote." Brock waved a hand. "Zip-lining?" Hands went up. "Waterfalls?" Jodi and Garth raised their hands, but the others outvoted them.

Brock looked at Yvette and Trevor, neither of whom hadn't taken a vote. "What about you?"

Yvette answered quickly, "I'll do whatever the majority chooses." Just as she'd told Brock this morning, before that deliciously sexy quickie, she just wanted to be with the girls. Brock, of course, would do whatever she did.

And they'd have another glorious day together.

Trevor smiled, taking Lorna's hand in his, kissing her knuckles. "I'll stay with my wife." Even across the table, Yvette saw the stars in his eyes.

She wanted Brock to look at her that way right now. If she'd let him, he would. But she couldn't. Not with Adeline here.

"In fact," Trevor added, "I'll take you ladies for a drive around the island."

"That's so thoughtful of you, dear." Irritation bristled in Adeline's eyes, despite the words. Lorna could no longer be her victim with Trevor there to intervene.

Although Yvette's talk with Lorna last night had shown that the woman could handle her mother-in-law.

"Then it's decided," Brock said. "Zip-lining today, and the day after Christmas, we'll do the waterfalls." He glanced at Garth and Jodi, and they nodded agreement.

The result made everyone happy. Including Darryl.

The makeup of the two parties suited Yvette. The kids would naturally gravitate together, and even as much as she enjoyed her daughters' company, that would still leave her and Brock with more time together.

WITH TEN OF THEM, THEY DROVE THREE JEEPS THROUGH the small towns. Here on the wet side of the island, the foliage sometimes seemed to grow right into the houses.

Over the Jeep's roaring engine and the sound of the wind, Yvette called to Brock, "It looks like all the houses are under construction. And yet it seems like people are living in them."

Brock noted that in every house nestled close to the road-side, one room was of plain cinderblocks and lacked any windows. He called back, the wind through the Jeep making it necessary to shout, "I read that the taxation is based on completed construction. So they all leave one incomplete room to avoid the higher taxes."

Yvette's laughter curled around his insides. He wanted to hear that laugh for the rest of his life.

"Of course you would have read that somewhere," she shouted. "And I love it. A nice way to get around the government."

They arrived at the park fifteen minutes later. The kids tumbled out of the Jeeps, racing up the stone steps as if they were all under the age of ten. Brock stayed behind, helping Yvette out of the Jeep even though she needed no help. But he wanted the excuse to touch her. And that touch was electric. Even though he'd made love to her twice in the night, then again in the early morning, he wanted her again. Right here under the jungle canopy.

He would have leaned in for a surreptitious kiss, but Yvette gave him the evil eye, glancing over her shoulder, in case one of the kids had turned back.

"No one's looking," he muttered.

But she fended him off with a hand on his chest. "If you wait now," she said in a seductive voice that made him hard, "you'll get double later."

He laughed even as he ached. "That definitely sweetens the pot. And worth a bit of blue balls now."

She pushed past him, laughing.

They joined their children, pretending they were just the slowpoke old folks.

On his phone, he pulled up the tickets and waited for the attendant to scan them all.

A lovely young woman with dark skin, she smiled widely after the task was done. "Hello and Merry Christmas. Thank you so much for joining us on your holiday. Since there are so many of you, we will take you all in one group. I am Nacheline, and I will be one of your guides. Now please follow me."

Her English was excellent. Brock had found that most people here on the island spoke excellent English.

Christmas ornaments hung from the palm trees and foliage surrounding the hut she led them to. And carols played softly from a speaker mounted above them. But it was warm and slightly muggy, nothing like the Christmases of his past.

No. This one was better. He felt almost as if it were his first Christmas with Yvette.

"I am glad none of you are wearing flip-flops or open-toed shoes," Nacheline said. "And those of you with long hair, please tie it back. We do not wish for you to get it caught in the zip line." The young women obeyed, and Nacheline went on. "Now, if you line up, we will hand out your gear."

Two other attendants assisted Nacheline, a young man handing Brock a harness, while the other provided one to Yvette. The kids were already scrambling into theirs as Brock stepped into the contraption. But Yvette looked nonplussed as to what to do. He'd been zip-lining before, and after buckling his harness, he said to her, "I can help."

Ahh, the perfect cover for touching her wherever he wanted. She put a hand on his shoulder as he bent down, holding the harness for her to step into. Once her feet were both on the ground again, he slowly stood, dragging the harness up her body. He almost laughed when he realized how fast his breath had become. Standing tall again, he noticed the rapid rise and fall of her chest and knew she felt the same. With her arms in the harness, he busied himself buckling her up, his fingers brushing her breasts until her nipples peaked. She licked her lips, and if ever there was an invitation, that was it.

As he leaned in to strap on her helmet, though she needed no help with that, he whispered, "You'll pay for that tonight." And he shot her a wicked grin.

She laughed, perhaps a little too loudly. Jodi turned to look at her, and Yvette covered their display by saying, "This will be so much fun."

Following a group of noisy tourists, their guide, Nacheline, led them along a steep path to the cable cars that would take them up to the zip line. The young woman turned. "Be sure to look at the gardens we have here. You might even see a python in the bushes or the trees."

The kids naturally turned that way, but Yvette clung to his arm. "You'll protect me, won't you?"

God, how he loved her flirting. Nacheline said to Yvette, "You need not wear the helmet until we get to the actual zip lines. The cable cars are perfectly safe."

Yvette took it off. Brock had only put it on so he could touch her, and he murmured close to her ear, "Now I'll have another excuse to touch you."

"There's one," Darryl called out, grabbing the railing and pointing.

A fat python coiled at the base of a tree, having found a sunny spot, its body as thick as his arm. Darryl picked up a broken branch from beside the path and once again leaned over the railing as if he intended to poke the snake.

Nacheline shouted at him, her voice sharp, "Never poke a python. And get back on this side of the railing."

Brock wanted to smack the young man upside the head, but Nacheline's voice was chastisement enough, and seemed to embarrass even Darryl. He snapped the stick over his knee, throwing it on the ground before he marched up the hill.

Jodi muttered, "Idiot." And Garth added, "What a dick."

Brock heartily agreed. But Kacey rushed to join her boyfriend and furious whispers ensued between them. Brock hoped, as he was sure Yvette did, that Kacey was chastising for him for his reckless behavior.

The lift was a cross between a cable car and a chairlift, the car open air, with three rows, enough to carry six. Two groups waited ahead of them, and Yvette stepped over to photograph a cable car coming down. The car swung slightly as it chugged down the hill on the cables, then turned around the small terminus and disgorged its occupants, a mixture of kids and adults, two of the children hooting and saying, "Can we go again? Please, please!"

A man ruffled a blond boy's head. "Maybe another day."

Full once more, the car rumbled up the hill, just as another was coming down through the jungle canopy. The surrounding vegetation was lush, with blooming rhododendrons and magnolias.

Nacheline followed his gaze. "Something is always blooming up here. All year round. It is a beautiful spot."

"It's gorgeous," Yvette said. "And it seems like you have a lot of tourists."

The girl smiled. "This is our busiest time of year. But during the rainy season and the heat of the summer, everything calms down."

Brock could imagine. The summer humidity and heat would make the day untenable for northerners.

Finally their turn, Ethan and Francine, Malcolm and Iris, along with Kacey and Darryl, scrambled onto the cable car, and Nacheline said, "We will get on the next one and meet the rest of your party at the top, where we can all do the zip line together."

Off they went, Darryl sitting in the back and punching his fist in the air. "Too bad, suckers!"

When the next car arrived, Garth and Jodi sat together in the two front seats, leaving the back for Brock and Yvette. Nacheline took the middle seat.

"Are you the only one guiding us on the zip line?" Brock asked.

She shook her head, smiling a perfect, bright smile. "Oh no. You will find guides on each of the platforms."

Fragrant blooms filled the jungle canopy. The greens were so green, the pinks of the flowers brilliant. He turned to Yvette and thought the vivid jungle was almost as beautiful as her.

Nacheline jutted her chin beyond them. "Look at the scene behind you."

Both he and Yvette turned. The ocean was a surreal aquamarine, another mountain below them outlined against its crystal waters. A massive cruise ship steamed by, much too big to dock in the island's small harbor. Puffy white clouds drifted across the sky, hiding the sun for a moment, then moving on to allow its brilliance to shine again.

"It's unbelievable." Yvette held up her phone to capture photo after photo, finally turning the camera on Brock and taking one of his face. "Look at the ocean. I want a profile."

As soon as he heard the shutter click, he pulled out his own phone. "Let me do the same with you."

As she stared out at the amazing colors of the Caribbean Sea, he snapped a picture that made his heart flutter. She made his heart flutter with everything she did.

When they reached the top, the rest of their group waited at the upper turnaround.

"We have a quarter-mile hike to the first platform," Nacheline informed them. "It's just down the trail." She pointed the way.

Darryl bounded ahead before she stopped him. "I will take the lead." Her voice held a sharp edge, as if, after the python incident, she'd figured out Darryl's nature and didn't like it.

The overhanging trees covered them as they walked the narrow path, and without the clamor of the cable car, Brock heard birdsong in the branches, even over the jingle of their harnesses. The snug fit between his legs made him think sensual thoughts about Yvette. Having taken the last position, with her in front of him, he enjoyed the sway of her beautiful rear end. People always added *for a woman of her age* after a description of a lady passed her fiftieth year, as if she was somehow less beautiful than someone ten or twenty years younger. But Yvette was toned, her calves taut as she walked in her sturdy boots. There was no *for a woman of her age* about her. She was flat-out beautiful. She always had been, always would be. Especially to him.

Five minutes later, they reached the first platform, where two sturdy young men helped the girls climb the steps. Once they were all on the platform, Nacheline stood on the block from which they would launch themselves. In a raised voice, she said, "First, we will give you a short list of safety instructions."

At the groans from the younger generation, she asked, "How many of you have been on a zip line before?"

Everyone raised their hand except Yvette. Brock had taken all five, his kids and Yvette's, to the Mount Hermon zip line in the Santa Cruz Mountains, then the steam train at Roaring Camp after that.

Yvette hadn't gone on that trip, but he couldn't remember why.

Nacheline didn't single her out. "The safety training is for everyone, not just those of you who have never done it before. Everyone needs a refresher."

She went through the same the drill he remembered from Mount Hermon: wait until the previous person is done before starting, lift your legs high before touching down on the opposite platform, don't let go or you'll start to rotate, and so on.

She finished with, "Now that you are all up to speed—" Brock realized she must have learned a lot of American colloquialisms because she used them often. "—put on your helmets. Who would like to go first?"

Yvette secured her helmet with no help from him this time—too bad—and Jodi turned to her. "You should go first, Mom, since you've never done it before."

Yvette backed up, bumping into him and holding out her hands as if she were warding off Jodi. "I'll watch some other people do it before I get up there."

Darryl called out, "Chicken."

If anyone else had said it, Brock would have laughed at the good-natured ribbing, but from Darryl, it made him want to smack the boy.

But Yvette wasn't cowed. "You go first, Darryl, so I can watch your expertise."

Darryl smirked, completely missing the sarcasm in her voice, and jumped onto the block. "Don't mind if I do."

The guys hooked him in and he launched. It was a straight shot down the steep slope to a massive tree at the other end. He shouted all the way. Letting both hands go and spreading his legs, he twirled, flying faster and faster. It was exactly what Nacheline told him not to do. But of course, Darryl did whatever he wanted.

Jodi muttered, "What an ass."

Two guides stood on the platform at the other end, and he barreled right into them, his momentum taking him past the block where he should have stopped. But the two were seasoned, and they grabbed him, setting him on his feet.

"I'll go next," Kacey said. "Since Darryl's already there."

Her flight was more sedate, though her delirious laughter filled the canopy. Yvette snapped pictures as she went, then zipped her phone back into her pocket so it wouldn't fall when she was flying down the line.

"I'll do it next," Brock said before anyone could step in.

"You come after me," he said, jutting his chin at Yvette. He wanted to be on the other end to catch her if she needed him.

She smiled. "That would be great. Then I can take a picture of everyone else coming in." Her smile grew. "Instead of having all your backsides as you go down."

The family chuckled with her.

Brock got up on the block and launched. It was an amazing ride. Flying through the air, the wind beat at his face, the jungle sounds pounded against his ears. And Yvette called out, "Go, Brock!"

He'd forgotten the delirium of flying suspended only by the harness, the sense of being airborne as if he were a bird in flight, the sense of being secure yet nothing between him and the ground but air.

All too soon it was over, and he landed on the block, the two guides helping him unhook his harness from the line. He stepped out of the way, turning to wait for Yvette, needing to watch her sail through the air as if she were flying right into his arms.

## ❧ 13 ❧

Yvette climbed onto the wooden block as if it were an executioner's stone.

*Don't be ridiculous*, she whispered inside her mind. She would not be afraid. It was just a zip line. And Brock was waiting for her.

But she couldn't help the trepidation that made her heart beat faster and her palms sweat. She wondered if she could hold on to the trolley handle at the same time. Not that it would matter if her hands slipped, since she was still attached to the line.

Nacheline said softly, so no one else could hear, "You have this. Enjoy the ride. By the time you get to the second line, you will love it."

Yvette launched, the woman giving her a slight push. She stifled the scream when she went airborne, feeling as if she were falling until the zip line took control. The jungle had been slightly muggy, but as she flew through the air, the breeze blew cool across her face.

A kind of euphoria took hold of her, and she leaned back to gaze into the canopy overhead. Spots of blue sky and white clouds seemed to rain down on her through the leaves. It was a freedom she'd never known, and it seemed to go on and on, even though when she'd watched the others, especially Brock, they'd reached the other side so quickly.

She heard him calling to her. "You go, girl." As if she were a teenager. As if she were her daughters' ages. As if she still had her whole life ahead of her.

Then she looked down at the tree and the platform coming up at her.

A sliver of fear took over again. What if she went in wrong? What if she didn't land on the block, and she broke her ankle or her leg?

Then it was so close she no longer had time to think. Her feet miraculously landed on the block, and the two young men steadied her and unhooked her. She almost fell into Brock's arms.

She would have thrown herself at him, let him wrap her up in his arms, hold her. Kiss her. Only at the last moment, when she was inches from him, did she remember Darryl and Kacey on the platform, and all the others looking on.

They were all cheering her, even Darryl. But it was Brock's smile that curled around her. She smiled in return. "I did it."

"I got a picture of you doing it," he said with a smile. She thought of the subtle sexual innuendo in that. The picture of her in his mind as he made love to her.

As Jodi started down the line, she wiped it all from her mind. She shouldn't think about that now. But she smiled to herself. Because she would think about it later tonight.

Jodi squealed all the way down. It was only at the end, after taking so long to get her phone out of her zipped pocket, that Yvette snapped a picture of her daughter having the time of her life. Garth came next. His hoots and hollers filling the canopy and then he landed, throwing himself at

Jodi and twirling with her in his arms. "That was so *effing* amazing."

Jodi bounced on the balls of her feet. "Totally."

Yvette looked at Brock, knowing that they used *effing* instead of the *F-word* for her sake.

Standing next to him, she whispered, "Oh yeah, it was *effing* amazing."

His muscles bunched, and she felt his need to throw his arms around her. If they were alone, he would have done it. But there was always that hesitancy between them whenever they were around other people, always making sure they never touched if anyone else could see, just those sexy surreptitious brushes of their hands or legs under the table. Or when he buckled her into a zip-lining harness.

It was all because of her fear of being discovered. They couldn't even hug the way they had before all this started, like brother-in-law and sister-in-law. Like she hugged Trevor. Like Jodi and Garth could dance around the platform after a fabulous flight down the zip line. She and Brock couldn't have that. And yes, that was because of her too. Her and her fears.

As much as she loved his arms around her at night, as much as she loved his kiss, his touch, the stroke of his body inside hers, she missed those familial touches.

And instead of touching him the way she craved, she joined Kacey and Jodi, shouting encouragement to the boys and their girlfriends as, one after another, they launched themselves into the air and flew down the zip line.

"Oh my God," Yvette said. "I should have gone with all of you when you went to Mount Hermon." Her need to distance herself from Adeline had made her miss so much. She'd even distanced herself from her nephews.

This time, Brock touched her, just a hand on her shoulder, but the heat of his palm made her imagine everything he'd do to her tonight. "We'll do it again. And this time, you'll come."

He could have been speaking of tonight.

Jodi punched the air. "You go, Mom. Let's do it."

They continued down each zip line, sometimes with her going before Brock, sometimes after, but always together. She loved the pictures she took of his beatific face as he flew down the line. The experience was exhilarating, the sky above, the earth beneath, the trees surrounding her, the bird calls, the scent of flowers, the feeling of flying and never having to stop.

As they worked their way steadily downhill, Darryl always did something a little over the top. She'd learned that was his nature. He needed the attention. If her daughter stayed with him, she hoped he'd curb that need for attention. Oddly enough, Kacey merely smiled at his antics. She never berated him for being an idiot or unsafe. Yvette realized that wasn't like her daughter either. Kacey wasn't weak. So why did she want to believe in Darryl so much?

It was an unanswerable question. Their relationship would have to play itself out. And when it ended—Yvette didn't even feel disloyal hoping that it would end—she would be there for Kacey.

They were on the sixth zip line, and Brock had gone before her. It wasn't as steep as the previous ones, and though she'd pushed off as heartily as she had from the other platforms, she didn't feel as if she had the same momentum. Sure enough, she stopped short of the platform, hanging there, nothing moving, and she called out. "How do I get down now?"

The guide on the platform said, "Turn around and grab the cable." Brock added, "Just pull yourself in hand over hand."

She did as instructed, turning herself around so she faced the platform she'd jumped from, putting her hands up to the cables. And those steel rollers. What if she slipped, or she moved too fast and they rolled right over her fingers? They'd cut them off.

Then Darryl—of course it was Darryl—called out, "Don't be weenie, Yvette."

She was not a weenie. And when she got down to the platform, she might have to bop the kid on his nose. But she pulled herself hand over hand down to the platform, never letting the wheels chop off her fingers. The two guides helped her turn around, unhooked her, and hugged her after she jumped down.

Then she stalked to Darryl and poked him in the chest. "Who are you calling a weenie, Mister?"

"Well, it got you down, didn't it?" he quipped.

She ended up laughing. Because she had to admit his taunt had gotten her moving.

Flouncing to Kacey, she threw her arms around her, hugging her as they jumped around the platform. Then she pulled Jodi into their hug. And God, it felt so good to be with her girls. To be with her family.

To be with Brock.

YVETTE'S EXHILARATION TURNED HIS BODY HARD. THERE was something about her utter enjoyment, of zip lining, of being with the girls, with family, even being with him, that made him want her so badly he could have dragged her off into the jungle. Of course he wouldn't. But he could dream about it.

And a plan took shape in his mind.

With the final line, they flew into a clearing near the bottom where they'd stepped onto the cable car. Brock zipped before Yvette, and as she soared down to him, the mental picture of her joy burned itself forever into his mind.

The guides steadied her as she landed—though she was getting quite good at it and needed little help—then let her step away.

After only a short walk to the hut where they'd received their gear, Nacheline said, "And now you may take off all the harnesses. I hope you had fun."

"We did," Ethan called out, the other kids adding their voices to the clamor.

Brock had already shed his harness, and he reached for Yvette. It was another perfect excuse. No one was looking. They were all busy removing their own harnesses.

Smiling, he said softly, "Here, let me help you." And he touched her liberally.

"You shouldn't do that," she hissed, but he heard the husky note of desire in her voice. She wanted him to touch her, especially with her blood high after the exhilaration of the zip line.

As he bent over to unclasp the hooks, he used the excuse to whisper in her ear, "I want you so bad right now. You better be ready for tonight."

Her breathing ratcheted up, and he scented how much she wanted it too. But she pushed him away, saying with a glacial tone, "I'm fine. I can do it myself."

He saw the fire in her eyes and knew she'd use it on him tonight.

He couldn't wait.

It was only then that he noticed Jodi's gaze on them. And he realized he was pushing the limit. He needed to cool it, at least in front of the kids.

Jodi couldn't know they were lovers. But maybe she suspected an attraction. It wasn't horror in her gaze, merely curiosity. He could live with that. Maybe he could even get his niece on his side.

With all the harnesses collected, Nacheline twirled on her

heel. "Follow me. You now get a drink of your choice, and you will taste test some products we sell in our store. And a Merry Christmas to all of you."

Brock hung back, letting Yvette precede him, and Jodi looped an arm through her mother's. He heard her say, "Wasn't it awesome, Mom?"

Yvette skipped a few steps with her. "That was so amazing. I can hardly wait for the waterfalls tomorrow. I've never had so much fun in my life."

Jodi hip-bumped her. "We should do this kind of stuff more often. And I'll teach you how to ride a horse when we're back home at the big house, I promise. You'll love it. And there's lots of other fun things we could do around the Bay Area."

Yvette said, "I'd love that." Emphasis on *love*.

"They're expecting a superbloom this year out at Carrizo Plain National Monument. You'd love all the flowers. You should come down for that. It's pretty close to school. And San Luis Obispo has some great restaurants."

"Thank you for inviting me, sweetheart. I'd love that." Brock made out the gratitude in her voice. What college kid wanted their mom to come down just to hang out? But that was Jodi.

The girls went to Cal Poly in San Luis Obispo. With the family's money, they could have afforded a more exclusive school. Yvette would have taken the money if she had to, but Cal Poly had a well-respected interior design school, which was what Kacey had wanted to do. Their business administration school was also highly respected, and Jodi had chosen a concentration in accounting. He hoped she'd come into the company, but that would be her choice.

Though his sons had gone to Berkeley, there was nothing wrong with Cal Poly. If they'd wanted to be doctors or lawyers, it would have been a different decision for Kacey and

Jodi. But as it was, they'd chosen well. And they hadn't needed to dip into the trust funds their grandfather had set up for them. Yvette had used money out of her 401(k), which is what she'd been saving it for. The trusts were for the girls to use as they wished after they'd graduated. Then the choice of how to spend it would be theirs.

When they entered the open-air shop, the kids, including Jodi, headed to the bar on the back patio. A small Christmas tree stood on the cobblestones, and Christmas carols played softly. They seemed to cater to Americans escaping the winter cold.

Instead of rushing to the bar like the kids, Yvette sauntered through the shop—of course Brock followed her—examining the delicacies she could sample. She stopped by a basket of tortilla chips with three bowls in front.

The young woman standing beside the table said, "This is banana ketchup." Then she waved a finger as if she were chiding them. "Please do not turn up your nose." Her use of the terms was spot on. "We put banana ketchup on everything here." She pointed to the tortilla chips. "Try. I promise you will never go back to American ketchup again."

The side of Yvette's mouth quirked. "I'm game if you are."

When Brock nodded, she dipped into the chips, then scooped out the banana ketchup. Not a tiny morsel, but something that truly gave her a good taste of it. She chewed thoughtfully, the crunch of tortilla chips audible. And finally, she closed her eyes, a moan falling from her lips.

It was enough to send his body into orbit. She made that exact sound when he had his mouth buried against her, or his body filling her.

She glanced at him with a twinkle in her eye, and he wondered if she'd made that sound on purpose just to drive him wild.

She held out a chip dipped in the ketchup. "Oh, you've got to try this." Then she fed him.

Christ, it was sexy. He wanted this all the time. He wanted to be with her on these fun excursions, not just in the middle of the night, not just on business trips. But all the time.

The ketchup burst with flavor on his tongue, as piquant as her luscious taste. Sweeter than ketchup, with a hint of banana, the condiment was an odd but delightful combination.

He let the smile grow on his face. "That," he said, elongating the word, "is delicious." He looked at Yvette, long, hard. "And I need it again. Over and over."

He didn't look to see if the young woman blushed, or even glanced their way. But she would have to recognize the intimacy in his tone and the sensuality of his words. And Yvette blushed.

"We'll take five bottles. I'm pretty sure we can't get banana ketchup back home."

"Thank you, sir." The young woman smiled as wide as the moon. "It is on the shelf right over there." She pointed. "I can put them behind the counter if you would like to get your drink."

"That would be perfect. Thank you."

He wanted to take Yvette's hand, walk with her to the bar. But most of the kids already had their glasses, and they would notice whatever he did.

Christ. He didn't care, but Yvette would.

Jodi watched them as if she'd seen the byplay over the ketchup tasting. Was that knowledge in her gaze? But she said nothing.

He knew instinctively that Yvette would hate the speculation. It wasn't cool to keep pushing it. Especially since it was against her wishes. And he backed off.

"You guys have to try that banana ketchup," Yvette enthused, as if she were trying to hide her embarrassment. And Brock added, "Yeah. It's tasty."

"Ewwe," Francine said, and plugged her nose.

But Ethan told her, "Listen to Dad. He always knows about the good stuff."

Brock ordered an alcoholic passionfruit punch. And even after telling himself he needed to back off, he couldn't help leaning closer and saying softly to Yvette, "Passionfruit. How appropriate."

The concoction was delicious, with the tang of rum. The drinks weren't strong, and they'd all be safe to drive home. "Can we get the passionfruit juice here?" he asked the bartender.

The young man smiled. "Of course, sir. And you will want to try the guava juice as well. The guava has been infused with banana. You will enjoy it. Here, let me make the lady's drink with the guava juice." He poured a glass for Yvette, then, with a smile, added, "You should share, taste each drink."

When Brock would have bent down to sip from her drink, Yvette handed it to him. And he groaned the way she had over the banana ketchup. "You're so right. They're both delicious. Thank you for the recommendation," he told the bartender. "We'll need to get a few bottles of this to enjoy while we're here."

"I've seen the bar back at the house," Yvette said. "And we're stocked with enough alcohol for five bottles of juice."

"That's it then," he said to the bartender. "Five bottles of each."

Yvette laughed. "I was joking about the five bottles."

"I wasn't. We'll want this with breakfast."

"Big spender, Dad," Malcolm called, standing at one of the cafe tables.

"You'll be glad I am when I get all this back to the house."

Everyone laughed, agreeing with him.

"Grandmother will refuse to try the banana ketchup," Ethan proclaimed.

"Then there's more for all of us."

And tonight, he had big plans involving passionfruit and the woman who held his heart in her hands.

•.

## ✣ 14 ✣

---

## ADELINE

"Your brother is ignoring me," I drawl.

Trevor shoots me a sideways glance as he drives. I'm almost positive that is a smirk on his face. He drives competently enough. When I got in the car, it wasn't even a question that I should take the front seat and Lorna the back. After all, I'm his mother. She's just the wife.

"You're being ridiculous," he says. "Brock isn't ignoring you." I hear a sigh puff from his lips, as if he's humoring me.

"He hasn't spent a moment with me on this island other than mealtimes. He didn't go shopping the other day. And he didn't want to go for a drive today." And I need to know why, though it wouldn't do to say that aloud.

"He's here to enjoy time with the boys, Mother."

Trevor has a certain way of saying *Mother*. As if he doesn't mean it as a term of respect, but one of sarcasm. Mostly he calls me by my name, which I prefer. Especially when he uses *Mother* in that tone. A mother has favorites. It doesn't make her a bad person or a terrible mother. And Trevor is my least favorite. Perhaps because he was the last of my children. By that time, Harris and I were completely at odds. I'm not sure how we even spawned Trevor. Perhaps I'd had too much to drink one night.

"He's spent enough time with them," I snap. "And they're doing young-people activities. Honestly." I would roll my eyes like one of my granddaughters, but that is beneath me. "I mean, really, horseback riding, zip lining, sliding down waterfalls?"

Trevor says, without even having the nerve to look at me, "If Lorna wasn't pregnant, we'd both be out there doing those fun young-people things too. And you'd be all by yourself."

If he were still a child, I'd smack his bottom for such impudence. As it had been when I was a child, I instructed all the nannies not to hold back. Unfortunately, Trevor had been an exceptionally good boy and never received a spanking. Unlike Pierce, who always tempted a spanking. The thought makes me smile. He'd been such an incorrigible child. I admired that about him. It reminded me of myself when I was a girl.

But all I say is, "They could at least choose group activities that are designed for older adults as well. I've read on my tablet that there is a brilliant bird sanctuary on the coast a few miles from here. We should all go there. I would love to see the birds. I'm sure the children would love it too."

Is that a snicker from the back seat? It can't be Lorna. I'm coming along so well with her training. She'd never do such a thing.

Trevor says, "I'll take you to the bird sanctuary." He glances in the rearview mirror, adjusting it so he can see his wife. "Lorna would love that too."

It's almost as if they're designing a schedule to exclude me from family activities.

I want to know why.

## 15

I t was late. The kids had quieted down. If they were still outside, Yvette couldn't hear them. She sat on the bed, going through the day's photos on her phone. The scenery was gorgeous, the foliage lush, the kids laughing, everyone wearing smiles.

But there was that picture of Brock in profile, the one she'd taken on the tram. He was so beautiful. A man in his prime. Her heart flip-flopped just looking at him. And he was hers.

At least late at night when no one else was around.

As if she'd conjured him, Brock toed open her door, holding a tray laden with bottles and glasses and boxes.

She gaped from her cross-legged position on the bed. "What have you got there?"

Excitement pumped through her the way it did every night, whether or not she knew he was coming. After the magnificent meal Olive had prepared—steamed crawfish, lionfish tacos, and the ubiquitous peas and rice and fried plantains—Yvette had taken a long, luxurious bath. Then she'd smoothed lotion onto her shaved legs, and even that had sent her senses reeling. Now she was wet and ready for him.

But Brock obviously had other things in mind first.

She'd thrown the cover and top sheet off the end of the bed. She wanted the door open for the breeze, though she'd still drawn the curtains in case anyone came close. It would mean she had to be quiet, but sometimes that was sexy too.

He set the tray on the bed, then sat cross-legged, mirroring her position. "I had a chat with the bartender at the zip line store. He told me how to prepare passionfruit punch." He smiled wickedly. "And I thought of a way to use our banana ketchup."

She leaned over the tray, her negligee hanging open for him to see her peaked nipples. She brought it for him, even though she'd told him she always slept naked.

"Witch," he whispered. "You're trying to distract me." He twisted the top off the rum.

She gazed at him innocently. "I see you absconded with a bottle out of the bar. What did Olive have to say about that?"

"She told me to take two."

"Liar." They laughed together. She didn't care what Olive had said. His idea was perfect.

"First, we've got rum punch. One made with guava and one with passionfruit which we'll share." He'd already filled the tumblers with ice, and now he poured a generous jigger of rum, then added the juice. He held up a glass. "You get the passionfruit first." He waggled his eyebrows with deliciously naughty intentions. "Operative word, *passion*."

She touched herself then, fingers to the peaked nipple clearly visible through her lacy lingerie. "I don't think I need any more inducement."

He swore. "We'll never get to the rest of this if you don't stop teasing me."

She laughed, loving the power she had, loving the way he

had to adjust his shorts over his erection. She loved knowing she could do this to him.

And he did it to her just as easily. Because she was wet. But she wanted this, the buildup, the tease.

After a long swallow of the passionfruit punch, the alcohol speeding through her veins made her weak with need. He handed her his glass, a slight lip print on the edge where he'd slugged back a quarter of it. "This is the guava."

They drank together again, feeling the rush of alcohol mixed with desire.

"And here's the rest of our treat." He spilled crackers onto the tray from a box imprinted with the label of the tramway and the zip line. "First, we have crackers." He unwrapped a triangle of cheese, the name written in a language she didn't understand. "The salesgirl told me this is the perfect pairing with the banana ketchup." He tore off the plastic wrapping and scooped out a nugget of the soft cheese with what looked like a butter knife. "Now I'll prepare a cracker for you." His eyes blazed with his desire; the alcohol, the treats, her negligee, her scent. They all had their way with him.

He added a daub of the yellow banana ketchup. "Now open up for me."

She was always open for him, for whatever he wanted. He fed her the cracker, and while he watched her, he prepared another for himself.

Tipping her head back, she savored the sweet ketchup on the creamy cheese, a cross between brie and blue. Even the crunch of the cracker between her teeth seemed erotic.

"Is it good?" he whispered.

"So good," she answered. Because everything about him was so good. So perfect.

He bit into his cracker, crumbs dropping onto the bed. After swallowing the last bite, he asked, "Will you kick me out of bed for eating crackers?"

She answered him with a cheeky smile. "The only way I'll kick you out of bed is if you don't make love to me right this second."

His eyes grew dark and his voice husky. "Christ, you are so tempting."

Then he handed her the passionfruit, tipping the glass when she would have stopped drinking. Then he drank from the guava cup. The weightiness of the alcohol once again blasted through her blood.

And she wanted him. "Are we done yet?" Her words rushed out with all her desire, all her feeling.

"Oh, we are so far from done."

And she would never be done with him. "I meant the cheese and crackers."

"Why?"

"Because I can't wait. I want you now."

He whisked the tray to the floor, and the moment he was back on the bed, she jumped him. She didn't care about cracker crumbs, her fingers tearing at the buttons of his shirt, then she stripped his shorts down. When he was naked, she fell on him, holding his erection in her hand. "All I want to feast on right now is this." Then she took all of him. The only sounds in the room were his groans. And they were like music to her ears.

YVETTE MADE LOVE TO HIM IN EVERY WAY POSSIBLE, WITH her mouth, her tongue, her hands, her lips, and finally, her whole body taking him. They had more of the spiked fruit punch and the crackers slathered with cheese and banana ketchup. After they'd fed each other, he feasted on her. Over and over. They slept, they woke, they made love, and slept again.

Brock wanted this every night of his life. He wanted her. She was so willing to do anything he wanted. If only he could get her to channel all that willingness into taking his hand in marriage.

The day dawned, and it was Christmas.

And that was his Christmas wish, for Yvette to risk Adeline's wrath and marry him.

But he wouldn't hold his breath in case he turned blue and expired before he ever got a ring on her finger.

THE KIDS BURST INTO THE HOUSE, CALLING OUT IN ECHOES of, "Merry Christmas!"

Christmas morning in the tropics. No snow, no rain, no cold. Yvette and Brock were the last inside, with Brock several steps behind her, as if they hadn't spent the night together and watched the sunrise.

Yvette surreptitiously set a bag of small gifts by the back of the couch, just something for each person to open. Since it was Christmas. Though the actual gift was this vacation.

"Oh my God." Jodi put her hands to her mouth as she took in the living room. Then she and Kacey hugged each other, hopping around the room.

The boys were more subdued, as if what Brock had arranged didn't tickle them the way it did the girls.

Adeline, Lorna, and Trevor were already seated in the living room, while Olive set a tray of steaming beverages on the big driftwood coffee table.

But it was the massive Christmas tree in the corner the girls squealed over.

Jodi broke away from her sister and threw her arms around Brock. "How did you manage this, Uncle Brock?"

He saluted Olive. "This dear lady helped me arrange it. So, in fact, you have Olive to thank."

The gracious woman smiled. "It was my pleasure. We often have people here for the Christmas holidays. I like to be prepared," she said in her lilting accent. Then she pointed to the boxes around the tree. "We keep the ornaments packed away. And now you shall have a party for the decorating." She waved a hand over the tray of creamy coffees as if she were waving a wand. "I believe in your country you call this Irish coffee." Whipped cream with chocolate sprinkles floated on the top. "But I have added my own special flavoring. A bit of amaretto." Then she smiled again. "And a touch of cayenne. I hope you find them delicious while you are decorating the tree."

The girls, including Malcolm's and Ethan's girlfriends, pounced on the boxes, tearing them open and finding delicate glass ornaments, garlands, and even silver and gold tinsel.

Trevor stood, holding out his hand to Lorna. "Let's help decorate. We have to get used to it for the baby."

Although Adeline always had a tree at Christmas, she hired professional decorators, and allowed no one else to touch the tree.

Now she sat on the primly on her chair, her legs crossed at the ankles. Yvette picked up a cup of the Irish coffee and offered it to Adeline. The woman stopped short of wrinkling her nose. "Olive is making me a cup of tea. Imbibing in alcohol this early in the day isn't good for the digestion."

"I'm sure you'll enjoy your tea," Yvette said. Then she took a sip of Olive's delicious brew. "Oh my God." She sounded just like Jodi. "This is wonderful." The coffee, the sweet, almondy amaretto, then the kick of the spice. She closed her eyes to savor it. Besides, she didn't need to see Adeline's pinched face.

Brock took a mug, stepping close to clink glasses. With

Adeline behind her, Yvette allowed herself to beam at him. "This is amazing. I don't know how you and Olive arranged getting a Christmas tree here." Especially since he'd spent most of the night making love to her. "Thank you. I know the whole family loves it." She glanced at her girls, who took sips of the delicious coffee drink between hanging delicate ornaments on the tree. Each of the blown-glass balls was painted with a different Christmas scene.

Garth was already throwing tinsel, and Jodi batted at him playfully. "You're supposed to do that after the tree is completely decorated, dunce."

He laughed at the good-natured ribbing. He was a beautiful man, just like his father.

They both had beautiful children, almost as if they'd created them together.

But Brock took little credit for the undertaking. "Like I said, Olive had all the contacts and all the ornaments."

"Where did you get the tree?"

Brock put a finger to her lips. Thankfully, her back was to her former mother-in-law, and she gave his fingertip a kiss as he said, "I won't spoil the magic by telling you how it was done."

Olive, followed by the maid Samara, carried trays of Caribbean small bites, the conch fritters, conch-stuffed mushroom caps, even bites of French toast drizzled with syrup and powdered sugar.

Everything was delicious, and they ate, sipped their coffees, and decorated the tree. All except Adeline. After winding garland around it and throwing tinsel all over the branches, Jodi stepped back with a sigh to survey their efforts.

"Best Christmas ever," she declared.

Kacey was still rummaging through the leftover boxes. "Look. There's an angel for the top". She handed it to Brock, the tallest man in the room. "Please put it on for us, Uncle Brock."

Setting down his glass, he did the honors, and without even needing to stretch, he slid the angel into place on the tree's crown.

"It's beautiful," Jodi said in a dreamy voice.

And it was just what they all needed, the Christmas spirit.

Brock began stuffing all the tissue paper that guarded the Christmas treasures back into the boxes. Trevor helped, and together they carried everything out to the kitchen. Only minutes later, they returned, this time carrying brightly wrapped packages.

Adeline said sternly, "It was my understanding that this trip was supposed to be the Christmas gift to us all."

Brock grinned at her. "It's not Christmas without presents under the tree. Even if we are in the Caribbean."

She harrumphed, even as he placed a small box on her lap.

The kids went through everything, separating the boxes into piles by name. And when Brock sat next to her, Yvette said, "I didn't want to say it too loudly, but I thought the same thing. This vacation was our present."

He looked as if he wanted to kiss her, perhaps just the tip of her nose. But neither of them moved. And he smiled. "There should always be more presents. And don't think I missed that bag of presents you set over there." He pointed behind the couch.

She couldn't help smiling. "Busted. But it's just small stuff."

While everyone else sorted the gifts, Garth stood, holding his hand out to Jodi. Taking it, she followed him to the back porch, almost as if they thought no one would see them. Maybe Yvette and Brock were the only ones who did.

Trevor pecked Lorna on the nose and said, "I'll be right

back." Then he took the stairs two at a time to the second floor.

Adeline said sharply, "You should have told me. Now I have nothing to give anyone. It's embarrassing."

Yvette didn't let her attitude ruin the Christmas spirit on this lovely Caribbean morning, and she sipped Olive's special Irish coffee to keep the spirit alive.

Trevor was back in a flash, carrying more presents for everyone, especially one for his wife and one for his mother.

Then Jodi and Garth burst through the door with carrier bags filled with still more presents. They had something for everyone. Small boxes, yes, but the thought was delightful. When Jodi handed a package to her, Yvette said, "Thank you. You didn't need to do this."

Her daughter said, like her Uncle Brock had, "It's not Christmas without presents."

But Jodi had already given her the best present by inviting her down to San Luis Obispo for the wildflower superbloom. Her daughter's thoughtfulness had touched her more than she could say. And now there was this. Jodi was such an amazing girl. Though she had to give credit to Garth, too, for being part of it.

Then everyone dove into the packages beside them. Nothing was terribly expensive. Yvette had purchased a box of petit fours for Adeline, a scarf for Lorna, a blanket for the baby, for Trevor, a leather travel roll for all his chargers, gift cards for all the kids for their favorite stores, and for Francine and Iris, a simple Visa card they could use anywhere.

The girls gave her a body lotion gift pack from her favorite shop. She opened each bottle to sniff the scent. "Gosh, these smell so good. Thank you."

She'd finished her small pile long before the kids did. With only one gift left, she knew it was from Brock. For a moment, her stomach turned over with the fear that he'd gotten her something suspiciously extravagant. But she opened the box to find a set of bath bombs, and laughed, almost in relief. "I guess all of you know what I like."

Jodi waved her hand in the air. "I told him what to get you."

"Well, then, I thank you both."

A card lay inside the box that she ignored until the others were all busy with their own gifts. Then she read his note. *I got these because I want to watch them sizzle against your skin in the bath. Then I want to breathe you in with their scent all over you.*

She looked in the box to find one bath bomb had been removed and replaced by another slightly misshapen one. What did it mean? Of course she wouldn't ask now, but she looked at him. "Thank you for listening to my daughter's suggestion."

He didn't say a word about the mismatched bomb. "You're welcome. Thank God for your daughters or I never would have known what to get you."

But oh yes, he knew. He knew everything.

Then he reached down for his last package, the one from her. And inside were two silk ties that would look scrumptious on him. She loved a man in a suit with a silk tie over a white shirt. He held one up. "Ties. Two of them. Thank you." Then Brock opened the note she'd written, and his eyes blazed as he read. He definitely got the message.

Kacey flapped her hand at Yvette. "Really, Mom?" She rolled her eyes. "A tie? You could've thought of something more original."

But Brock said, "A man can always use two good silk ties." And the heat in his eyes was enough to send Yvette's pulse rate skyrocketing.

## 16

After opening presents, they all sat around the coffee table, drinking Olive's spicy Irish coffee and singing carols.

In Adeline's house, the holiday was much more staid. Christmas carols played on the stereo, and if anyone sang along, it was almost under their breath. But not this Christmas in the Bahamas. They were loud and off key and boisterous. They played rowdy games of Rummikub, using three sets so they could all play. The winners, Garth, Brock, and Jodi, had a playoff.

Brock loved Yvette's boisterous cheering for her daughter, sometimes leaning over to give her advice. He had the temerity to put a finger to her forehead and push her back, the touch electric as he said, "No helping from the peanut gallery."

A little after midday, Olive called them over for dinner, serving early so that she and Samara could go home to their families for the rest of the holiday.

The two of them carried in dish after dish and platter after platter. As the family took their seats at the table—

Brock making sure Yvette sat next to him—Olive introduced everything they were about to eat. Pointing to a soup tureen, she said, "We have smoked turkey soup with red beans. As your other starter, I have prepared a crab salad. For your main course, we have our traditional baked ham glazed with brown sugar mustard."

Brock noticed Adeline's lips thin, but she said nothing.

Olive continued. "Your side dishes include our peas and rice, as well as baked macaroni and cheese. And here in the Bahamas, we love our root vegetables. We have pumpkin, yams, and dasheen. Dasheen is like your taro, and we cook it with garlic and onions and smoked pork belly." She rushed on to say, "Think of it as bacon, oven roasted and cut into pieces. Then we add a bit of scotch bonnet pepper for spice and top it with scallions. It looks like potatoes, but spicy and smoky." She looked at Adeline. "Of course, for those of you who don't want the spice, I've also prepared cassava, another root vegetable, which has a mild, nutty, sweet flavor. It is very much like mashed potatoes. Be sure to add a wedge of butter. And of course, we have our steamed vegetables." She clapped her hands and cried out, "It is Christmas, and there are no calories today." Which seemed such an American thing to say.

As always, Adeline went first. Once Olive and Samara had returned to the kitchen, Adeline passed his seat, saying, "We were supposed to have roast beef. That's Christmas tradition."

Brock answered her mildly. "I told Olive to make us a traditional Bahamas feast. Next year, you can have your roast beef."

She harrumphed, and he wanted to laugh. Bypassing the soup and crab salad, she added a healthy portion of ham to her plate, some of the cassava, and a lot of the steamed vegetables. Back at her seat, she scraped the mustard glaze off the ham. Typical Adeline.

He held back while everyone else helped themselves, and with a foot beneath the table, he held Yvette back as well. As the line grew shorter, he gave her a subtle nod, and they rose together. He said, loudly, mostly for Adeline's sake, "I'm dying to try the smoked turkey soup with red beans. As well as the crab salad."

She gave him the evil eye, but he thought there was a hint of humor in there too. Yvette echoed him. "I'll try both the soup and the crab salad to start."

Everyone else had piled their plates high, taking a bit of everything, carrying both plates and soup bowls back to the table. Brock took only the first course.

With Yvette once again beside him, the way he always wanted her to be, he tried the soup. It was smoky, a tad spicy, and thick with mashed beans and some left whole. "This is freaking delicious," he said to the table at large. His sons and his nieces nodded, but they were all too busy eating to speak. "The crab salad is excellent too." Then he shook his finger. "Never tell Mrs. French I said this, but I believe Olive is her equal."

At the other end of the table, Adeline harrumphed, still working on her ham and cassava. With another foot tap against Yvette's calf, he rose to dish up his main course and sides, saying, "How's the ham?"

"It's to die for, Uncle Brock," Jodi called out.

He was happy, maybe even giddy, the words of Yvette's note sizzling in his veins. Over the chafing dishes, he leaned close to her, saying softly, sure no one else could hear, "So, two ties are better than one for what you have in mind."

She gave him a closed-lipped smile, her eyes dancing.

"And exactly *what* do you have in mind?" he pushed.

She zipped her lips, sliding a piece of ham onto her plate,

and telling him, "Move along, you're holding up the line." But the sparkle in her eyes promised everything.

He took both cassava and dasheen, wanting the dasheen's spice as badly as he wanted Yvette's spice.

The note was making him crazy. He was sure that was why he'd lost the Rummikub playoff. He wanted whatever Yvette planned, wanted it so badly his brain felt fogged. And his dirty mind was telling him to grab her up and whisk her off to his cottage. He might have, had Adeline not barked out, "What are you two whispering about? It's vulgar to whisper."

Brock shot back, "We weren't whispering. We were talking softly so you wouldn't hear me say you're crazy for not trying the dasheen. It smells amazing." He held up the serving spoon. "Are you sure you won't try?"

"You must be joking," she drawled. "It will give me indigestion. The way it will give all of you indigestion."

Garth laughed. "I haven't had indigestion since we've been here."

Adeline always had a comeback. "That's because you're used to eating ramen noodles and chili out of the can. You have a cast iron stomach." She shook her finger at him. "In twenty years, those poor habits will catch up with you."

Everyone enjoyed all the offerings, but Brock made sure he wasn't stuffed by the time Samara removed all the dinner plates and Olive brought out their dessert.

"The holidays here in the Bahamas are nothing without our special rum cake." She set the cake, already sliced, in the middle of the table along with dessert plates and forks. "I want every crumb eaten, do you hear?" She shook her finger at them, her eyes lit with a smile.

"Oh my God," was all Jodi said as she tried the first bite.

"I could get drunk on this," Trevor added.

There was a definite kick to the bite Brock swallowed, but damn, it was good.

Adeline snorted. "Lorna, you're not allowed to eat it." And she slapped at the woman's hand as Lorna picked up her fork.

"The alcohol cooks off," Trevor said with a snort. "Eat as much as you want, sweetheart."

"Adeline's right," Lorna said. "I don't think all the alcohol is gone."

Adeline harrumphed, this time in triumph.

But Olive was back, another dessert plate in her hand. "I have made you and the baby my special coconut duff." She smiled down at Lorna as she set the rolled cake in front of her, then dropped her voice to add, "And I promise there is no rum in the sauce."

Lorna held her hand for a moment. "Bless you, Olive."

And Brock added, "Our thanks to you and Samara for this fabulous meal. We appreciate you taking the time away from your families to prepare it for us."

Olive put her hands together and smiled, accepting the thanks. "It was our pleasure. But we will take our leave of you now. Except for what remains on the table, the dishes are all done. Merry Christmas."

A chorus of, "Thank you," and, "Merry Christmas," followed her out to the kitchen.

They spent the rest of the day in laughter and fun, games, walks on the beach, swimming, and even a rowdy volleyball match on the sand.

"Can you imagine doing all of this on Christmas back home?" Garth asked no one in particular while they sat around the fire pit that evening.

"We'd need a wetsuit to go bodysurfing," Jodi answered.

Brock raised a toast to his family, minus Adeline, who'd already retired. "Best Christmas ever," he repeated Jodi's earlier sentiment. And there was so much more to come.

For him and Yvette, the night had barely begun.

IT WAS LATE, THE NIGHT QUIET. SHE'D WAITED FOR HIM. The tub in her cottage was barely big enough for two, but Brock stripped down to all his beautiful naked flesh and climbed in with her. The water was probably too warm for the balmy night, but she loved it hot.

He pulled her snug against his chest. And finally, he opened the box of bath bombs she'd set on the side of the tub. He plucked out the misshapen one, and, putting his arms around her, he held it out. "Try this one."

Yvette held it to her nose. "Mango, I think."

She tested it in the water, watching it froth. Moving her legs as she lay between his, she swished until the water turned orange. Then she cupped the ball, enjoying the foam as the water released the bath bomb's fragrance. Dipping it beneath the surface again, and then again, it fizzed against her palm, growing smaller.

Brock leaned forward to nip between her shoulder and neck in a sexy love bite. "I love the way you smell. I love the way your scent clings to me after we make love. I love the way it lingers in my office after you've walked out."

She answered him with, "I love the way you feel against me." She wriggled back, rubbing the hard ridge of his sex against her spine. "And I love the way you feel inside me."

Dipping her hands again, this time something gold peeked out of the foam. "Oh my God," she whispered. "What did you put in here?"

"I had this bath bomb made especially for you."

With one more dip in the water, the last of the bath crystals crumbled away and a gold necklace lay in her cupped palms. A choker with a red stone. "It's gorgeous. Thank you. What's the stone? It's not like anything I've ever seen before."

"It's a cabochon ruby. I saw it." He bent to kiss her neck.

"And I knew I needed to make love to you while you wore only that ruby."

She held it out to him. "Put it on for me." The chain made of chunky gold links, it felt slightly heavy against her collarbones as he fastened the choker around her throat. She touched the ruby, the weight of the necklace against her skin. "It feels so beautiful. But I can't see it." She moaned as he kissed her ear, his warm breath making her shiver.

"I like it on you. "

"Thank you. But you didn't need to get me anything."

"But I want to. I want to cover you in jewels."

"I don't need them," she said, wanting him to know that what was between them was never about money or about the jewels he could buy her.

He trailed a hand from the necklace to her breast and pinched a streak of heat from her nipple straight down to her center. Then he followed its trail down into the water, finding her core. With her body pressed to his, the scent of mangos all around them and the bath bomb turning her skin to silk, he brought her to a shuddering full-body climax.

The water was lukewarm when they climbed out, but her body was hot. He stood her in front of the mirror, toweling her dry with a bath sheet. And his gift glowed against her skin, tinged pink with the heat of his touch.

"It makes me look beautiful," she whispered.

He leaned close, his breath across her ear. "You make the necklace look beautiful."

When they were dry, he picked her up in his arms and carried her into the bedroom. He must have entered while she was running the bath, because the covers lay at the end of the bed.

"I'm assuming that's why you gave me two ties instead of one." He pointed to the head of the bed, where he'd knotted a tie around each of the bedposts.

She laughed. "That's exactly what I had in mind." When he set her on her feet, she turned in his arms. "I want to tie you down and have my wicked way with you."

"It sounds much more fun if I tie you down and make you come until you scream."

"My gift, my way," she whispered, trailing her fingers down his chest to his erection.

"If you insist." Then he took her with a kiss that seared her soul.

Breathless, she pulled back and pointed. "Now stretch out on the bed."

He spread-eagled himself, and she climbed over him, taking each hand and looping the ties around his wrists. He could easily pull free, but he wrapped his fists around the silk, stretching it taut from the bedpost. "Now," he murmured. "I beg you to have your wicked way with me."

"I love the power of sitting astride you."

His body twitched against her core. She leaned down, her hair falling over them, and kissed him for long, delicious minutes, their tastes mingling, their tongues swirling. Then she crawled down him, torturing his small nipples with licks and bites and pinches until he groaned, "I like your torture."

"Oh, it gets worse."

She kissed her way over his abdomen, then curled her hand around him and took him in her mouth. She pleasured him until he bucked against her, his body seeming to react of its own accord. He moaned, he writhed, and then he swore, "I need inside you, God, please."

Only then did she rise above him, sliding down, taking him deep. His lips stretched with a guttural groan, his fists tightened around the length of silk binding him, and his words came out in a growl, "Torture me some more. Please. I'm begging you."

She gave it to him exactly the way he wanted it, riding

him in slow torture, using him to stroke herself on the inside. Falling over him, she braced her hands on the mattress, and the new angle became a glorious, seductive torment even for her. The climax built inside her, and she reached for it, grabbed it, exploded on him.

Hanging on to the ties, he took over the ride, his body pounding up into her, the bed slamming into the wall with the rhythm of his thrusts. Then he swore through gritted teeth and his body throbbed inside her, filling her, words bursting from his mouth as he burst inside her. "Christ, I love you. I love you so damn much."

HE SLIPPED HIS WRISTS LOOSE OF THE TIES. IT HAD BEEN SO sensual, letting her do whatever she wanted. He liked the way the necklace clung to her throat like a brand, a symbol of ownership for all the world to see.

He whispered to her as she lay nestled against him, "You're mine."

She curled her fingers in his chest hair. "And you're mine."

"We belong to each other."

He didn't ask her to marry him. He didn't even beg her. But she was his. The time would come when he would never have to leave her. Because he couldn't live without this, without her. And whatever he had to do to keep her forever, he would.

What he felt for her gave him no other choice.

## 17

---

## ADELINE

"I insist you go to the waterfalls, Trevor," I say to my youngest son.

We stand on the front porch, the Jeep engines roaring, and I take Lorna's hand. "Your wife and I will have such a pleasant day without you," I tell him, as if chocolate would melt in my mouth. Once they are gone, perhaps I'll send Lorna to the store while I sit on the back porch with a nice fruit punch. Brock brought home some of the most delicious guava and passionfruit juices from the zip-lining jaunt the other day.

But Trevor says, "I'd rather stay with you, Lorna. The waterfalls don't interest me."

Damn the boy. "Lorna doesn't want you to miss out on all the fun." I turn to his wife. "Correct, my dear?"

The girl merely smiles. Not even attempting to make up Trevor's mind for him. So many lessons to teach her, the first of which is that you *always* make up your husband's mind for him.

I feel it imperative that Trevor go with his brother. I lay awake all night thinking about this. As impossible as it seems,

I fear that something is happening between Brock and Yvette. How long can it have been going on? It occurs to me I rarely see them together. In fact, until this holiday trip, I haven't seen Yvette since Thanksgiving. She avoids me, for the most part. Even now, it's nothing I can put my finger on. Just a look here, a glance there. They never touch, they don't even truly speak to each other. Except for all that whispering over the Christmas buffet yesterday. Perhaps that is what's bothering me. I sensed a sizzle in the air between them. Like father, like son. My teeth grit. Trevor needs to be a mitigating force between the two of them. Just like he is on the way to work every morning, since they all drive together.

Trevor's presence will keep whatever is growing between them at bay.

At least I hope it will.

If only he will do exactly what I tell him to do right now.

Instead, he takes his wife's hand. "Have no fear. I plan on having plenty of fun with you and Lorna. And today, we should go out for a lovely lunch. There's a resort on the other side of the island. And the food looks amazing." Then he adds, and I see him squeeze his wife's hand and look into her eyes like a sickeningly sweet puppy in love. "Would you like that, sweetheart?"

And Lorna, in *another* sickeningly sweet gesture, wraps her arm around his waist, leans her head on his shoulder, and places his hand on her belly. "Oh, we'd all love that."

*Speak for yourself,* I want to say. But then I know she is speaking for her and the baby.

It turns out my youngest son is immovable when it comes to his wife.

And I let the rest of them go without him, Yvette in the front seat next to Brock. Why isn't she sitting with one of her daughters?

The only thing I can do for the moment is tell myself that

Brock can't be so foolish as to fall for her wiles the same way his brother did. He won't dare.

They made the half hour drive to the waterfall park, where the attendants assigned their lockers and handed out life vests and helmets. Cameras weren't allowed since the company couldn't take responsibility if they were ruined in the water. Yvette chattered with the girls, with Brock's sons, with their girlfriends, and any of the other six tourists joining their group. Then they all trekked up the trail to the top of the falls. Just as there had been seven zip lines, there were seven waterfalls.

She was gorgeous in the dappled sunlight falling through the trees, and all the things they'd done to each other in the night came back to him. His breath came heavier, his body reacting to the memories, to her. She would always do this to him, always make him hard and hungry. If he were honest, she always had, but he'd buried the feelings so deep, denied them so harshly, they were almost nonexistent. Until every single need and emotion erupted like a volcano in the months after Corrine divorced him for another man.

Perhaps that was why he hadn't cared when his wife was gone. He hadn't cheated, hadn't thought about cheating, hadn't admitted any feelings for Yvette were even there. And yet they had lain dormant inside him, like magma waiting to bubble through the cracks of his resolve.

And now he couldn't get enough of her.

Their water shoes crunched on the gravel path.

It was like the crunch of his heart every time she stepped on it. Every time she refused to marry him or even admit to the family that they were lovers.

It didn't matter that he understood her reasons. It still broke him.

But this holiday was his chance to show her how good they could be together. All the time. During the day. Long into the night. Over breakfast, lunch, and dinner. On excursions with the kids or just walking on the beach at sunrise. And tomorrow, he had a very special day planned for her.

Maybe it would be her tipping point.

CLIMBING A SET OF SOLID WOODEN STAIRS, THEN TAKING another that trailed slightly down, Yvette heard the rush of water below them. The sound rushed through her veins like the alcohol she'd drunk last night. Like the taste of him in her mouth. Like the feel of him deep inside her.

Waterfalls? Or making love with Brock? Which was more exhilarating?

Definitely Brock.

Stepping off the wooden walkway, she landed on a relatively flat rock, worn smooth with thousands of footsteps. She felt Brock at her side as she leaned over the edge to look down, whispering, "Oh my," as vertigo hit her and she had to pull away.

Brock whispered back, "That's what you said last night."

She should have elbowed him, but she laughed and

murmured for his ears only, "I said a lot more than that last night."

"Gather round," called Kristiano, their guide. Just as for horseback riding, they had two guides, José taking up the rear and Kristiano leading.

Kristiano told them, "The rocks are very smooth, especially with the water constantly running over them. But this is important. Cross your arms over your chest and keep your elbows in as you slide down. You will be jostled, and you do not want to hit your elbows on the rocks. Then you will plunge into the water and go deep. But with your life vest, you will come up quickly." And finally, he asked, "Who wants to go first?"

Darryl, naturally, raced to the edge. "I'll do it. The rest of these guys are all weenies. I need to show them how it's done." Two of the guys who were not part of the family group grumbled at Darryl's characterization.

José guided him to the top of the waterfall and tapped on his shoulder. "Down on your butt. And just slide."

The water gushed over the edge, providing a smooth ride down the rock face. As José pushed Darryl off, the rest of them automatically leaned over the side railing to watch. While he started with crossed arms, when Darryl was almost free-falling, he put his hands out, giving a great whoop as he fell.

The crack of his elbow was audible even over the crash of the water.

Kristiano said nonchalantly, "That is going to hurt."

When Darryl hit the water with a massive splash and plunged beneath the surface, appearing a few seconds later, José called down, "Are you all right?"

"I'm great." He waved an arm, but not the one with the cracked elbow, Yvette assumed.

"Are you sure you didn't break your elbow?" Brock yelled down at him.

Darryl raised both arms this time, waving them in the air as he treaded water, then sank beneath the surface again. When he popped back up, Kristiano called once more, "Okay. Then get out of the way for the next guest."

Kacey went next, screaming, her arms crossed, elbows in, and splashed down in the water almost on top of Darryl, who hadn't moved as far as he should have. She came up spluttering, and they threw their arms around each other. Then Kacey fluttered her feet, pulling them farther out of the way.

A girl who'd joined their tour—Yvette couldn't remember her name—stepped up next, and Kristiano said, "You must take off your sunglasses."

"But they're prescription," she said, fingers tight on the stem as if Kristiano might tear them off her face. "How will I see everything if I don't have them on?"

Kristiano smiled widely. "If you keep them on, you will not find them in the water once you land. Then you will not see anything for the rest of your vacation."

Accepting the logic, the young woman slipped them into the baggie Kristiano held out. She squealed as she went down, and when she bounced back up to the water's surface after her dunking, she screamed her pleasure. "That is so cool."

When Yvette would have stepped forward, Brock held her back. "Let's go last." She had a feeling why when Jodi finally took her turn, and they were the only two left. The moment José pushed Jodi off the top of the waterfall, Brock leaned into Yvette for a deep kiss.

They stood far enough back from the railing along the rock ledge that no one would see, and the kiss was delicious, spiked with the heat of his desire.

When they heard Jodi's shriek from below, he pushed her to the edge. "Your turn."

She sat in the flow of water, crossed her arms, elbows in, and José pushed her.

It felt like that last kiss from Brock, like free-falling without a parachute. Nestled in the slick curve of the rocks, she plummeted along with the warm water, and screamed with the utter exhilaration.

Pointing her toes, she hit the pool below, plunging deep, until the pull of the life vest shot her back to the surface. Though she'd tied her hair back in a ponytail, some had come loose and fell over her eyes.

"Wasn't that incredible?" Jodi grabbed her arm, pulling her out of the way as Brock sat on the rocks above.

"Outstanding." Especially with the bliss of Brock's kiss still rushing through her veins.

Then he was sliding down, his powerful arms clasped in front of him, his mouth wide with an exultant shout, and he hit the water with a force that drove her back into Jodi.

Popping up moments later, he punched a fist in the air. "That was incredible."

His sons laughed, Garth swimming forward to hug him the way Yvette wanted to.

And they had six more waterfalls to go.

Kristiano and José took their turns down the falls, then led them to the next waterfall.

After three more, they entered a canyon with steep sides, the water too deep for her feet to touch the bottom. She swam through, the buoyant vest making it easy.

She slid off the next falls, screaming her pleasure. This was what she'd loved about making love with Brock in her house, the big house a quarter-mile away. Where she could scream like this and make the pleasure so much more intense.

Whenever he could, Brock held her back where the

others couldn't see, kissing her, then shoving her towards the rocks. But other times, the ledge wasn't wide enough. One even had a ladder to get to the waterfall.

Finally, they came to the last drop. Below them lay a crystal blue lagoon, its water so deep the bottom was invisible. On a small beach beyond it, couples, families, and kids sat on the sand watching the spectacle.

Yvette stood at the edge of the viewing platform. This drop was probably twenty feet, which didn't sound like much when you said it. But when she looked down from above, it seemed so far below.

Kristiano said to the group, "Have no fear. The water below is very deep. You will not hit the bottom."

Darryl's elbow was red, already turning purple around the edges. But he didn't seem to notice, and he went first. But this time, as he had on the last five falls, he kept his arms tucked.

Yvette watched. The outcropping hung over the water, and there were no rocks to slide down this time. It was a straight drop, the falls careening down over Darryl's head. Then he hit with a massive splash, plunging deeper than she could see.

Could she do that?

As if she spoke aloud, Jodi said softly, "You can do it, Mom. You can do anything."

She wanted to laugh. Because there were so many things she couldn't do. Like stepping up to Adeline and saying, *I love your son. And we're getting married.*

Could she even say it after the girls moved out?

A couple from below scrambled back up the rocks, finding handholds that seemed designed for that purpose. When they got to the top, the man said in German-accented English, "Awesome. We have to do it again."

But José held them off since his group was still making

their first drop. She and Brock went last, everyone on the beach looking up at them.

He couldn't touch her. He couldn't kiss her. But he gave her a look that said, *You've got this.*

She sat on the edge, the water seeming so very far below.

"You are ready," José said softly in her ear. And she nodded. Though she wasn't ready. Maybe she never would be. But she had to take the plunge.

Maybe that's what she had to do with Adeline. Just take the plunge.

And José pushed her. She kept her toes pointed, her arms tucked, even though there were no rocks for her to hit. Then she closed her eyes. And suddenly she relished the weightlessness of a free fall that seemed to go on forever. Maybe time even stopped.

And God, yes, it was exhilarating.

Then she hit the water. It went up her nose, pushed past her eyelids, even between her lips. She came up spluttering, plugging her nose, spitting out what had gone into her mouth. Kristiano had been right, she never hit the bottom. Then she opened her eyes to see Brock far above her.

She swam backwards through the water to give him room. It was amazing how quickly he fell, while she had seemed to take forever. The splash created waves in the lagoon, pushing her closer to the sand. Then he was up and swimming hard toward her.

She knew deep in her gut what he intended. And she turned, swimming as fast as she could for the shore, scrambling up the sand.

Then he was on her, wrapping his arms around her, and twirling with her on the beach, laughing, shouting his joy.

She felt his joy deep inside. She wanted so badly to let go of the fear that their kids were watching. Finally, when he set her on her feet, he was laughing, turning to the family, his arm still slung around her shoulders. "Wasn't that the most incredible thing you've ever done in your whole life?"

Jodi threw herself at him, as if she didn't even see her uncle's arm around her mother. As if she didn't care. As if it meant nothing.

When the truth was, it meant everything.

AFTER THE FABULOUS DAY AT THE WATERFALLS, THE FAMILY gathered in the living room for a pre-dinner cocktail.

"Trevor took us to a terribly exclusive spa," Lorna enthused. Her cheeks glowed from a facial.

"It was ridiculously expensive," Adeline said sharply, as if she hadn't enjoyed a single moment.

But Lorna took her hand, squeezed, and with a smile, she said, "You know you loved it. You even said your deep tissue massage relieved so many aches and pains."

Adeline merely snorted. "I said that so Trevor wouldn't feel bad."

Lorna laughed, a tinkling sound. "You're such a hard case," she said through a smile.

Adeline didn't even bite off her head. It amazed Yvette what Lorna could get away with. Was that because of her pregnancy? Although Adeline had never cut Yvette a single millimeter of slack when she was pregnant, not with either of the girls.

Good Lord, she actually sounded jealous.

Brock had pulled Trevor aside, talking earnestly with him in the corner, highball glasses in their hands.

What about? Yvette would have to ask later.

"They even had couples' massages." Lorna was beaming.

"I hope you didn't take your clothes off in the same room with your husband and a massage therapist," Adeline groused, then sipped from her whiskey glass. She took it neat. She hadn't tried any of the sweet island drinks. Adeline had always preferred one small glass of the strong stuff.

Lorna freed that tinkling laugh again. "Of course we were naked. How else could they massage every part of our bodies?" Then she winked at her mother-in-law. "But I promise you a towel covered all the naughty bits."

The kids gathered around, laughing with her. They loved their aunt. From Brock's boys to Yvette's girls, they thought Lorna was wonderful. Perhaps it was because she was closer to their age, almost an older sister, rather than a parent.

"That sounds like fun," Jodi said. "I haven't had a good massage since I started university."

"Oh, you'd love it." Lorna smoothed a hand down Jodi's arm. "We were so pampered. They had fruit-infused water, fruit plates, and vegetable trays. They even had fat-free vegan baked goods. The carrot cake was delicious." She closed her eyes and licked her lips.

Adeline merely huffed. "How can a cake be fat free and vegan and still taste delicious?"

Lorna gave her a playful slap on the shoulder. "That's because you didn't try it. You should have. You would've loved it."

The play slap once again flabbergasted Yvette. Adeline didn't say a word about it. She didn't even brush off Lorna's touch.

Either Adeline was mellowing in her old age, or Lorna was a miracle worker.

Yvette's attention skipped back to Brock and Trevor. There was something fishy about this one-on-one discussion. Brock was planning something. She'd have to ask him later. And not let him weasel out of telling her.

Olive entered then, carrying a sizzling platter of something that smelled divine, and called out, "Dinner is ready."

And of course, everyone rushed to the dining table, dying to see the amazing meal Olive had prepared this time.

Adeline didn't take her customary place as first in line at the buffet. Instead, hand on the back of the sofa, she waved at the kids, who grabbed their plates and dug in.

Returning with another plate, Olive said, "I have something very special for madame. No extra spices. Just a deliciously flaky fish that I think you will love. Along with steamed vegetables and brown rice." She set the steaming plate in Adeline's place, then took the old lady's arm and walked her to her seat.

Adeline graciously accepted the help from Olive. "I appreciate that you've made a special dish for me, Olive. It's very considerate of you."

The miraculous chef smiled her pleasure.

Getting in line behind Brock, Yvette used the cover of leaning over to check what was in the warming tray to ask, "What were you and Trevor talking about?"

Brock merely smiled, saying smoothly, "Just about the waterfalls and how amazing they were. He didn't want to talk about it in front of Lorna in case she felt bad that he gave up the excursion to be with her."

But there was a gleam in his eye, and she didn't believe him.

She was sure he and Trevor had been planning something.

## ✿ 19 ✿

---

### ADELINE

The fish is indeed flaky, as Olive predicted, while also being moist. Grilled, it's topped with some sort of lemon sauce that doesn't stick to the ribs. The steamed vegetables are done to perfection.

I have trained our chef here well in what I like. Just plain food, nothing spicy, nothing fatty, nothing deep-fried like the kingfish the rest of them are enjoying. Though the accompanying mango salad looks quite delicious.

Brock commands everyone's attention. "What do we all want to do tomorrow?"

Obviously, it will be something I'll have to exclude myself from.

The boys shout almost in unison, "We want to rent ATVs."

I'm well aware that ATV is the acronym for an all-terrain vehicle, and just as I have guessed, they choose something I can never do. But let them have their fun. I still have more work to do on Lorna. She's becoming a bit too familiar with me, sometimes ignoring what I instruct her to do. I do believe she was even laughing at me when we told the family about the spa trip. I could have slammed her down, but it will be so much better to find a private moment for that.

"So is ATVing the consensus among all of you?" Brock asks.

All the young people raise their hands.

Then he rubs his lower back. "My fifty-eight-year-old body won't like it. I'm already aching from those waterfalls today. Not to mention the zip line the other day. So I'm out for the ATVs."

Brock isn't old. He can handle an ATV. He often goes horseback riding. How can it be any worse?

Then he adds, "I'd like to do some shopping in town and get a few souvenirs. Who wants to join me?"

I can't help but pooh-pooh the idea. "Lorna and I have already gone shopping. We don't need to go again."

But he turns to Trevor and Lorna as if they will consider doing something I don't want to. "What about you two?"

With a broad smile, Trevor says, "I've already made plans to take Adeline and Lorna to the bird sanctuary Adeline talked about. Everyone is welcome to come. What about you, Brock?"

It looks as if, for a moment, Brock considers it. But then he says, "No. I'd rather have lunch in town and do a little shopping." He juts his chin at Yvette. "How about you? Bird sanctuary or shopping?"

She rolls her lips between her teeth and bites down. As if she has to think about it.

And I say, "Yvette wants to see the bird sanctuary, don't you, dear." It isn't a question.

But something smolders in the woman's eyes. Perhaps I shouldn't have told her what to do because she says, quite defiantly, "I want to go shopping. I like to find one of those embroidered blouses we've seen the local women wear."

Which meant they will go alone. Together. That is

completely unacceptable. "All right then, if you want to go shopping, we'll all go shopping too. We can do the bird sanctuary another day."

But Trevor shakes his head. "I've already bought our tickets. And you're the one who suggested the bird sanctuary. You're coming with us. No arguments about it."

"You'll love it." Lorna pats my hand like I'm a child or a very old lady. I want to snatch it away. Or slap her. "You said that was a place you wanted to go," she adds.

I'm being outnumbered and outmaneuvered.

What is going on here?

The boys are colluding to get me out of the way. But Brock can't possibly be scheming to spend time alone with that woman. He simply wouldn't dream of doing that. Never. Yet why is he so protective of her, vetoing every plan I have for putting her out of the gatehouse and giving it to Trevor and Lorna?

Is he actually attracted to her?

Then Brock looks once again at Yvette. And he says, without a single inflection in his voice, "I guess it's just you and me then. Is that okay with you?"

Yvette answers, "I suppose I can handle it."

And something horrible and cold slithers down my spine.

T he following morning, Brock headed out with Yvette. Just the two of them.

"This isn't the way to town," she called over the Jeep's engine, her voice turning into a squeak when they hit a pothole.

"No," he said, reaching over to put his hand on her thigh. "I have a surprise for you."

The jungle grew denser, almost swallowing the road, the canopy above obliterating all but the most persistent rays of sunshine. Brock even had to turn on the headlights.

"I'm not sure I'll like this surprise." Her trepidation came out in her voice. "It's scary back here."

He just laughed, squeezing her leg. "I guarantee you'll love it. A lot more than the bird sanctuary with my mother."

She had to laugh. "Anything would be better than spending a day in Adeline's company." She eyed him then. "This is something you and Trevor cooked up together." She should have known when he told her to wear her swimsuit under her dress, just in case. And he'd worn his board shorts.

He glanced at her, his smile wide, his eyes hot. "I wanted a bit of alone time with you."

Her blood froze despite the muggy heat beneath the canopy. "You didn't tell Trevor anything about us?"

"I didn't have to. He's known about us for months."

She was suddenly cold all over. "He couldn't possibly know. We've been so careful."

Brock shook his head, seemingly unperturbed that his brother had guessed their secret. "He has a keen eye, and he's watched us interacting together, on the way to the office, at the office, on the way home..." He trailed off.

"Is he threatening to tell Adeline?" She wanted to throw up.

Brock snorted a laugh. "You've got to be joking. Of course not. He thinks we should get married."

The flush didn't just creep into her cheeks; it came in a rush, setting her skin on fire. "What?"

"He thinks we should just get it over with. Tell Adeline and get married." He stroked her thigh, as if it were a promise of nights to come, so many married nights. "Which, you know, is exactly how I feel. You're the only holdout."

She thought of her daughters. She thought of the havoc Adeline could wield. And she was almost hyperventilating. "You told him not to say a damn thing to your mother, right?"

Brock scoffed from deep in his throat. "Trevor's not stupid. He knows it's up to you and me to tell her. But he's okay with us getting married. Maybe Adeline will surprise you too."

She shook her head, almost violently. Another pothole jammed her teeth together. It felt as if the jolt cracked open her heart too.

"I told you, the girls." The words came out breathless and so fast she almost couldn't finish the thought. "I don't know how fast Adeline can react and try turning them against me."

The canopy opened up before them, assaulting her with a gorgeous view of a wide expanse of white beach, the turquoise water beyond it, and waves lapping at the shore. It would have stolen her breath, if she'd had any left after Brock's declarations.

He stopped the Jeep and cut off the engine, but the sounds went on. Bird song, parrots squawking, insects chirping, wildlife rustling in the jungle, her heart pounding against her ears.

"It's a private beach. I've rented it for the whole day." He climbed out of the Jeep, and coming round to her side, he held his hand out. "It's all ours."

She couldn't help but put her hand in his and let him help her stand. Then he reached into the back and plucked out a picnic basket she hadn't noticed.

"I had Olive fix a picnic."

"How did you know about this place?" she asked, as breathless as when he'd said Trevor knew about them.

"A little research. It's a private cove people can rent for the day, a group or a family." He raised her hand to his lips, kissed her knuckles. "Or a couple."

Two lounge chairs with thick cushions sat beneath a tent, the flaps pulled back to let the sea air pass through. "It looks amazing." Awe-inspiring.

He kicked off his deck shoes and said, "We have a whole day of body surfing in the ocean—" He held up the picnic basket. "—eating amazing food and just relaxing together."

When had she ever had a day with him? A whole day that wasn't work, that wasn't about opening Christmas presents while Adeline judged her, a whole day that wasn't about meals with the family presided over by Adeline. And on business trips, meetings and evening meals with customers or vendors took all their time.

She'd never had him all to herself for a whole day.

All her worries about Trevor and what he would say to Adeline melted away.

If there was something to worry about, she'd worry about it later.

HE SAW THE CHANGE IN HER, THE SOFTENING IN HER features, the fear washing away. Brock took Yvette's hand, leading her across the sand to their cabana.

The empty beach beckoned them. He'd paid for privacy. No families with kids building sand castles, no teenagers splashing in the water. No one but them.

The champagne bucket stood at the foot of the lounge chairs, the ice cubes still fully intact, as if it had only just been filled. He set the picnic basket on the nearby table, and opening it, he fished out the champagne he'd had chilling in a thermos cover. Two flutes sat on a small table next to the ice bucket, and he made quick work of popping the cork.

Pouring two glasses, not losing a drop, he handed one to her, then held up his own. "Here is to the most amazing day together."

He wanted to show her what life could be like if they were open about their relationship. If they could spend their days and nights together without worrying what anyone saw.

She tapped her glass to his, the tinkle of crystal wafting through the ocean air. "I can't believe you did this. That's what you and Trevor were talking about, how to get Adeline off to the bird sanctuary so you and I could come here."

"There are advantages to Trevor knowing about us. And this is one of them."

He'd been searching online for a venue to take her to. After Trevor had made his proclamation, he'd enlisted his brother in helping him plan everything. It almost went awry when Adeline decided she'd go shopping too. But Trevor hadn't let her get away with it.

Did she suspect something? His mother wasn't stupid, but she couldn't know for sure.

And maybe her suspicion was exactly what he needed to galvanize Yvette into finally realizing they had to come clean and tell the family so they marry.

He wasn't stupid either. He knew his mother would put up a fight. But she couldn't win.

And Yvette wouldn't lose her daughters either. He would make sure of that.

He wished now that he'd asked Yvette to bring the ruby necklace she'd hidden away after their Christmas night together. Here, she could wear it without fear. Of course, she would have been suspicious, and he'd wanted the day to be a complete surprise.

"What would you like first? A swim? Enjoy your champagne? Sunbathing?" Or making love on the beach? He could have said it aloud, but the thought went without saying.

She took another long swallow of her champagne. "A swim." She reached down to the hem of her sundress, pulled it over her head.

And stole his breath. Her body was slim in the one-piece, her breasts pert. His mouth watered for her.

"Last one in is a rotten egg," she called as she sprinted across the sand.

He tore off his shirt and raced after her. Then they were splashing into the warm sea-blue water. She swam hard and fast, coming up breathless several meters out. "Oh my God, this water is glorious."

Reaching her, he wrapped his arm around her waist, pulling her in, kissing her until they were both breathless.

Then she pushed him away, swimming along the shoreline with strong, sure strokes.

He let her go for now. After all, they had the whole day. And he had so many plans for her.

THE WARM CARIBBEAN WATERS CARESSED HER, BUOYED HER. Yvette could have stayed in the sea all day.

She and Brock body-surfed, tumbling in the waves when they hit the shore. She had sand up her bathing suit, down between her breasts, in her hair, but she didn't care. It was too much fun. Out in the water, waiting for the next big wave —they seemed to come in threes—Brock grabbed her to him, and she felt his rock hardness against her backside. He dropped a kiss on the tender skin between her neck and shoulder. Then he bit down lightly, sending a shiver racing through her body.

"I want to take you out here. In the water. Fill you up." His hands closed over her breasts, squeezing until her nipples peaked against her suit's bodice.

She turned, wrapped her arms around his neck, hanging on like a limpet, while she curled her legs around his waist as they bobbed. "But we'd lose our bathing suits in the water," she said, hiding a smile.

He laughed. "Who cares? We're all alone out here. We don't even need to wear suits."

He was already stripping the straps off her shoulders, until his lips latched on to her breast, and she arched against him.

The sensations were glorious, the warm water lapping at her body, his mouth on her, his erection rubbing between her thighs.

"But this is my favorite suit," she complained, not caring one whit if she lost it.

He treaded water, keeping them afloat, the waves bobbing them up and down, over her shoulders, over their heads, until he pushed them up and they could breathe again.

"I'll buy you a new suit."

Then he stripped her, diving below the water to drag her suit down her legs until she was naked. He rose above the surface, the straps of her swimsuit looped over his arm. "There, you won't lose it."

A giant wave crashed over them, tumbling her away, and she came up sputtering, laughing. Brock was right there again. "We've got three more waves until the next big one. Come here. I want you."

He pulled her to him, and she wrapped her legs around his body, splaying herself for him beneath the water. He held her with one arm banded across her back, and then he delved deep into the water, deep into her, touching all her private places, skimming back up to rub the sensitive nub between her legs.

"Oh my God." It was excruciatingly good. She held on, not caring if her mouth and nose dipped beneath the water because they always came up again. Breathing deeply, she tipped her head back, and let sensation rocket through her body. She didn't hold back as she cried out her pleasure, and the sounds seem to drive that pleasure on forever.

Then another wave crashed over them, tossing them into the shore. On the beach, as the water pummeled them, they rolled in the waves. He threw her suit onto dry sand, then wriggled out of his board shorts and tossed them too. They held each other, loved each other, like Deborah Kerr and Burt Lancaster kissing on the beach in *From Here to Eternity*.

Only this was so much more. His hands everywhere, she cried out again, the carnality of it overwhelming her.

Reaching between them, she curled her fist around him. "I'm getting sand in every crevice where it shouldn't be," she said through her laughter.

But she stroked him anyway, hot and hard in her hand.

Laughter laced his whisper. "I don't want to get inside you with sand all over me."

He rose, pulling her to her feet, and they dashed into the waves again, cleaning off, until finally, naked as the day they were born, he took her hand, and ran with her across the hot sand.

Throwing themselves on a lounge chair, it was a tight squeeze, but Yvette didn't care about that any more than she cared about the sand on their feet. There was just Brock, his hard body, his steel erection, and then he was filling her.

One foot braced on the sand, he lifted her bottom to just the right angle, until it was perfect. He took her slowly, the way she loved, skimming over her G-spot and making her crazy. She clutched his arms, digging her nails into his skin, holding on as if she'd never let go. Until another wave of pleasure crashed through her, and her body clenched tight around him.

He drove deep then, taking her hard, taking her fast, taking her to the moon, to the stars, to the universe beyond.

THEY LAY PANTING IN EACH OTHER'S ARMS FOR LONG moments, his body draped over hers, probably crushing her, but she didn't seem to mind. Brock loved the feel of her beneath him, her body still milking him with an occasional clench that felt glorious around him.

Sex had never been as good as it was with her. Making love. That's what they did. That's why it was so goddamn special. Because of how he felt about her. And how she felt about him.

She pushed him, a laugh in her voice. "I need something to drink."

He pulled off her, leaving his seed inside her. In their younger days, he would have hoped for a baby, their baby. But it was too late for that. They both loved the children they had with all their hearts, and that was enough.

Naked, he stepped away to grab the champagne bottle and the two glasses, holding them both as he poured. She lay deliciously splayed on the lounge chair, going up on her elbows to take the glass, thirstily slugging down half.

Reaching into the wicker basket, he pulled out two bottles of water, handing her one. She drank half of that too. And he powered half his bottle. He didn't want them getting drunk or dehydrated from heat stroke.

As he stood over her, naked, she stroked a hand down his flank. "You are so beautiful," she murmured. "I love your body. I love what you do to me with your body. I love the way you taste." She licked her lips. "I love the way you feel inside me. I love the way you kiss me, the way you stroke me, the way you put your head between my legs and make me come."

Her words brought him to life again, and he wagged a finger at her. "You better stop that talk or we won't get anything to eat."

She laughed and sat up, reaching down for her sundress and pulling it over her head.

"You don't have to dress. We're the only ones out here. No one will see."

She shrugged. "Call me old-fashioned." And there was the secrecy. She couldn't let it go, not even out here. They did everything in the dark, so her lights wouldn't shine in the middle of the night.

But he loved her nakedness. He missed it when the dress fell into place over her lap. When he felt her nerves and embarrassment taking over. So he ran down the beach, grabbed their suits off the sand and took them into the ocean to wash them out. He didn't care if anyone saw his naked ass.

Back at their cabana, he wrung the water out and hung her suit over a nearby tree limb.

Then he pulled on his board shorts even though they were wet. She would want it that way. And they would dry soon enough. Sitting on the edge of her lounger, he pulled the wicker basket closer. "Let's see what we have here."

The wicker disguised the cooler inside, and he pulled out the goodies Olive had prepared. Opening one package wrapped in wax paper, he found lightly fried chicken.

"I shouldn't be hungry after that breakfast," she said, grabbing a drumstick.

"But you are, after all that swimming." And all the love-making, he thought. He would make her hungry again, for him, for his touches, his kisses, his mouth between her legs.

He pondered the myth of menopause, that a woman lost her libido. It was so not true for Yvette. Maybe it was just the two of them together. Maybe they were the spark that kept her desire alive. Maybe it was how often they made love, almost in desperation, afraid it would be the last time. Maybe it was the illicitness, hiding it from their families. Whatever the reason, he wanted her. He was already hard again. And she wanted him. He scented her arousal, her sensuality. And he tore into a chicken wing, tearing it with his teeth.

He'd never been so famished in his life, for food, but mostly for her. They'd been together every night since they'd arrived, and still he wanted more.

"What else is in Olive's magic picnic basket?" she asked, sipping her champagne.

He delved deeper. "We've got fruit, cheese, cut vegetables, crackers, meats."

She leaned forward. "What kind of meat?"

He opened the wax paper. "Salami, ham, roast beef."

She groaned. "I'd love salami and cheese on a cracker. With a chaser of grapes."

"Oh yeah." He prepared the cracker for her, held it out, and she leaned close, taking the entire bite into her mouth, barely missing his fingers and laughing when she did. After she chewed and swallowed, he popped the grape chaser into her mouth. She tipped her head back to savor the sweetness.

"Any more grapes?" she asked.

"How about mango?"

She looked at him, groaned. "Oh my God, yes. Mango."

He fed her the pieces, letting her take small bites until her lips kissed the tips of his fingers. Then she picked up a mango slice and fed him.

It was an orgy of food and touching and kissing and feeding each other. He licked the mango juice off her chin, drizzled champagne into her mouth, then kissed her throat as she tipped her head back. It was an erotic feast, of everything in the basket, of each other, of their lips, their skin, their bodies.

Pulling down the straps of her sundress, he rubbed mango juice over her breasts, licking them clean until she writhed beneath him. He pushed her back on the lounge chair, flipped up her skirt, and laid the mango between her legs, feasting on it, and on her sweet taste too. She cried out, and he fit two fingers inside her, forcing to her to ride the pleasure for long moments.

Until she collapsed on the lounger. "You are deliriously crazy."

Then she yanked at his shorts, pushing them off until he kicked them aside, not caring about the sand. Her breath washed over him, turning him as hard as the stones scattered on the shore.

Reaching into the basket, she came out with another slice of mango. It was long enough to wrap around him, and she laughed. "This is how I want to eat you."

His head fell back as she took his crown into her mouth,

sucking on him, driving him closer to insanity. He wanted to throw her down on the chaise and fill her up. Yet he wanted this. She ate her way down the mango slice, down his hard shaft, swallowing and licking, grazing her teeth over him and the fruit, juice trickling down between his legs. When she'd eaten the fruit, she licked the juice from his thighs, off his balls, then sucked him again, all the way in, all the way out, then teasing just the crown the way he'd shown her he loved. They'd taught each other what they liked. She did it just the way he needed until he felt his mind explode. He filled her mouth, coming hard, and she drank every drop of him as if he were the sweetest champagne.

Collapsing beside her on the lounger, he laid his head in her lap while she stroked his hair. And finally, he opened his eyes, turning slightly to look up, her hair falling across his face. "You're so damn amazing. How do you do that to me?" His words were a rough rasp.

And she smiled. "How do you do that to me?"

He stroked her bare thigh beneath the sundress. "Because we were made for each other."

He knew that with every bone in his body, with every cell in his brain, with every beat of his heart.

The day had been magnificent. They swam, ate, lay in the sun, made love. She'd even gotten used to being naked with him, throwing aside her fear that someone might come upon them in their secluded cove.

No one had. They lay in each other's arms on the lounge chair, Brock pecking kisses to her temple, her forehead, stroking her hair.

Yvette wondered how they could eke out a vacation like this. Just the two of them. For a week. Or even a long weekend. Yes, they could do a long weekend. No one would know if they were both gone. No one would put it together.

She wanted it so badly her heart ached.

With his arms tight around her, she asked, "What would you have done if Adeline had insisted on going shopping with us rather than to the bird sanctuary with Trevor and Lorna?"

His answer was a whisper of breath across her hair. "I'd have found another day. We were meant to do this. And after the idea came to me, I wouldn't let anything stop me."

That was his way in business and in life.

It was his way with her as well. Not allowing anything to stop him.

She knew then, in his big, strong, beautiful arms, that he would never give up the idea of marriage until he got what he wanted. And maybe someday, she would give in.

When they arrived back at the compound, the kids were already there enthusing about the details of their incredible ride around the island on their ATVs. Lorna and Trevor had passed around their phones with pictures of the colorful birds they'd seen.

All Adeline had said, in the driest of tones, was, "It was worth the visit." Then she narrowed her eyes at Brock. "You should have come with us. It was so much better than shopping." Was that a snide note in her tone? "And what did you buy?"

Brock said easily, "I didn't see anything I wanted." He looked at Yvette. "And Yvette couldn't find the blouse she was looking for."

Adeline harrumphed, and Yvette couldn't tell whether that was suspicion or lack of interest.

After another amazing dinner provided by Olive—Yvette wasn't hungry for the conch salad after all the goodies in the picnic basket—the family gathered around the fire pit on the beach. The sun had gone down an hour ago, and from somewhere, Brock had secured a keg of some amazing island beer.

"When we were up on a ridge," Kacey said, "We could see the horses swimming in the ocean."

Jodi jumped in, "I loved the ATVs. We got to see so much of the island, and it's all so different depending on where you are. But the best thing we've done so far was swimming with the horses." She looked at her sister. "I wonder if we can do that somewhere at home."

Garth laughed. "In a wet suit. The water is way too cold up north."

Jodi gave a little pout. "I guess so. Maybe we'll have to go down to Newport Beach or even San Diego."

Yvette felt Adeline's eyes on her in an intense stare. It was the first time Adeline had joined them by the fire. And that stare was unnerving. Why was the woman looking at her that way? She couldn't know anything.

The conch salad, the little of it she'd eaten, curdled in her stomach. Adeline couldn't know. But maybe it was worse that she was guessing.

Yvette shivered at the thought. She and Brock needed to cool it for the rest of the trip. No more days out. Maybe she should even tell him not to sneak into her room at night. They were safer at home.

Screwing his beer mug into the sand, Brock clapped his hands. "Okay, we haven't picked out what we're doing tomorrow. How about I rent the catamaran and we can spend the day on the water, swimming and snorkeling?" He looked at Lorna. "You can do that, right?"

After she nodded, he looked at his mother. "And so can you, Adeline."

The lady snorted. "I don't need to get skin cancer by lounging around in the sun." Her words were so caustic, her tone so harsh that the group spirit immediately dipped.

But Brock laughed. "You don't need to sit in the sun, Adeline. There are usually tarps stretched over the back for people who want shade."

She harrumphed again, and Yvette had no idea what that meant. Before the standoff could degenerate into an argument, Jodi jumped into the breach. "We wanted to ask you something, Uncle Brock."

He jutted his chin at her with tacit permission to speak, as if he were running a meeting.

Jodi rushed on. "After we heard about that spa Uncle Trevor took Grandmother and Aunt Lorna to, we all decided we'd like to do that. Go for massages, facials, body scrubs. And there's a steam room, a cold plunge, all that stuff." She stared at him with wide eyes, as if afraid he'd come down hard on her.

But Brock smiled widely. "Sure. Is that what you all want?" The rest of the gang, including Kacey, nodded their heads. "Then we'll do the catamaran and snorkeling another day. No problem."

He didn't look at Yvette, but she heard his thoughts as if he'd said them aloud. This would give them another day together.

But Yvette was looking at Adeline. Another day was a bad idea.

Jodi's voice rose with excitement. "We can all go." She turned to Adeline. "Wouldn't you like to go again, Grandmother?"

Adeline sniffed as if she'd smelled something rotten. "I've already indulged, dear. I don't need to do that again so soon. And Trevor and Lorna have already gone as well."

Jodi didn't let it go. "But don't you want to go again, Aunt Lorna? It will be so good for the baby."

Lorna, a hand on her baby bump, smiled. "I don't think so, Jodi. We've had such a long day today walking around the bird sanctuary. I'd like to rest."

"But a day at the spa would be so relaxing," Kacey cajoled.

Then Trevor put an end to it. "We'll stay with Adeline, if that's okay with you girls. When Lorna says she needs her rest..." He trailed off, shrugging and raising his hands. But he gave Lorna that stars-in-his-eyes look.

"Then that's settled," Adeline said. "You young people can go to the spa, while we *old folks*," she drawled, not meaning a word of that, because Adeline wouldn't allow herself to be considered old, "will take a nice relaxing drive somewhere. I don't know where. We'll figure it out. Right, Brock?" She stared him down.

Until Brock said, "I prefer a spa day. I haven't had a massage in weeks." He stretched an arm back to massage his shoulder. "My back could use it too." Then he turned to Yvette. "What about you?"

She knew what he wanted, and the heat in his eyes stole her breath. She thought how wonderful today had been. And she wanted it again. Her heart and her desires won over her common sense. But it would be good to get out from under Adeline's eagle eye, who couldn't suspect anything if they were with the kids. Besides, Yvette didn't relish a day spent in the car driving around the island with Brock's mother.

"Yes," she agreed. "A spa day would be perfect." She wondered if Brock would finagle a couples' massage when no one was paying attention. "I'd love a facial. If you don't mind the old folks coming long," she parroted Adeline.

Jodi cooed, "You're not old folks. It'll be so much fun."

Brock smiled at his mother. "That's settled then, Adeline. Trevor and you and Lorna can go for a relaxing drive, have a pleasant lunch somewhere, and we'll go to the spa."

Adeline's brows knit. Yvette easily read her expression. She knew she'd been tricked. And she didn't like it.

YVETTE LAY IN BROCK'S ARMS, THE DARKNESS surrounding them. When he come to her door, she hadn't the will to turn him away. But now she said, "I think we need to cool it around Adeline. You shouldn't come to my room every single night. I think she suspects something."

He stroked the tangled hair back from her face and tipped her chin until she looked at him. "She doesn't suspect a thing. You worry too much."

But she didn't worry unnecessarily. Adeline had tricks up her sleeve that even Yvette couldn't anticipate.

"Even if she does suspect," he said, "it doesn't matter. I want her to know. I want everyone to know. I want to stop sneaking around. I want to *be* with you."

"I just don't think I can take it." A frisson of fear shimmied through her.

"I'll be there for you."

He meant Pierce *hadn't* been there for her. It was true. Pierce had pooh-poohed her anguish every time Adeline played her nasty mind games. He claimed his mother meant nothing by it, that Yvette had a thin skin. Maybe she had. Maybe she still did.

Maybe Brock's nonchalance regarding his mother finding out about them was like Pierce pooh-poohing her fears all those years ago.

Brock thought he could fix anything.

"I still think——" she began.

He shut her up with a kiss. She could never resist his kisses. She could never resist anything he did to her. And even after making love three times during the day, then again when he came to her room tonight, she wanted him again.

God, how good it felt. She wished she'd discovered how good sex could be when she was much younger. When she wasn't worried about wrinkles or bulges or crepey skin. And she let him do everything he wanted, relished every touch, every kiss, every pump of his body into hers.

But she woke up in the morning with all her fears crashing over her again.

IT WAS ALMOST ELEVEN THE NEXT MORNING WHEN BROCK watched Trevor herd their mother into the car. "Let's have lunch in town," Trevor said. "I found another interesting restaurant that Lorna wants to try." He glanced at his wife. "Don't you, sweetheart?"

She punched his shoulder lightly. "I was the one who found it."

From the front seat, Brock heard Adeline complain, "We'll all get fat. We're eating too much. We don't need another fancy lunch out." But Trevor closed the car door on her comments and walked around to the driver's side. Then the car rolled down the drive and out of sight.

As the kids piled into the Jeeps, Brock put his plan into action. Though Trevor had started it by making sure Adeline was out of the way before the kids left.

Garth asked, "Shall I drive, Dad?"

Brock smiled, rubbing his hand through his hair and ruffling it as if he were in deep thought. "You know, I've changed my mind. I feel like relaxing on the beach today. I've had little chance to do that so far."

"You're kidding." Jodi jammed her hands on her hips and turned to her mother. "What about you, Mom? Are you still coming?"

Indecision crossed Yvette's beautiful face. He'd sprung his plan on her. She'd either agree and stay with him. Or she'd let her fears take over and go with the girls.

Finally, after a long moment that had him holding his breath, she said, without even looking at him, "I think I'll take a beach day too. You'll enjoy the spa much better without me. You'll just be worrying about what I want to do and if I'm having enough fun and I'll just drag you all down." She made it about her without mentioning Brock at all.

"Mom," Kacey whined.

Yvette laughed. "You know it's true. That's why none of the rest of you are saying anything." She waved a hand at the boys and their girlfriends.

Darryl said, "If she doesn't want to go, Kacey, she doesn't have to. Don't force her."

Kacey shut her mouth.

But Jodi said, with a hint of sadness, "If that's what you want, Mom."

Yvette nodded her head. "What I want is for you guys to enjoy doing whatever you want without worrying about me."

"All right, already," Darryl called out. "Time is wasting. Let's go." And they took off with a roar, gravel spitting from beneath the tires.

Yvette turned on Brock the moment they were out of sight. "You planned that."

Grinning, he didn't need to say a thing.

"You're so bad."

He took a step closer. She took a step back.

"My mother's gone," he murmured. "You don't have to worry about her knowing we're here by ourselves. Trevor won't bring her back for hours. And the kids will be gone until evening." He took another step. She backed up another. "So now we have the entire afternoon to do whatever we want." Before she could back off again, he lunged, grabbing her up in his arms and swinging her around. "I intend to spend the whole day in bed with you."

She looped her arms around his neck, locked her legs at his waist. "I want to do some swimming and sunbathing first."

He waggled his eyebrows. "Oh yeah, I love stripping you out of your bathing suit in the water."

She held her finger up in front of his nose. "You will not strip off my bathing suit. We aren't alone here like we were in the cove. No funny business until we're in the room."

When she would have slid down, he carried her along the pathway to her cottage. "Wear that sexy suit with the gold buckle right between your breasts."

Hauling her up against her door, he kissed her, already hard, thinking about everything he wanted to do to her.

BROCK PINNED HER AGAINST THE DOOR, KISSING AWAY ALL her objections and all her guilt about not going to the spa with the girls. There was something thrilling about being the total focus of this beautiful man's attention. Even if they'd been together for months now.

But when you were sneaking around, hiding what you did, could you call it "being together?"

Yvette couldn't care about that right now as Brock's lips trailed a path from her earlobe down her neck to the slope of her shoulder. He cupped her breast, and her nipples begged for his mouth while her body ached for him to be inside her.

But she pushed his hand away. "Anyone could see us from the house." Wriggling out of his arms, she held him away and slipped inside her cottage before he could follow her. But she heard him laughing. They both knew he'd have his way with her eventually.

After they'd both changed into their swimsuits, they frolicked in the water for half an hour. Until she ran up the beach and climbed onto the big turquoise hammock swing to let her suit and body dry in the sun.

Of course, Brock joined her, and the wait had only made him hotter, harder. Their bodies rolled together on the swing. She didn't think they could be seen from the house. Olive wouldn't look anyway. And God, how she loved teasing him. How she loved lying here with his arms around her. Loved his kisses, his touches.

If she wasn't a scared mouse, she'd let him make love to her right here on this swing, the turquoise cushion the exact shade of the Caribbean Sea.

Hadn't that been her fantasy the first night?

He licked her ear, then blew a warm breath that made her shiver with desire.

"If you don't want them to see me pick you up," he whispered, his breath shooting a shaft of need straight through her. "And carry you back to your room where they'll definitely know I plan to ravish you, then you better get up and head there yourself."

His eyes were ablaze with desire when he pulled back to look at her.

"Are you ordering me about?"

He shook his head slowly, his face so close she could see all the shades of blue in his eyes. "Not ordering you," he said, his voice harsh. "I'm begging you. I want you so bad that if we wait, I might take you right where you lay." He grinned. "And I know you don't want that."

Oh yes, there was something so exciting and erotic being the focus of this sexy, incredible man's attention.

She sat up and fluffed her hair nonchalantly. "If you insist. We can't have Olive and Samara or the gardeners scandalized by your overactive libido."

He laughed loudly. She stood, dabbed her legs dry, her arms, her throat, her breasts, then wrapped the towel around her hips. Sashaying, slowly, very slowly, to her cottage, she slipped across the back porch, knowing he watched every move. And drooled.

Inside, she found Samara had already cleaned the room. Yvette stripped the covers to the end of the bed, then turned the air conditioner to high. She'd have to close the sliding glass door so no one would hear her scream when Brock made her come over and over.

And no one would hear him shout out his climax.

He was through the door in less than five minutes, sliding it closed behind him and locking it. Yvette pulled the curtains over the glass, shutting out the sun on the sand. And Brock tugged the towel from her around her waist, throwing it on the nearby chair. When he hauled her against his taut frame, every inch of him told her what he wanted.

Then he devoured her mouth, going deep with his tongue, sucking the breath right out of her. She clung to him, savored every taste, every scent, every hard muscle, every steel inch.

He swore, and lifting her high, he tossed her on the bed, dropping on her like a caveman or a predator. "I want you. I'm going to have you. And I'll make you scream when I do." His words were guttural, welling up from deep within him, filled with so much feeling her skin burned.

This was how women wanted to be wanted. This was how Yvette needed to be craved. To be desired above all else.

He bent then, licking her right through the buckle of her swimsuit. His fingers found her nipples, teasing them to a ripe fullness. Yanking the straps down her arms, he dove on her, licking her, sucking her nipple into his mouth while he pinched the other, shooting fire straight to her core.

"Brock," she cried out, fingers gripping his shoulders, nails digging into his flesh.

He groaned, the throaty sound against her nipple making her arch into him. Then he stripped her down, dragging the suit past her hips, down her legs, before he dropped his trunks on the floor and climbed over her again.

Hands under her armpits, he hauled her up the bed, until his mouth was level with her spread legs. And he swore again. She loved the word on his lips, the strain on his face, the huskiness of his voice. He buried his face against her, licking, filling her with his fingers, taking her to heights she might never have known, even with him. Because every time was better, sexier, hotter.

She exploded in a blaze of colored lights, her throat

aching with the screams she couldn't stop. Until finally her tense body relaxed against the bed, and she laughed. "I don't know how it gets better every single time, but it does."

He crawled up to cover her, his hard chest to her soft breasts. "That's because we get better together. We're meant for this. We're meant to be together."

But were they together if all they did was sneak around? He wasn't the one who wanted all the secrecy. She demanded it.

Now wasn't the time to think about it. She turned with him, sprawling on top of him, smiling. "I can think of another way to make it better right now."

She shimmied down him, trailing her lips over his tight male nipples, loving the thrum of his groan, licking a pathway down the line of hair that headed straight to the erection she was dying for.

Laughing, she reached back and drew the covers over her head, leaning down to him in the sudden darkness, taking his solid length in her mouth, sucking hard on the tip. His hands reached beneath the sheet to tangle in her hair, and he guided her. This was part of what made it good for him, the feel of her hair beneath his fingers, the need for control, even as they both knew she had all the control right now.

She sucked him, hard, deep, his body arching off the bed and those first few luscious drops bursting on her tongue. Relishing every moment of the act, savoring every groan, every growl, she loved the way his thighs tightened around her body, squeezing, releasing, exactly the way she knew her body squeezed him when he was deep inside her.

She felt it coming, his explosion, his need overwhelming him. Just before he let loose, he hauled her up, pulled her beneath him, the covers twisting around them, trapping them together.

His eyes were cerulean pools of need as he demanded, "Open up for me."

Spreading her legs wide, she didn't need to guide him. He was like a missile, heading straight for her, and he plunged deep, filling her. Screaming, not with pain but with the glorious sensation shooting through her, she felt him in every part of her body, surrounding her, the throb of him inside her matching the beat of her heart.

And she shot to the pinnacle right along with him.

HE SWORE AS THE FEEL OF HER BODY CLUTCHING HIM MADE him crazy. He pounded her hard, harder than ever before. But he wanted her so badly. Needed her. She scored his back with her fingernails, leaving welts he knew would show tomorrow when he took his shirt off to go swimming. Her body clenched tight, dragged him deeper, pushed him higher, and she locked her legs around him, gripping his ass, taking him as much as he took her.

From somewhere, he heard rapping, heard his name. Maybe it was the headboard against the wall and her crying out for him. And he couldn't stop. He was sure she wouldn't let him stop.

He whirled out of control, trapped with her beneath the sheets, his blood high, his skin hot, her body squeezing him, begging him, killing him.

And even when he thought he heard another call, something like *Mom*, he told himself it was his imagination, blocked it out. He had to take her now. Had to claim her, stamp his ownership on her the same way she had stamped ownership on him so many months ago.

He bellowed his release as he felt her body spasm around him.

He arched into her, giving her everything, every drop of who he was, of how much he wanted her, needed her, loved her. Until finally he collapsed on top of her.

And a scream that wasn't hers suddenly ripped the air.

I t was a scream of horror, a scream of fury.

And it came from outside of them, from the short hallway that led to her front door.

Yvette went rigid beneath him, her eyes tightly closed. She'd heard it too. And she knew what it meant.

Brock turned his head because he couldn't hide from this. Maybe it was what he'd wanted all along. No maybe about it. He'd wanted them all to know.

But not this way.

Kacey stood framed in the hallway, both hands to her mouth, her eyes wide with shock. Just behind her, Jodi and Garth. Brock couldn't bring himself to ask where the others were.

Garth said, "Holy hell."

And Brock felt Yvette shudder around him, through him, taking him down. Because while he'd wanted their relationship out in the open, she would never forgive him—or herself —for the way it happened.

He did the only thing he could. "Get the hell out," he bellowed through crunching teeth and bared lips.

Grabbing Kacey's arm and pulling her away, Garth threw his words over his shoulder, "Yeah, but there's a problem. We need you, Dad." Then Garth herded the two girls out of the room and slammed the door.

Eyes tightly closed, Yvette whispered, her voice weak, "Wasn't the door locked?"

Still buried deep inside her, still craving her, he muttered, "We came through the back door. I thought the front door was already locked."

She covered her eyes with her hand as if, even with her eyes closed, there was too much light on them. "I don't know. I don't remember. I came in to change into my suit. But I don't remember about the door." She dropped her hand, and tears leaked down her temples.

"It'll be okay," he murmured, trying to soothe her. "I promise."

She shoved him off her then, scrambling out of the tangled blankets, backing up against the wall, so beautiful in her nakedness. And yet her face was a mask of horror.

"Get dressed," she snapped at him in a voice he'd never heard before.

He grabbed his trunks off the floor. She pushed past him to her closet and dragged out another sundress, pulling it over her head, then grappled with the drawers until she found a pair of panties. Stepping into them, she kept her back to him.

She would never forgive him for this.

Bare-chested and pulling on his trunks, he said, "I'll talk to them. You can stay here."

She whirled on him. "I'm not a child you need to protect. I can handle this." Then she poked him in the chest. "I told you this would happen. But you wouldn't stop. You wouldn't listen."

His own anger welled up. "You didn't sound like you hated

what I was doing to you. In fact, you loved it." He recognized the danger immediately. This was what would break them apart, the anger between them, not everyone else's horror.

She slapped the flat of her hand against his chest, not hard, and yet he felt rage and fear seething in her. "I wanted it when it was a secret. When it was just us. When the world didn't have a say in it," she said, each word clipped, her voice harsh.

He grabbed her wrist, pulled her close. "Don't let this ruin us." His voice was softer, his heart aching at the spitfire in her eyes.

"I don't know what it'll do," she said through clenched teeth. "I just know I need to talk to my girls. Now. Before Adeline gets back."

That was her greatest fear, what Adeline would do, what weapons she would use against Yvette. And if the girls were angry because of this, he wasn't sure his prediction that her daughters wouldn't mind could stand up to whatever Adeline dished out under these circumstances.

The absolute worst circumstances.

HER LEGS TREMBLED. IT WASN'T JUST THE FEAR OF OPENING that door and having to look at her daughters' faces.

It was him. It was what he'd done to her in that bed. The way he made her feel. The glory of it still trembling through her limbs.

And as angry as she was, as angry as she wanted to stay so she could deal with it all, she could never forget how good they were together. Because she loved him.

God help her.

Would she have to sacrifice her daughters to keep what

they had? Or would she have to sacrifice him to keep her daughters?

"I'll do the talking," she murmured, not wanting him to pick up on the panic in her voice or the shudder that ran through her body.

The kids were out there, milling around just off the path. Thank God Adeline wasn't with them.

A thundercloud darkened Kacey's face. Yvette couldn't bear to look at Jodi's reaction. She kept her voice as calm as possible. "We need to talk."

Kacey slashed an angry hand through the air. "Look." Her voice sliced through Yvette. "Right now, I don't care who you're screwing. I don't care if it's Uncle Brock or anyone else. I don't even care if it's Uncle Trevor."

The words slapped Yvette across the face. But even worse was the movement on the driveway. No gasp, no cry. But she knew Adeline was back. And when she turned, her former mother-in-law lasered her with a look that stripped every ounce of flesh from her body and gutted her like a filet knife.

But she had to concentrate on her daughters. "Kacey—"

Kacey didn't let her get another word out, not even a sound. "The only thing I want from you now is Uncle Brock. We need his help."

Yvette couldn't help saying, "Why didn't you call?" Mired in her own guilt and fear, she didn't even ask what was wrong.

Angry red splotches marred Kacey's cheeks. "I tried. I called you both. Over and over. And now I know why neither of you answered." Her words came out through clenched teeth.

Yvette could barely swallow down her bile. Her daughter had needed her; it didn't matter why. And she hadn't been there. She remembered the deliberately taunting sashay she'd made on her way back to the cottage, willing Brock to follow her. She hadn't even thought about the phone she'd left on a table by the lounge chairs. Brock's had been there too.

She was guilty of so many bad decisions.

Maybe she deserved whatever punishment Adeline would mete out.

Then Brock took over. "What's wrong? Why were you trying to get hold of me?"

For one moment, Kacey stared him down. Then she burst into gasping sobs, her fists screwing into her eyes. Jodi threw an arm around her sister's shoulder, and Yvette couldn't bear to see the look of censure in her eyes.

"Tell me what happened," Brock insisted.

Garth answered, "Darryl got arrested."

Brock muttered, "What the hell?" Then he threw his hands up. "Why?"

"We don't know," Garth admitted. "Suddenly there were all these island cops there. Then they marched him out and shoved him in a car." He gave a helpless shrug. "I was in the steam room," he added. "I heard a commotion outside and when I went out there, it was all about Darryl." He lifted his shoulders in mystification, his hands out.

Then Kacey said amid her sobs, "They just took him away. No one would tell us why."

Brock was all business. "Where did they take him?"

Jodi rubbed Kacey's back. "To the police station in town. When we couldn't get hold of you, Malcolm, Ethan, and the girls followed the cops in the other Jeep so we'd know where they were going. They're waiting for us there."

So that's where the others were. Yvette hadn't even bothered to ask. She hadn't thought about it in her concentration on her daughters.

"And we came back here to get you." Garth glanced at Yvette, and she felt his unyielding gaze pierce right through her.

Oh God, what had she done? She wasn't there for her girls. She'd left her phone outside. No mother should ever do that. It didn't matter how old your kids were, you always had your phone with you.

And you never put a man or sex above your children.

Brock shoved his hands through his hair, already a tangled riot after what they'd done in bed. She winced at the memory. He swore. "All right. I'll change, then we'll go over there." He looked at his son, already strategizing. "Trevor's back. We'll take the Lincoln. That'll give a better impression than the Jeep." He waved a hand, indicating Garth's shorts. "You should change too. Wear a button-down shirt and slacks."

"What should I wear?" Kacey asked, the tremble still in her voice.

Almost as if it were automatic, Brock said, "You stay here. We want to make this look official."

"I'm going," she snapped.

He raked her with his boardroom gaze. "You asked me to help. And it's my opinion that it's detrimental to have an emotional young woman right there while we talk this out."

"I'm not emotional. I'm just mad." She shot a glare at Yvette.

Brock was already moving, decision made. And she saw the marks she'd left on his back. She prayed no one else noticed. He waved a hand at Trevor, who was walking over to them.

Didn't Brock even get that Adeline had seen them, had probably heard everything?

There wasn't an ounce of fear in his voice as he called out, "There's a problem. Darryl's been arrested. We don't know why. But he's in town at the jail. You and Garth need to go over there with me." Then he pointed a finger at Trevor's casual shorts. "Wear something more formal. Slacks, at least."

He marched to his cottage door just as Adeline called out in a strident voice, "What on earth is going on?"

Lorna put an arm around her shoulder. "Let's go inside and have Olive make us a nice cup of tea. Then Yvette can tell us why the men are going to the jail."

That's when Adeline smiled. It was like Hannibal Lecter smiling at Clarice Starling through the bars in *The Silence of the Lambs*.

And it chilled Yvette to the bone.

## 23

---

## ADELINE

ood riddance to that little mushroom. I hope he rots in jail. He was never good enough for my granddaughter. I should have talked her out of dating him the first time she brought him to the house. But sometimes you have to let a relationship run its course, because sooner or later it will die out on its own anyway.

Except for Pierce and Yvette.

It was only because of Harris and Yvette's dirty little pregnancy trick that their affair hadn't died after the first few weeks.

We're all seated in the living room where I preside. Just the women of the family, not those two hangers-on clinging to Ethan and Malcolm because they both know a gold mine when they see it.

I have to act as if there isn't glee in my heart. But I couldn't have orchestrated this scenario any better. Even if I want to murder my eldest son for sleeping with the enemy.

It should be a book title. Oh wait, it already is.

Brock, Trevor, and Garth drove into town to meet up with Ethan and Malcolm at the jail. The big tough men going off to do battle with the local authorities. I could have handled it far better. But then, I don't want to.

"Drink your tea, ladies," I order. Olive has brewed two pots exactly to my specifications.

"We can't just sit here and do nothing." Kacey's voice wobbles.

I turn to her, softening my tone, because coming across as a hard case right now won't benefit me. "You know your Uncle Brock will take care of everything." I need to show that I am on her side. On Jodi's side.

And the three of us are sitting on the opposite side from their mother.

"He has all the connections," I go on. "He'll get this sorted out. But in the meantime, you need to calm down."

Then I turn to Yvette, the true villain of this debacle. And my victim. "You and Brock were at the spa with them. How could you let this happen?" I have eyes and ears, and I know what we'd walked in on as soon as the car rolled into the driveway. Guilt was written all over the two of them. And it still stains Yvette's cheeks. But it suits my plan to pretend I haven't guessed.

My darling granddaughter jumps in with the damning words. Better Kacey says them rather than me. "They both said at the last minute that they didn't want to go. That they wanted to stay behind and soak up the sun."

I smile inside, not a flicker of it showing on my lips. Instead, I look aghast. "You let them all go on their own?"

I expect her to fight back. And she does. "They're adults, Adeline. They can go to a spa on their own."

"So you could—" I spread my hands, fluttering them as if I just can't grasp the truth. "So you and your brother-in-law could enjoy the sun?" My tone got harder with every word.

Yvette can no longer say a word. There is no defense.

I'm not surprised at the scene we came upon once we'd

returned to the house. I could hardly *not* hear Kacey say that word. *Screwing*. That's what they'd been doing. Thank God Kacey called me when she couldn't get hold of her mother. She'd been in tears. Garth had taken over the phone, saying he couldn't get hold of either Brock or Yvette. It was fortunate Kacey made that call. If it had been Garth, he'd have called Trevor first. At that point, I'd immediately directed Trevor back to the house.

So the scene we came upon wasn't a shock, not at all. It was obvious after Trevor herded me into the car the way he did. Something was up. Though I hadn't known exactly what, I did know my two sons were colluding against me.

Thank goodness for Darryl and whatever horrific thing he'd done.

And again, I smile deep inside. It's just so perfect.

Especially when Kacey says, "And they weren't just sunbathing, Grandmother." She sends her mother a glare that shreds Yvette to pieces. "They were in bed together."

If I were her mother rather than her grandmother, I would slap her for that tone. No one talks to me that way. But right now, she's doing and saying exactly what I need her to. Because that means I don't have to be the bad guy.

The harlot gives a horrified little gasp. But that traitor Lorna jumps in as if she's suddenly taken on the role of peacemaker. "Kacey, sweetheart, they're consenting adults. They can do whatever they want."

Kacey spits out exactly what I want to say. "It's disgusting."

I see Yvette breaking down, bit by bit, first her fingers digging into the chair arms, then her eyes turning to blurred pools, and finally her bosom heaving as if she can't make her lungs work. I'd broken her once, long ago, and it had sent her running down to the gatehouse to live. Although she hadn't left Pierce the way I'd hoped.

I will break her again. And this time when she runs, that will be the end of her. I can wash that girl right off my hands.

But Jodi isn't chiming in. I need her to back up her sister.

"I'm sure you were both shocked." I set my watery gaze on my two granddaughters and play the mediator. "But your Aunt Lorna is right. They're adults." Then I give my youngest granddaughter a needed push. "Are you all right, Jodi? You haven't said a word. Please, we all need to talk this out."

Jodi opens her mouth, but Kacey jumps in before her sister can speak. "This is all your fault," she shouts at her mother.

Good, very good. The more blame cast about, the better.

"Darryl told me there was something going on between the two of you." She points her finger at Yvette like the bony hand of judgment. "I wouldn't believe him. But now I wouldn't put it past you to send the police to arrest him because he knew what was going on."

Oh my. I want to clap my hands. I want to cheer. She is marvelously off the rails, to use an old but very apt cliché. And I say softly, "Please, Kacey, you need to calm yourself." Of course, when you tell someone to calm down, that just works them up even more.

Kacey doesn't calm down, and she hurls the words at her mother. "I hate you for what you've done."

Ahh, this is perfect.

But I do wonder why they arrested that little mushroom, Darryl. Not that it matters. I don't care one whit. It would be even better if we left him here. He isn't our responsibility. Let his parents bail him out.

Jodi stands, puts her arm around her hysterical sister. "Come on, Kacey, this isn't doing any good. Let's go back to your room. Maybe you can sleep. Or take a shower. That'll help you feel better."

Kacey bursts into tears again, and her sister leads her

away. I expect Yvette to melt into a miserable puddle on the floor after what her daughter said.

But the harlot is glaring at me with the venom of a rattlesnake in her eyes. "You're a witch."

No. I'm a python.

And I will suffocate the life out of this relationship she's forged with my son if it's the last thing I ever do.

Yvette left the house after Adeline rang her annoying bell for Olive, telling their chef it was time to take the Christmas tree down. No one felt like celebrating anymore. It was the only thing on which Yvette agreed with Adeline.

Once away from that vicious woman, Yvette knocked on the front door of the girls' house. And heard Kacey scream, "Go away," the words and the tone slicing off several more pieces of her heart.

Adeline had made it all worse, of course. Yvette hadn't a clue how to stop her. Maybe there was no way to stop Adeline. Kacey had been too distraught to see reason. Her boyfriend was arrested for no discernible reason, and right after that, she caught her mother in bed with her uncle.

What could be worse?

She shriveled inside, dying right there on the path before the unopened door. Reaching out, she tried to handle. But they'd locked her out.

It was everything she'd ever feared. She never should have slept with Brock. She never should have kissed him, touched him. And she certainly shouldn't have fallen in love with him.

Pulling her phone from her dress pocket—Brock had given it back to her when he'd retrieved his from the beach—she found it filled with missed calls from Kacey and Jodi.

Her finger hovered over the call button, Jodi's number. Should she let them calm down first?

God, she had no idea what to do.

And she pushed the button, because what more could she lose? She'd already lost it all.

Jodi answered, no words, just her breath.

"Sweetheart," Yvette whispered.

"Look, Mom, I'm taking care of Kacey. Can you just back off for a while? She's not ready to talk about anything yet."

"Are you?" Yvette's voice trembled, making her sound weak.

Jodi took so long to answer that Yvette's breath stopped in her chest.

"Mom, we just need the uncles to solve this problem with Darryl. When that's all settled, we can talk. But not right now." Yvette couldn't tell if there was anger or just resignation in her daughter's voice.

She wanted to ask if Jodi still loved her. But terrified of the answer, she couldn't get the words out. "All right." The only good thing she could hang onto was that Jodi said, "Bye, Mom," before she hung up.

Yvette couldn't go back to her room, couldn't look at that bed, couldn't remember the sound of Kacey's shriek when she'd burst in on them.

Walking down between the two houses, she stepped onto the beach, heading away from the turquoise swing where she'd put the day's events in motion with that sexy little sashay back to her cottage.

She never should have let him kiss her on that Chicago

waterfront. She never should have let him into her hotel room. She never should have let him come to her night after night after night, making her feel all that pleasure, all that wonder. All that love.

Because she'd known this would eventually happen. And now she'd lost her daughters.

Finally, she sank onto the sand, out of sight of the houses and the cottages. As if she were hiding. Maybe she was. Legs tight together, she hooked her arms around her shins and laid her head on her knees. It was hot, even here in the shade. But she didn't care. She couldn't stand the air conditioning of her room.

Not with the bed and all the reminders still there in its rumpled sheets.

Her phone rang, and when she looked, she saw Brock's icon. She wouldn't have answered except that she needed to know was happening with Darryl. And what Brock was doing about it.

"Hello." Her voice came out weak and strained.

His was as solid and controlled as ever. "How are you doing?"

*Dying*, she wanted to tell him.

"I'm on the beach, just taking a respite from all the drama." She sounded so mild, so unaffected.

"We'll fix this." His words came out in a rush.

"I guess it depends on what Darryl's done."

"I was talking about us."

It felt like raking her heart over a bed of coals when she said, "There is no us. We can't do this anymore. We never should have started. Now it's over."

His voice broke on his words. "We'll never be over. At least I won't be over you."

"But I have to be over you. This had to end. You know it. I know it."

His voice was harsh against her ear, as if he were standing right next to her. "You love me. I love you. We're not done. We will never be done."

She closed her eyes against the bright sun reflecting off the ocean. "What we feel doesn't matter. Only our children matter. And they need us now."

"They need us united."

"We'll always be united in protecting them. But what we've been doing hasn't protected them." She slashed a hand through the air as if she were cutting the ties that connected them. "I won't talk about it anymore. Tell me what's happening with Darryl."

As if he heard the resolve in her voice, he sighed. "The kid is an idiot."

"But what did he do?" Neither of them had any doubt that Darryl had done something.

Brock sighed again. "He propositioned his masseuse. All he wanted, and I quote, was a happy ending."

She exhaled as heavily as he had. "Well, I hope this helps Kacey see what he's really like. But honestly, he got arrested just for a proposition?"

"He probably wouldn't have been arrested if he'd stopped with just that. But he rolled over, and apparently there was some intimate physical contact involved which she didn't appreciate."

She flopped back, not caring about the sand in her hair. "You're right. He's an idiot."

"It's hard to get a concrete answer out of the kid. He just keeps saying he didn't do anything. But she ended up running out screaming and the spa security arrived. They called the cops." He actually laughed. "They hauled him away wrapped up in just a towel."

Okay, she couldn't help an answering laugh. "Oh my God,"

she breathed out. "I hope he'll have learned his lesson by the time you get him out of there."

"It won't be easy. They take a thing like this very seriously. It's assault and attempted rape."

She gasped. "What will they do to him?"

"He could go to prison for years. I've already got a lawyer coming over from Nassau. Because we need someone local. And our US lawyer is also flying in."

"Can you fix this?" Or should they leave Darryl to his just rewards?

"I don't know. Part of me doesn't want to fix it," he said, echoing her thoughts. "But since it's Saturday, we can't get into the courts today anyway. He won't go in for arraignment, or whatever they call it down here, until Monday. That might not be a bad thing. It will give Trevor and me time to strategize with the lawyers tomorrow. But the New Year's holiday is coming up, which could cause a further delay."

"How am I going to tell Kacey?" Her stomach curdled when she thought about it.

"Trevor and I will be home soon. But we can't keep it a secret from Kacey. That would make everything worse. She's an adult."

Yvette agreed. "I can't shelter her." But bringing this news would make everything worse.

Kacey already blamed her for not being able to contact Brock as soon as it happened. Not that it would have made any difference. Darryl had already committed the crime.

But Kacey would still hate her for everything that happened.

BROCK COULDN'T THINK ABOUT WHAT YVETTE HAD SAID. He wouldn't believe it. They were not over. She was just reacting to a bad situation. She'd remember later that they were meant to be together. And nothing would stop them.

Except she'd torn his heart into so many pieces he could never sew them all back together.

He saw her sitting in a chair on the front porch of the main house when he and Trevor drove up. Ethan, Malcolm, Francine, and Iris were on their way in the Jeep, but Garth sat in the back seat of the Town Car. His son hadn't had a lot to say. Except to call Darryl every name his grandmother would have boxed his ears for saying.

Now, before they got out of the car, Garth asked, "What will we tell Kacey?"

Trevor gave an immediate answer. "We'll tell her the truth."

Garth slumped in the seat. "That'll break her heart."

"Her heart will break anyway," Brock said. "Because I know my niece. And she won't stop questioning us until she knows the truth." Her heartbreak was inevitable.

Maybe his was as well, even as he kept telling himself Yvette would change her mind. But the thing she'd feared most had happened. Her daughter hated her. Maybe later, Kacey would get over it. But for now, when she heard about Darryl, Kacey would take out all her anger on her mother. And probably him too. Though Yvette would take the brunt of it. And there was nothing he could do to stop it.

Yvette rose from the chair as they all climbed out of the car. When she was close enough, she asked, "Will he be all right in jail over the weekend?"

"We got him a single cell. And they gave him some clothes instead of just the towel. There's food and water. They won't starve him. He'll be fine."

"Although," Trevor added, "putting the fear of God in that boy would be a good thing."

In a beaten voice, Yvette said, "I knocked on the girls'

door earlier to see if I could talk to Kacey, but they won't let me in."

His heart broke for her. This pain was all hers. His sons didn't care. Garth had even said they could leave Darryl in jail for all he cared. It was Yvette's girls who would feel the most pain. And therefore, so would Yvette. He wanted to wrap her up in his arms. But at this moment, that was the worst idea. He had only one thing to offer. "I'll talk to them."

As Yvette crossed her arms and meandered closer, he caught her scent, a mix of him and her and their love.

"She's already hurting." Her chest rose with a deep breath. "Just make it gentle."

When his vocal cords wouldn't work, Trevor said for him, "We'll tell her as easily as possible. But she needs to know the truth."

She closed her eyes, swaying on her feet. Brock wanted to grab her, hold her steady. But looking once again at Trevor, she said, "I know you're right."

As he and Trevor turned, Garth put an arm around her shoulders. "It'll all be okay, Aunt Yvette."

He could have kissed his son for doing the thing he couldn't. As Yvette laid her head on Garth's solid shoulder, he felt her lap up the forgiveness buried in those words.

Brock knocked on the girls' door. A thin, angry voice carried out. "I told you to go away, Mother."

Brock wished he could take the impact, but Yvette heard. All he could do was call through the door. "It's your Uncle Brock. I've been to the jail. We need to talk."

The door opened instantly, with Jodi standing there, as if she'd been waiting for him.

The Jeep roared up then, spitting gravel, Ethan at the wheel. Moments later, Iris and Francine rushed the doorway, barreling past him, sparing quick hugs for Jodi, then dashing into the living room.

Kacey sat on the sofa, a box of tissues in front of her, several gripped in her fingers. Her pink-stained cheeks matched her nose and red-rimmed eyes. Tears still clotted her eyelashes, but she managed a weak voice. "What's happening, Uncle Brock?"

Her animosity for him was nothing compared to what she'd dished out to Yvette. Wasn't that the age-old way of things? The woman always bore the shame. Or maybe Kacey just wanted an answer before she attacked him.

A hand on Jodi's shoulder, he said, "Why don't you sit with Kacey?" His niece obeyed immediately, hugging close to her sister.

But when Yvette stepped over the threshold, the venom in Kacey's voice shocked even him. "I don't want her in here," she spat through clenched teeth.

Brock stood his ground. "This is family business. And your mother is part of this family. She'll be here the way everyone else is."

Kacey burst into tears again, and Jodi pulled her sister's head onto her shoulder. She might be the younger one, but she had the compassion of a woman years older.

Yvette said, "I'll wait outside." But Brock reached for her. "No. We all need to know the stakes." He pleaded with his eyes. She couldn't run away. If she did, the chances of Kacey and Jodi forgiving them would shrink to nothing. Yvette had to face the truth, just the way Kacey did.

Brock took a seat on the chair facing Kacey. Standing by the other end of the sofa, Yvette was as far from him as she could get. Garth perched on a sofa arm next to the girls. He squeezed Jodi's shoulder, eliciting a gentle smile from her, not a happy one but a thankful one. Crossing his arms, Trevor remained standing by the coffee table. Brock could have left the tale to his brother, but this was his battle. He was the reason the two girls blamed their mother. He couldn't back down any more than he could let Yvette back down.

"This will be hard," he said in a tone he hoped would gentle the girl. "If I could spare you, I would. But I can't. Darryl was arrested for solicitation and..." He didn't quite know how to say the words. The stark reality of them would break her. But it had to be said.

And yet Garth finished for him. "He was arrested for attempting to rape his masseuse."

Was it any wonder Kacey burst into another round of sobs? In a tear-filled voice, she asked, "What exactly did he do?"

Brock had known he'd find the story hard to tell. But her swollen face and her misery tore at his heart as viciously as Yvette's words had. "He asked her to give him a happy ending. You know what that is?"

She nodded. Kids knew everything these days.

"When she protested, there was some unwanted touching involved."

"She should have squeezed him hard enough to make him scream," Jodi snapped.

The boy certainly would have learned his lesson if she had. At least for a little while.

Trevor took over then. "She called Security. Then the police came."

"But what is Darryl saying?" Kacey wanted to know, probably *needed* to.

Brock answered honestly. "He said all he did was ask her. But he didn't touch her. He just rolled over." He had to lick his lips before he added, "It was quite clear what he wanted, and somehow there was a touch involved, but it was an accident." An accident, yeah right. But as much as he and Trevor pushed, Darryl couldn't—or wouldn't—say exactly what that meant. Maybe the lawyers could get it out of him tomorrow.

She looked at him with wide eyes. "Do you believe him? That whatever happened was accidental?"

The truth? Or a lie to save her feelings? He considered which for a moment. But his niece deserved the truth. "I believe he did something, I'm not sure what, and it was completely unwanted on her part."

She jumped up from the couch, dashed around the end, and ran for the sliding glass door to the beach. But there she stopped. Yvette made a move toward her, but then she looked at Jodi and something passed between them. And Jodi went to her sister.

Brock told them the current situation. "We've got two lawyers coming, one from Nassau and one from the US, since it's an international matter."

Though she muffled her voice against Jodi's shoulder, he made out Kacey's words threaded through her tears. "I wanted a couples' massage. They brought you fruit and cheese and champagne and chocolate. And there would be two massage therapists. But Darryl said it cost too much money, and he told me I should get a facial instead. Because I couldn't have both a facial and a massage."

Brock wanted to smash the kid's face. It hadn't been a spur-of-the-moment thing. He'd planned it. He'd thought the spa was some sort of sex club where he could ask for sexual favors. Whatever "accidental" thing happened was on his head.

He turned at a noise behind him. And his mother's voice rang out. "We should leave him exactly where he is. In jail. Perhaps the punishment here in the Bahamas is castration."

## ❦ 25 ❦

---

### ADELINE

The nerve of them. They cut me out of the family meeting.

I don't move quickly these days. And sometimes I hold on to a chair back or two. But no one stops me as I make my way to my granddaughter.

I can't miss this opportunity. Eying Jodi until she steps back, I wrap my arms around Kacey. The girl clings to me. I count on that.

Then I stand back, holding her shoulders in my disgustingly frail hands.

Are these *my* hands? How many of us think we're still thirty-five? Until we look at our crooked fingers and the age spots and remember all the aches and pains in our joints.

"It's been a terrible day for you, my dear. First, that horrible boy getting himself arrested for betraying you." I let my voice rise only slightly, but enough to make sure everyone hears. Especially Jodi. "And then you come home to find your mother's treachery."

Brock jumps to his feet. "Adeline." His voice snaps through the air.

## CHAPTER 25

The girl needs a reminder that it isn't only her boyfriend who has betrayed her. So has her mother and her uncle. *Especially* her mother. Kacey begins to cry. She has so many tears ahead of her before this is all over.

And when it's over, I will make sure she never speaks to her mother again.

I expect Brock to drag me away. Even Trevor might do it. Yvette is too stunned. She's always been a weakling. She never deserved to be a Donnelly.

But it's Jodi who leans close to me and says, "You're making it worse, Grandmother."

I can't believe I hear censure, not from her. After all, it's her mother and her uncle. Yet a surprising amount of battle light shines out of her Donnelly-blue eyes, and she adds softly, perhaps so no one else will hear, "Stop making trouble, Adeline."

*Adeline*. It's the first time the girl has ever called me anything but Grandmother. Or spoken with anything but respect.

The girl has gumption. I'm suddenly proud of her. Because Jodi is just like me.

I have to consider how I can use that to my advantage.

## ❧ 26 ☙

**Y**vette wanted to hug her youngest daughter for standing up to Adeline.

But Francine asked, "So does this mean we're not going out on the catamaran tomorrow?"

For a moment, there was stunned silence.

Even though Yvette was the furthest thing from laughing right now, she wanted to laugh. Young people. Sometimes the gravity of a situation didn't hit home. But then it wasn't Francine's boyfriend who'd assaulted his massage therapist and gotten himself thrown in jail.

Brock, however, laughed. "You can go out on the catamaran. Garth can take care of it."

Garth stood taller. "I'm staying with you and Uncle Trevor to deal with the lawyers." Of course. He wasn't a boy; he was a man. And he wanted to be down in the trenches with the other men.

Ethan said, "I'll take care of everyone." Followed quickly on the heels by Malcolm adding, "We can both do it."

Through her tears, Kacey ground out, "I can't believe you guys." Then she raced up the stairs. On any other day, Yvette would have run after her, but as she heard a door slam upstairs, she knew it would be a long time before her daughter ever let her in again.

Jodi swiftly followed Kacey. "I'll go make sure she's okay."

Francine raised her hands in the air, asking, "What did I say?" as if she didn't get it.

Adeline turned to Yvette, her smile saying, *My work here is done*. Heading for the sliding glass door, she stepped out, closing it gently behind her.

At the front door, Lorna said, "Olive is holding dinner for us. I think we need something to eat. Come on, everyone."

Trevor went to her, sliding an arm around her shoulders as they turned back to the big house.

Garth, the boys, and their girlfriends followed. Suddenly, it was just Brock and Yvette.

His laughter faded, and the lines of his face were strained. "We need to talk."

She held her palm out toward him, warning him off in case he tried to touch her. "There's nothing to talk about. We can't keep on doing what we were doing."

He closed his eyes. As if the words hurt him as much as they did her. Then his haunted gaze cut through her. "You know it's not over."

She didn't know how she would have fought him, because all she wanted to do was throw herself in his arms and cry out her anger, frustration, and fear.

But Jodi appeared at the top of the stairs. "Can I talk to you?"

She didn't call her Mom. But her gaze made it clear who she was talking to. Brock mouthed, *Later*, before he followed the rest of the family.

Jodi slowly descended the stairs, but instead of sitting on the couch, she opened the back door, stepping out and kicking off her flip-flops before she walked onto the sand.

As the sun dipped, the day was cooling off, though the air remained balmy. Instead of begging her daughter's forgiveness, she asked, "How's Kacey?"

They strolled down the beach a long minute before Jodi finally answered. "She's angry. Upset. She feels betrayed."

Yvette closed her eyes against the pain. She deserved that. "I mean," Jodi said, "we all knew Darryl was an ass. But now she gets slapped in the face with it. And that hurts."

Of course. Darryl had betrayed Kacey as well. Consumed with her own guilt and her roiling emotions, Yvette had concentrated only on what *she'd* done, not how Kacey felt about Darryl's infidelity.

Did that make her selfish? Of course it did. And it made her a terrible mother. But it also made her human.

"At least she's seen the light," Jodi went on. "I didn't want it to happen this way, but now she can be done with that douche bag and find someone who's worthy of her."

Yvette couldn't help adding, even with a little smile, "You're right. He's a total douche."

Jodi laughed.

Her daughter would never know how good that laugh felt. That Jodi could still laugh with her mother meant the world. It meant there was a chance.

"The only reason she's so angry with you and Uncle Brock is because of Darryl." She turned, spread her hands as she walked backwards, looking at Yvette. "I mean, when they took him away, she was like a crazy person. We had to hold her back. Then she was calling you guys frantically, and no one answered. It just made it worse for her."

The only thing Yvette wanted to ask in this moment was if Jodi would get over finding her mother and her uncle together. She was afraid Kacey never would. But Jodi? Yvette could only pray.

"Kacey said we didn't know what he'd done." Jodi stopped on the sand, facing the sea, gazing at the sunset as the colors stretched across the sky. Then she turned to Yvette. "I mean, he was calling out, 'I didn't do it. I didn't do it.'" She snorted. "And there were all these whispers, and his masseuse looked so upset. She was out there, and both Ethan and Malcolm had seen her call his name when we were all waiting for our sessions. So it wasn't like we weren't *guessing* what happened. At least I wasn't. But Kacey just kept saying she couldn't understand why. But she knew. We all knew. She was just in denial."

"And when your Uncle Brock came back," Yvette added, "and told her why Darryl was arrested, Kacey couldn't deny it anymore."

Jodi nodded.

Yvette had to say it. She couldn't *not* say it, even as much as she didn't want to. "And to top it off, she found me with your uncle."

Jodi gave her a sideways glance Yvette couldn't read. "Yeah. She walked in on you." She sighed. "It was so much easier to spit all her anger at you instead of where it belonged."

Yvette's need to know tore her apart. "And how do you feel?"

"About you and Uncle Brock?" The question was an obvious stalling tactic.

"Yes," Yvette confirmed. "About us." Even though it felt as if there was no "us" anymore. No Brock and Yvette. There never could be again.

But Jodi snorted a laugh. It wasn't sad. It wasn't angry. It wasn't happy either. It was just a burst of sound. "Jesus, Mom. I've known about you guys for months."

It felt like a punch straight to her belly, but Yvette didn't collapse, didn't even bend over so she could breathe. Even though Jodi's words sucked all the air out of her. "What do you mean?"

An odd light filled Jodi's eyes. It might have been laughter. And a definite smirk creased her lips. "I see the way he looks at you. And the way you look at him. I mean, sometimes it's like there's no one else in the room but the two of you. You only have eyes for each other."

Sensation sizzled along her skin. Fear. But something else too. Hope. "Does it bother you?"

Jodi tipped her head back, staring at the sky, and tucked her hair behind her ears. Finally, she looked at Yvette. "At first I thought it was…" She shrugged. "Weird, I guess. Then I thought about how miserable you always were with Dad."

Yvette gasped. "I wasn't miserable."

Jodi rolled her eyes. "Are you really saying that you two always got along?"

Yvette swallowed hard. She'd tried to keep all that from her daughters. Obviously, she hadn't. "I guess not," she confessed.

"And after he was gone, it was like your life was so lonely. It was just go to work, come home, cook dinner for us."

"I love cooking for you. I love taking care of you and your sister. I even love doing your laundry."

Jodi snorted. "Yeah right. That's why you always asked us why we couldn't clean up our rooms and do our own laundry."

This time, Yvette couldn't help the bubble of laughter. "All right. That's true."

"Anyway, now, with us gone, you're all alone."

"I just want to be here for you when you are home. Vacations, holidays. Especially during the summer. Unless you go to summer school."

Jodi lifted her shoulders like a physical question. "What about when we graduate? When we've got jobs and our own apartments?"

Yvette sighed, bit her lip, still not answering the key question. "I suppose I could get a flat in the city. Something close enough to walk to work."

But Jodi said what Yvette couldn't. "Would you marry Uncle Brock?"

He'd asked her so many times, it shouldn't have taken her breath away. But this was her daughter. Finally, when she could breathe again, she said, "Would you be okay with that?"

Shaking her head, Jodi said, "You must think I'm some sort of ungrateful cow."

The words shocked Yvette. "Of course I don't. You should never say that about yourself."

Jodi grinned, her hand to her chest. "I never said *I* felt that way."

"Well, I certainly don't think you're an ungrateful cow. And neither is your sister."

Jodi tipped her head to one side. "So, would you marry him?"

She suddenly felt like the daughter, and Jodi had become the mother. "I don't know."

"Why not? Because you think Kacey will hate you forever?"

Yvette couldn't help saying, "When did you become so grown up?"

"I've been a grown-up for a long time," Jodi said with a certain amount of sadness. "Who do you think takes care of Kacey at school?"

Yvette huffed out a breath. "And now you're taking care of me."

She looked at her beautiful daughter with fresh eyes. Jodi was so perceptive. It wasn't as if Yvette hadn't known that. She'd always felt her daughter was special. Both her daughters were. But Jodi had always seemed to be there when Yvette felt her lowest, asking if they could bake cookies or play a card game or watch a favorite show together.

It came to her then, in a way it never had before, that those times had never been about what Jodi needed. It had been about what Jodi thought Yvette needed.

The words fell out of her mouth. "Do you know how much I love you?"

Jodi shrugged. "Yeah, yeah, I know you love me."

"No. I mean it. I—" She touched her chest. "—love—" She pointed at Jodi. "—you."

Then she drew her daughter into her arms, hugged her tightly, and said against her ear, "I don't know what will happen between your uncle and me. I only know I can't make your sister unhappy because of me."

Jodi drew back. "She's unhappy because of Darryl. Because he's such a creep."

"Douche bag," Yvette said softly.

Jodi smiled. "She's just taking it out on you right now. She'll get over it."

"Did she guess about us too?" She didn't need to add more for Jodi to understand.

"She had her head buried in *The Book of Darryl*. Of course she didn't notice." She looked at the sand as if she couldn't say the words while her eyes were on her mother. "She's just lashing out at you so she doesn't have to face what a douche Darryl is. And she has to admit that before she can do something about it."

"She can't be thinking of staying with him after this?" It was almost a question. If Kacey hadn't found her with Brock, if she hadn't gone ballistic, that was what Yvette would say to her daughter now.

"You can darn well believe I won't let her stay with him. Right now, she's in denial. She's still trying to tell herself he's not guilty."

"Do you think I can talk to her?" Oh yes, they had reversed roles.

Jodi shook her head so hard her hair flew. "Not right now. But it might be soon."

It had to be soon if she didn't want to lose Kasey altogether. The longer this went on, the worse it would get.

Then she threw her arms around her daughter again, squeezed her with all the love bubbling up inside her. "I love you."

Jodi whispered, "I love you too." Then, after a breath, she added, "And Kasey will again."

Yvette loved her daughter for those words.

But she wasn't sure they were true.

BROCK STOOD OUTSIDE YVETTE'S DOOR. IT WAS LATE. NO lights burned in any of the houses in their compound, no fires on the beach, no rowdy drinking songs, no beer toasts, no midnight swims. Olive had even removed the Christmas tree. The holiday was over.

He knocked.

Yvette never answered. He'd hoped she would. But he'd also known she wouldn't.

Walking around the back to her small porch, he found her curtains closed. He knocked anyway, afraid it would be the same as it had been at the front door. Nothing.

Then Yvette opened a slit in the curtains.

And stole his breath.

She wore shorty pajamas that would have been called baby dolls in his day. Short shorts that showed off the long, tanned legs he loved to feel wrapped around him, and a sleeveless top that bared the shoulders he loved to kiss.

Through the screen-in porch between them, he said, "We

need to talk." There was no sound to the words; he didn't have the breath to make her hear.

She shook her head, her luscious hair falling over her shoulders. He loved to sink his fingers into those thick, silky locks.

He was afraid he'd never get to do it again.

Unable to hear her, he could only read her lips. "It's over," she said. "There has to be an end to this, and it's now."

He wanted to shout. He wanted to bang on the glass. He wanted to howl at the moon. "We'll never be over." She might not hear his words, but she would read them on his lips.

But the only thing on her kissable mouth was, "Go away."

Then she yanked the curtains closed across his face.

Deep in his gut and wrapped around his heart was the knowledge that they would never be over. He didn't care what her daughters thought. He didn't care what his mother said. He didn't care what the Board of Directors wanted. Yvette was his.

And he was hers.

He took out his phone and sent a three-word text message.

*I love you.*

She didn't answer.

THE LAWYERS SAT WITH BROCK, TREVOR, AND GARTH around the table in the big dining room of the main house. Kacey had wanted to attend, but Brock had firmly told her no. But there was no amount of firmness that would keep Adeline out. She saw herself as the matriarch, the ruler. And she sat at the head of the table.

"This is a very serious charge," the softly accented

Bahamian lawyer said. Romario Deveaux's dark skin was a striking contrast to his crisply white shirt. He was younger than Trevor, somewhere in his late thirties. "And this is not America," he added, "where a rich white man is automatically believed over the word of a young woman."

"Now wait just a minute," Grady Thompson began. The Donnelly lawyer was in his fifties, with steel-gray hair and a loud voice that carried well in a courtroom.

But they weren't in a courtroom yet. Brock held up his hand. "We're not questioning the young woman's sincerity." In fact, Brock believed her. But he still couldn't leave the kid down here to rot in a Bahamian jail for God knew how long.

"Can we just put him on a plane to go home?" Trevor asked. It wasn't Brock's preferred method, but the question had to be asked.

"You could do that," Deveaux said softly. "But there would be an immediate warrant for his arrest." He shrugged. "Of course, he would be fine as long as he stayed in the United States. But he could never leave the country because as soon as he showed his passport, he would be arrested by our authorities." His tone and his words were clipped.

"We have no intention of spiriting him away," Brock said.

Grady continued, "All we want is to ensure a sentence commensurate with what he did."

Gravely, Deveaux said, "I assure you what he did was quite serious. There was touching—" He cut himself off, glancing at Adeline.

Adeline gave him the full force of her stare. "Let him fry. He isn't good enough for my granddaughter."

Brock wanted to drop his head in his hands. His mother had always been bloodthirsty. But he said, "Darryl claims he wouldn't have gone any further when he realized she wasn't willing. She started screaming before he could say that."

Adeline harrumphed, raising her gaze to the ceiling and folding her arms over her chest.

Darryl was an ass, Brock had to admit. But he didn't believe the kid was a rapist. He believed him as much as he believed the young woman. Darryl was stupid, and he was arrogant. And no way in hell did he have a right to proposition a woman when she was only doing her job. But would he have forced her?

Elbows on the table, hands in the air, fingers splayed, Trevor said, "So." He paused, staring down Romario Deveaux. "Are you on our side? Or the prosecution's side?"

Deveaux smiled. "I am only playing devil's advocate here. That is what the government will say." He waved a hand to encompass them all. "We need to find a way to mitigate the charges. And bring the young man home again."

Adeline narrowed her eyes. "He better not get off scot-free," she said, her tone as pointed as her index finger.

"He won't get off scot-free, Adeline," Brock said. "We just don't want him staying down here in a foreign jail."

"And I want him out of my granddaughter's life." Her nostrils flared with her vehemence.

Brock wanted the same thing, but Kacey was a woman, not a child. Whatever she did would be her decision. That didn't mean he wouldn't steer her in the right direction if she started taking the wrong one. But he couldn't force her.

"Whatever happens between them is up to them, Adeline."

The only concern now was strategizing how they would keep Darryl out of a thirty-year prison sentence in a Bahamian jail.

Yvette should have sat in on the meeting since it was her daughter's boyfriend who'd committed the crime.

But Adeline was there. And Yvette couldn't have withstood the cutting remarks. Besides, Brock would do everything he could on Kacey's behalf, even if that meant doing something decent for Darryl.

No matter what, she wanted that young man out of her daughter's life.

She didn't know if Kacey had ever come out of her room —she certainly hadn't been at breakfast or lunch—but Yvette knew the longer this went on, the deeper the rift between them would grow.

Brock's sons had gone out on the catamaran, their girlfriends with them. When Yvette entered the girls' house, she found Jodi seated on the couch. "Why didn't you go with them?" she asked her daughter.

It didn't surprise her when Jodi said, "I wanted to be here in case Kacey comes out of her room."

"Has she?"

Jodi shook her head.

Yvette sucked up her courage. "I'm going up to talk to her." Then she asked, "Is her door locked?"

Again, Jodi shook her head. "Enter at your own risk," she warned.

The words brought a smile to her lips. Jodi, as a teenager, had put that sticker on her bedroom door.

Reminding her, Yvette said, "But you always let me in to get your dirty laundry."

Her daughter laughed, and it was so good to hear that beautiful sound. Maybe Kacey would never forgive her, but Jodi didn't seem to care one bit.

Still, Yvette had turned Brock away last night. Even as badly as she'd wanted to throw herself into his arms, wanted his comfort and his strength. As badly as she'd wanted to reply to his text and tell him she would never stop loving him. She didn't know how she would go on without him.

But today, there was her daughter. And Kacey needed her.

She started up the stairs. "If you hear things smashing, don't interrupt."

## 27

**E**ven as she climbed the stairs, Yvette wondered if this was the right time to talk to Kacey. Perhaps she should wait until after they knew what would happen to Darryl.

But waiting was the coward's way out. She should have gone to Kacey last night. And now, she couldn't let it go on for even another hour.

Upstairs, she strode to the only room with a closed door and knocked.

Kacey's reply was immediate and harsh. "Go away." She didn't even ask who was knocking. Yvette tried the doorknob and found it unlocked. She called out, "It's me, Kacey. I'm coming in."

Before the door was even halfway open, Kacey hissed, "I told you to go away."

The words and her daughter's tone scraped across her skin like steel wool, but she said, "I can't do that. You're my daughter, and I love you. We need to talk."

Kacey lay on the bed, her legs pulled up in the fetal position, her hair a tangled mess, her clothes the same she'd worn yesterday.

"I don't want to talk to you." The pillow she clutched to her chest muffled her words.

As much as the situation hurt her—she'd never experienced an argument this bad with either of her daughters— Yvette walked to the bed and sat down next to Kacey's feet. "I realize you don't want to talk. I know you're angry. But we can't let this fester between us."

Kacey scrunched even tighter into her fetal ball. "I hate you. I can't believe what you did. Get out."

Yvette wanted to scrunch into that same fetal ball, the pain of her child's words worse than even the harshest memory of Adeline's most callous remarks. But she was here, and she wouldn't stop now. "I'm sorry about Darryl."

Kacey didn't let her go on. "I'm not talking about Darryl," she snapped. "It's what *you* did."

What *had* she done? Fallen in love? Kept her relationship secret from her daughters? Made love to Brock in her bed with the door unlocked so her daughter could walk in on her?

It wasn't the crime of the century. It was just life. She'd known all along that her daughters would hate her. Jodi had astounded her by *not* hating her.

She didn't touch Kacey. But she didn't back down either. "I'm sorry you had to find out under those circumstances."

Kacey verbally jumped on her. "It was disgusting. And now everyone knows what you've been doing."

Yvette couldn't help it. She closed her eyes against the pain of her daughter's words.

But she had to deal with this now. If she let Adeline talk to Kacey before they worked this out, Yvette would lose everything. She gathered her courage from deep in her belly. "What bothers you the most? That I fell in love with another man. Or that the man is your uncle?"

It sounded so sordid. And yet there was nothing sordid about it. What she and Brock had found was beautiful. Didn't she deserve that beauty after all the years with Pierce while he'd grown to hate her?

But Kacey snapped, "All of it. At least you could've had the decency not to do it when we were on vacation and everyone was here." Her voice was so caustic it stripped a layer of skin from Yvette's body.

But she admitted the truth. "Maybe you're right. Maybe we shouldn't have done that." Then she drew in a deep breath and gave her daughter another truth. "But it doesn't change how we feel about each other."

Kacey shot out question after question. "How long has it been going on? Were you cheating on Dad? Did you always want Uncle Brock more than you wanted my father? Did you always want to marry him instead? I mean, honestly, if you thought everything was okay about it, why were you sneaking around? Why didn't you just tell us?"

If she told Kacey none of that was her business, it would be all over. So she spoke the truth. *Her* truth. "We've been together for nine months. I never cheated on your father. I never even wanted to cheat on your father, not with anyone." She didn't say that Pierce had no compunction at all about cheating on her. But impugning him now would only make things worse. "I didn't tell you because I was afraid of how you'd react." Exactly the way Kacey *had* reacted. But Yvette didn't say that either. And she didn't say that she'd been afraid of how Adeline would use the relationship to turn Kacey and Jodi against her.

"It makes my skin crawl to think of the two of you together."

Yvette's skin crawled hearing that tone in her daughter's voice. It was more than anger. It was disgust. It was hatred.

A part of her wanted to shrivel up and die, to drop on the

rug and creep out of the room like a beaten animal. But she'd started this. She had to finish it. No matter how it ended. She had to say what needed to be said. "I love you. My relationship with your uncle—" She could have called him Brock, eased the tension by not stressing the familial relationship. But maybe Kacey needed to feel a little stress. "If I have to, I'll give him up."

Hadn't she already given him up? Hadn't she already told him this was all his fault? Hadn't she refused to let him into her cottage last night, let alone into her bed?

Kacey didn't know any of that, and she said in a low, angry voice, "I don't care what you do. You can fuck him all you want."

That word on her daughter's lips sliced her straight through the middle, cut her in half, and left her bleeding right there on the edge of the bed. When Brock said it in the throes of passion, it was sexy.

But from her daughter's mouth, it was a travesty.

"That's not what we do." Risking her daughter's wrath, she added, "And don't ever call it that." She loved Kacey. She understood her anger. But even from her daughter, she wouldn't take that.

Then Kacey spat, "I'm not sorry I said it."

"But I am," Yvette whispered, loud enough for her daughter to hear. Then she said, "You and I are both adults. And neither of us has the right to question or criticize what the other does. I don't question you about Darryl and—"

Kacey sat up straight, the pillow hugged to her chest, her eyes blazing, tear tracks down her face. "Don't you dare talk about Darryl."

"I'm not. Because you have to make up your own mind about him. You have to decide if he's telling the truth. That's not up to me."

Instead of hurling more insults the way Yvette feared, her

beautiful daughter suddenly burst into tears. Throwing herself against the pillows, she sobbed.

There were no more words after that. Yvette sidled closer on the bed and stroked her daughter's hair until she fell asleep. Just the way she had when Kacey was a child.

BROCK KNOCKED ON YVETTE'S DOOR.

It had been a bitch of a day with Darryl's team. They'd gone to the jail to talk to the kid. After the lawyers asked several times in several ways, Darryl finally stated exactly what he'd done. He'd asked the girl for a hand job. When he rolled over, he was very erect, and her hand accidentally touched him. Then she started screaming.

The story the cops had given them yesterday was far more dramatic, that Darryl intended to force himself on her. The real question was Darryl's intention. If she hadn't screamed, would he have stopped?

"I swear," Darryl had said, "I wouldn't have touched her. If she didn't want me to, all she had to do was say no. She didn't have to scream."

But *would* he have stopped? It was a question Brock would never know the answer to. None of them would. The only one who knew for sure was Darryl. And the poor deluded kid, sure of his own omnipotence, maybe even he didn't know.

He waited so long, Brock was sure Yvette wouldn't answer his knock. Again.

He almost fell to his knees when she opened the door. "I know you went to see Darryl. What happened?" She didn't invite him in.

"He said he asked her, that she accidentally touched him when he rolled over, that he never made her touch him, and that he wouldn't have done anything if she'd said no. But she started screaming."

"Do you believe him?"

He rubbed his temples, then he looked at her. "Honestly, I do."

She stood in the doorway, blocking his way. But at least she'd opened the door. "Did he sound remorseful?"

Brock had thought about that on the way back from the jail. "He wasn't his usual swaggering self. And he was definitely scared. But whether he was sorry for what he'd done or because he'd gotten caught, I can't be sure."

"What do you think they'll do to him?"

Again, he shook his head. "I don't know. The lawyers say it all comes down to his arraignment tomorrow."

"I talked to Kacey today."

Now *that* surprised him. Kacey had been so angry.

"I don't think she believes he did it."

"Well, she'll have to face that he asked the girl to sexually gratify him. That he did for sure."

"If he gets out of this without having to do jail time, he could sound remorseful," she said thoughtfully. "And she might believe him." She let out a sigh. "She might even take him back."

He shot her a humorless smirk, one eyebrow raised. "If she does, she's not as smart as I've always thought she was. And I do think that girl is smart."

She looked down, concentrating on the pavers at his feet. "She is smart," she said softly. "But women have deluded themselves before."

He wondered if she was talking about herself and Pierce. Or about him.

He stepped into the void after she spoke. "Can we talk now?"

She looked up and gave him one simple word. "No." Then she closed the door.

YVETTE STOOD A LONG TIME WITH HER BACK TO THE DOOR, leaning against it in case he tried the knob. But he wouldn't. She knew that.

Just as she knew that if she let him inside, she would throw herself at him. She would make love with him.

But where that would get them? She wasn't sure what the right thing to do was. Jodi seemed accepting, but Kacey was still so angry. Yvette didn't know if she could ever get past that wall of anger.

Until she could figure it all out, until she knew what the girls truly needed from her, until the fallout had passed, she couldn't let Brock into her bed. Which meant she couldn't let him into her room. Or her heart.

Just as Kacey had fallen asleep after that long, hard cry, Yvette's eyes were wet and red with pain as she finally fell asleep.

THE NEXT MORNING, MONDAY, WAS A REPEAT OF SUNDAY. Brock, Trevor, and Garth were with the lawyers again, Darryl's arraignment scheduled for the afternoon. The kids went snorkeling, and this time Jodi had gone with them. When Yvette went up to Kacey's room, she found the door locked. And it stayed that way.

Now she sat on a lounge chair watching the waves beat against the sand and thinking about how they'd pummeled her life in exactly the same way.

She almost jumped when Olive said, "Madame would like to speak with you."

For a moment, Yvette didn't understand. "Madame?"

Olive's smile was full of mirth. "The old lady. I am not disrespectful. She is old. And she is a lady."

Yvette chuckled. "She's also very autocratic."

Olive nodded. "She wishes to speak with you up in her room."

Yvette followed the woman inside. On a table near the foot of the stairs, Olive pointed to a tray. "Here is her tea. And a glass of fruit punch for you." She leaned close to whisper, "It has a shot to ease the pain," she said in perfect American slang. "I think you will need it."

In little more than a week, Olive had figured out Brock's mother. And maybe she'd figured out Yvette as well.

"Bless you." She carried the tray, not bothering to climb the stairs in a rush. Whatever Adeline wanted, it couldn't be good. She decided not to even speculate. That way might very well lay madness.

Adeline's door was open, and Yvette didn't bother to knock. Passing over the threshold, she found Adeline in a chair by the window, her smile prim, her feet propped on a footstool, her legs uncrossed. Adeline said that crossing the legs caused varicose veins and swollen ankles.

The chair next to her was empty, and Yvette set the tray on the table between them. "Would you like me to pour the tea?"

Adeline snapped, "Absolutely not. You've never known how to pour a proper cup of tea." Adeline poured for herself.

Yvette noted it was no different from the way she would have poured, but she didn't say a word. What would be the point? "Olive said you wished to speak to me."

"Will you make sure the girl doesn't allow that boy back into her good graces?"

She didn't need further explanation. "Kacey is a grown woman, and she makes her own choices." Not that Yvette wouldn't have a talk with her daughter if she took Darryl back. Though it wouldn't do much good, not coming from her. She wasn't sure Kacey would ever listen to her again. But she wasn't about to admit that to Adeline.

"I'm not surprised you'd say that." Adeline sniffed. "After your disgusting behavior."

Yvette didn't allow herself to reel from the verbal slap. It was trademark Adeline.

Then she stepped right into the fight. It had been coming a long time. Not just since the day Kacey had walked in on them. And not just the last nine months when she'd been sleeping with Brock. But for years.

"And what disgusting behavior would that be?" she asked, her voice so calm, even sweet.

"You seduced my son and got him into your bed."

Yvette asked, "Which son?"

Adeline exploded then. "Both of them. You're a harlot. Just like your mother."

"Yes, I'm just like my mother. And neither of us were those things."

"I knew your mother far better than you did, girl."

Yvette tipped her head, not sure where this was coming from. "You mean when my grandfather was Harris's chauffeur?"

"Of course I do."

It was family lore. Her grandfather had been the Donnelly family chauffeur for years. Until Harris married Adeline. She'd hated that a mere chauffeur could be her husband's good friend. Harris had always enjoyed talking with Yvette's grandfather. And for years, even after Adeline had fired him, Harris had often dropped by to visit her grandfather. Harris said her grandfather was a wise man. And he had been.

She stood then, not willing to listen to one more moment of Adeline's vitriol. She knew exactly why the old lady had summoned her. "If you're going to tell me to stop seeing Brock, then I have only one answer for you."

She stood her ground, stared Adeline down. And she was done. Finally and completely done. She'd let fear get in her way far too long. She'd given Adeline far too much control over her life. But now her daughters knew her secret. Jodi approved. And Kacey would either accept or she wouldn't. Adeline couldn't do another thing. All the control she'd had for years was over.

And Yvette smiled. "My answer is no. I will not stop seeing Brock. I will not stop loving him. I will not stop sharing his bed. And this time, Adeline," she said with a sharp edge that chewed her former mother-in-law's name to bits, "you aren't getting in my way."

Then she left the room.

She hadn't even needed Olive's spiked fruit punch to give her the courage.

## 28

Darryl jumped out of the car before the tires even stopped crunching on the gravel. He ran for the girls' house just as Yvette walked toward Brock along the path from the big house. "You got him out already?"

Brock's heart thundered at the sight of her and the sweet sound of her voice. "We got a deal." He took her arm, leading her to the girls. "Let's talk about it with everyone inside."

With the front door wide open, Darryl called for Kacey. When Brock and Yvette stepped into the house, Kacey was already at the top of the stairs. Darryl stood at the bottom, looking up at her like a scene out of *Romeo and Juliet*. "You see, they let me out. I didn't do what they said I did."

Yvette said softly, "He didn't do *any* of it?"

Brock gave a slight shake of his head. "Let's see what he tells her."

Darryl tossed out his sob story. "She recanted everything she said. It was all a big lie."

"Now that's an even bigger lie," Brock muttered so only Yvette could hear.

Kacey didn't make a move from the top step. "She lied?

But why would she lie?" Her hair was straggly, as if she hadn't washed it for two days, and her puffy face revealed long crying jags.

Brock made his way into the living room. "Go ahead, Darryl. Tell Kacey what happened."

The kid looked back at him. Brock felt Yvette step closer, heat sparking between them, even if they weren't touching.

"She said I didn't attack her. That I didn't even touch her. She admitted that."

Brock stared him down, waiting for the kid to tell the truth. The room was full, though he hadn't noticed when they'd first walked in. Maybe the others had drifted through the screened-in porch along the back of the house after hearing the commotion Darryl made. By the sofa, Garth crossed his arms over his chest, Jodi beside him, death-glaring Darryl. Ethan, Malcolm, and their girlfriends stood next to them. And Trevor had entered the front door.

Kacey took only one step down. "But why would she lie?" she asked again, her tone far from Juliet begging for Romeo's protestations of love.

Brock willed the kid to tell the truth. If he did, it might show that he'd changed, that two nights in a jail cell had given him a different perspective.

Instead, Darryl said, "I don't know why she lied."

Brock felt forced to step in. "She didn't lie, Darryl. She never lied. Not even in the beginning."

Kacey looked at Brock, her eyes glittering as if the tears could come at any moment. "What exactly does that mean?"

Brock narrowed his gaze on Darryl. "It would be better if you said it, Darryl, rather than me, don't you think?"

His skin had turned pale, even after only two days behind bars. Or maybe it was the fact that Darryl felt cornered. "I didn't touch her. I didn't *do* anything," he said, making a very hard emphasis on *do*.

Because Darryl hadn't actually *done* anything.

When he failed to add further explanation, Brock asked, "But what did you *say*? And what happened when you *said* it?"

"I...I," Darryl stammered. Finally, because he didn't have a choice, the words rushed out. "I just asked her for a happy ending. That was all. I couldn't help it. It was a massage. And well, things came up."

"And?" Brock pressed. Because the kid just couldn't find the courage to admit it all.

"And—" Darryl gulped. "Well, then I turned over. I didn't know she was *right* there." He cupped his hands as if showing right *where*. "And her hand accidentally touched me—" He gasped in a breath like a fish thrown on the beach. "—there. Then she freaked, started screaming, and ran out."

The boy had gotten a hard-on when a beautiful woman had given him a massage. Then he'd asked her to jerk him off. And there'd been some accidental contact. Which was what the massage therapist had told the judge today. She'd admitted that she overreacted. She'd been afraid of what he *might* do, not what he actually did.

Kacey stared him down. And that glitter of tears morphed into a gleam of anger. "You asked her to give you a happy ending?"

"It was nothing, babe. I just needed a release, and I couldn't wait until we got home."

Now the entire family stared him down. Her voice tense, Kacey said, "But we'd made love the night before."

Brock felt Yvette cringe. Was it knowing that her daughter was having sex, something a parent doesn't want to think about? Or that it was Darryl, and nobody liked the kid?

"I know," he whined. "But it didn't mean anything with that girl. It was just a physical reaction."

Brock wondered how many men had said that. But sex

always meant something. It could have different meanings, but it always meant *something*.

Darryl pleaded then. "Look, I'm sorry. It'll never happen again. Please forgive me, baby. I need you."

Kacey looked at him, her puffy face a mask of anger and hurt. "I wish you were staying in my room. Because if you were, I'd march in there, throw all your stuff in your suitcase and dump it on your head." Then her gaze lasered in on Brock. "Is it possible to get him a flight out now?"

Brock smiled. "Oh yeah."

"Then I'd appreciate it if someone would get him out of here." She disappeared down the upstairs hall, and a moment later, her door slammed.

Garth punched the air. "Yeah." Then he stalked to Darryl, grabbed his arm while Malcolm grabbed the other, and they frog-marched him out of the house. Ethan, following right behind, said, "We'll help you pack your bags, buddy."

Trevor was right on the other side of the doorway. "I'll call for the helicopter." Which was how they'd all arrived. "They can take him to the airport in Nassau." Then he smiled. "We should make him fly coach, don't you think?"

Jodi said, "Mom?" Just that, with a definite question mark at the end. Then she added, "Maybe we should go up and talk to Kacey."

"I'll be up there in a minute," Yvette said. "I just need a few words with your uncle first."

Jodi waved a hand, then rushed up the stairs.

Yvette shifted to face him.

Without Brock even realizing it, they were alone in the living room. Francine and Iris had returned to their lounge chairs out on the sand.

"Is that what really happened? She took back her story?"

He shrugged. "She didn't take anything back. She just said that Darryl hadn't put her hand on him or held it there. That the touch was accidental, and she'd panicked, afraid because she was alone in the room with him. It was everyone else she worked with who got the story wrong, because of her reaction."

"And you believe it was an accident?"

"Yes, I do." The young woman had seemed sincere.

"So the judge just let Darryl go?"

Brock felt the smile grow on his face. "They charged him with solicitation and some misdemeanors and required him to pay a large fine. Then the judge told him never to come back to the Bahamas."

Her smile matched his. "It might have been better if they locked him up."

"But at least we're shipping him out."

And something burned in her gaze. "Can you still rent that cabana in the cove for tomorrow?"

His heart beat like a steel band drum. "Hell, yes."

Her smile turned sultry, downright seductive. "Then why don't you take care of that, as well as asking Olive to pack a picnic for us first thing in the morning?" She put a hand on his arm. "I'm giving tonight to the girls and a long talk with Kasey. And tomorrow, I'll have a long talk with you."

He didn't know what had changed. But he didn't care.

She was his again.

FOR OVER TWENTY YEARS, EVERY CHOICE SHE'D MADE WAS for her daughters, and that was as it should be. Before that, she'd taken care of her mother and her grandparents. She'd never done anything just for herself. Even sleeping with Brock, she'd thought about her daughters first, about how they'd feel, and she'd tailored their affair to her daughters' needs. And to her fear of Adeline.

She wasn't afraid of Adeline anymore.

Now, she had to tell Kacey she was proud of her for not accepting Darryl's lies. There would be other lovers. There would be the love of her life and marriage and children. While she might still come to her mother for advice, her life would be about her own family. The same was true for Jodi.

And Yvette needed Brock. Because Brock was the rest of her life.

Her girls deserved the truth, not secrets, not evasions.

Laying both hands on Brock's shoulders, she went up on her toes and kissed him on the mouth. It was passionate. And it was a promise.

Then she climbed the stairs to her daughter's bedroom.

Yvette gave herself one last glance over the banister at Brock. He still stood there, his face lifted to hers, their eyes meeting. Then he smiled, a smile so beautiful her heart turned over with more love than she had ever known.

Jodi had left the door open, but Yvette knocked anyway. Seated on the bed, her daughters were mirror images of each other, one leg bent, the other foot balanced on the floor.

Kacey faced the door. Yvette couldn't read a single clue in the look on her daughter's face. "May I come in?"

Jodi turned then, waved her over. Yvette thought she saw the slightest movement of Kacey's fingers, and she took it to mean agreement.

She had to. It was the only thing she could cling to.

Would Kacey ever forgive her?

She didn't sit on the bed but stood between them. She didn't fold her arms over her chest in a defensive posture but left her hands hanging limply. Honestly, she didn't know what to do with her hands. She only knew what she had to say.

"I want to ask both of you to forgive me for not telling you the whole story." She didn't use the word *lie*. Even though that's what she'd been doing for nine months. Neither of them spoke, and she carried on. "I'm in love with your Uncle Brock. And yes, we have a relationship."

Not a single flicker passed over Kacey's face. Nothing to show what she was thinking. But Jodi's lips curved slightly, giving Yvette hope.

"I didn't tell you about it because I was afraid you wouldn't approve." The whole truth and nothing but the truth. But still, she wanted to soften it. "Nothing happened when your father was alive. In fact, neither of us felt anything then. And not when Aunt Corrine was married to Brock either." The familiarity of his name just slipped off her tongue.

Still, Kacey didn't move, didn't say a word. Was she waiting for Yvette to hang herself?

"But nine months ago, we both agreed that feelings were growing between us." The truth. God. How did you tell your daughters the absolute truth? But she had to if she wanted to regain their trust. "We started sleeping together. Secretly."

Jodi was the first to speak. "Why did you do everything in secret?"

Why? It was such a simple question, just one word, and yet it held so much pain and grief and fear. She swallowed, and it went down hard, but she managed not to choke. "Because I was afraid. I knew your grandmother wouldn't approve, and I was afraid she might influence how you felt about it. And how you felt about me. So it was just easier to keep everything secret."

Again, it was Jodi who asked, "Are you going to marry him?"

Yvette admitted the truth. "He's asked me to marry him. What would you both think of that?"

Jodi had already guessed everything. The words were for Kacey.

"I'm okay with it," Jodi said. Then she looked at Kacey. "What about you?"

Had they already discussed it? They were sisters, and they were close. She was sure that her youngest knew exactly how her eldest felt.

"I—" Kacey started before she closed her mouth and didn't open it again.

So Yvette had to address the hardest part. "I know it was a shock when you walked into my cottage after the police arrested Darryl."

Finally, for the first time since Yvette had entered the room, Kacey reacted. She snorted.

The sound cut through Yvette, dashing all her hopes against the ocean rocks, while all her fears choked her.

Her daughter would never forgive her. And Yvette waited for Kacey's anger to rain down on her.

Kacey's voice was hard. "Hell, yes. I was shocked to my core." She put a hand on her belly. "I mean, he's my uncle. I've known him all my life. It just seemed so—" She shook her hands in the air as if she couldn't find the worst words to fling at her mother.

And she remembered the word she had used. *Disgusting*.

But Kacey said, "Unexpected."

It was better than anything Yvette could have imagined.

Kacey flopped back on the bed, staring at the ceiling. "I was so upset about Darryl. I wanted you to tell me everything would be okay. I wanted Uncle Brock to make it all go away."

Yvette's heart ached for her daughter.

Kacey blinked, and tears slid down her temples. "The worst was that I *knew* he'd done something. I didn't know what, but I was imagining the worst things he could've done. I just wanted to throw myself in your arms." She stopped.

Yvette finished for her. "You were afraid he'd betrayed

you. Then you walked into my room and thought I betrayed you too."

Kacey sniffed, sitting up to wipe the tears from her temples with two fingers. "Yes. That's how I felt."

Yvette wanted to throw herself on the bed by her girls, hug them. But she couldn't. Not yet. "I should have told you both. I shouldn't have kept it a secret. But even at fifty-three years old, people can be afraid. And I was afraid. But I never betrayed your father. I never broke a promise to you." She reached for both her daughters' hands, held them. "And I will never break a promise. I will always love you. I'll be here for you." She squeezed Kacey's fingers. "And I support you in whatever you decide to do about Darryl."

Kacey didn't squeeze her hand in return, but she didn't let go either. "Even if I decide to stay with him?"

It hurt. Because she wanted to fight for her daughter, and she knew Darryl wasn't the right man for Kacey. "If that's your decision, then I have to live with it. I might not think he's the best person for you, but you're an adult, and you're my daughter, and I have to trust in what you decide."

Jodi snorted a humorless laugh. "I'll accept your decision. But that doesn't mean I won't rag on you incessantly until you change your mind."

Kacey laughed through a sudden bubble of tears. "I know you will."

Yvette grabbed a tissue from the box on the bedside table and handed it to Kacey, who wiped her nose. "I'm not going back to him. We're done. Because a man who can say that sex means nothing isn't a man I want to be with." Finally, she looked at Yvette. "I think Uncle Brock loves you. I don't think he's using you." She swallowed, almost gulped. "If you want to marry him, then I'm okay with it."

Though it wasn't the most resounding endorsement, the ache around Yvette's heart fell away. She gathered her two girls against her and whispered, "Thank you." Then she stood back before she started crying too. "Let's do something fun tonight. Together. Whatever you want."

Kacey wiped her eyes. "Let's watch sappy romance movies like *Ten Things I Hate About You*."

"How about *Kick-Ass*?" Jodi said.

"How about both?" Yvette added. "We can watch all night long." She wanted to cry. She wanted to hug them. And she would always love them.

She should have told them about her feelings for Brock from the beginning. But maybe the time hadn't been right. Not for her, not for them. Not even for Brock.

Maybe they had to do this, face the bad so that they could find the good. Just as Kacey had to face the bad about Darryl before she could find the good in her life. Sometimes finding the good took a long, long time.

But Yvette had found it. And she knew her girls would too.

## 29

The cove was booked, the morning was gorgeous, the picnic basket was in the back, and Yvette was the most beautiful woman he'd ever seen.

And she wore the ruby necklace he'd given her for Christmas.

"How did your talk go with Kacey?" Brock wanted to ask so much more. If Yvette had changed her mind, if she forgave him, if she still loved him? If the necklace meant she wanted their relationship to be completely out in the open?

"Things went well," she said, and he glanced at her, finding a smile on her face, a good smile, maybe even a happy one, certainly not strained. It was New Year's Eve, she wore his necklace, and he wanted to believe they would soon have something to celebrate.

The Jeep bumped over the track, surprising a squeak out of Yvette. She held the top of her head as if she were about to bounce against the roof.

"I hope she dumps Darryl," he said.

She nodded. "I told her she was an adult and could make any choice she wanted, but I felt Darryl wasn't the right one.

And she said she was done with him." He felt her turn toward him, and he met her gaze briefly before concentrating on the rough road. "But who knows what she'll do when he talks to her." She sighed, the sound clear over the Jeep's engine. "Back at school, he might talk her into forgiving him."

Brock held the wheel straight as the track grew narrower, tree branches scraping both sides of the vehicle. "She's a smart girl, and now she has the full picture, she won't take him back."

With another glance, he saw her smile again, wanted to wrap it around him. And he missed seeing the looming pothole straight ahead, slamming the left front tire into it and jolting his teeth together. But that smile was worth it.

All he wanted was Yvette's happiness.

He could ask her now, but he sensed she had a plan. Hopefully she wanted to seduce him with food, champagne, and lovemaking.

She'd seduced him so long ago, even if he hadn't wanted to admit it. Even if he hadn't acknowledged it until that night nine months ago. And now he could never let her go. Through the trees, a sliver of beach and ocean appeared, and finally, he pulled into the small clearing that served as the parking lot. They were alone as he climbed out of the Jeep and reached in the back for the picnic basket.

"What did Olive make us?" she asked.

"She said it was a surprise." He held up the basket. "But I made sure she included champagne."

Yvette smiled. "It's never too early for champagne."

His heart beat hard and fast, the hairs on his arms raised with anticipation. Their cabana—he thought of it as theirs— stood on the sand, its curtains pulled down around the lounge chairs, open only to the view of the sea. Two towels sat on the end of each chair, and Yvette fluffed them before laying both neatly on the loungers.

"Swim first?" He didn't need to swim. He didn't need to eat. He needed only her.

But she said, "Let's eat. I didn't have any breakfast." She put her hand to her stomach. "And after the drive, I'm starving."

He couldn't help saying, "So am I." He held her gaze, signaling that he was starving for her more than the food.

But he opened the cooler, which doubled as the picnic basket, and pulled out the champagne. "Do you want to do the honors, or shall I?"

She took it from him. "I'll do the honors this time." Her smile was sexy and held every promise he wanted her to make. Just wearing his necklace, the ruby beautiful against her skin, seemed like a promise.

He unloaded food onto the table, a creamy dip with celery and green onion and chunks of conch, sesame crackers to go with it, hunks of cheese, a loaf of crusty dark bread. Olive even included a wooden board, a knife, and a cheese slicer. The woman thought of everything. In a thermal container, he uncovered conch-stuffed mushrooms, still warm from the oven.

Yvette popped the cork, sending it flying into the surrounding jungle. She poured expertly, not wasting a drop, tipping the glasses to the side and waiting till the foam died down before adding more. Then she handed him a glass and sat on the edge of her lounge chair. "To beachcombing in the Bahamas," she toasted.

He wanted more. But he sat beside her and said, "To the best trip I've ever had."

Yvette laughed. "Would you really call what happened with Darryl part of the best trip of your life?"

He wanted to pull her in for a kiss. "Maybe not that part. But the rest of it. Yeah, the best." He held her gaze as he added, "Ever."

His guts twisted as he waited for the words that would put him out of his misery. Instead, she picked up a mushroom and held it out to him. Only a bite, he took it from her fingers with his teeth, his lips touching her skin. It was good, lightly seasoned with the slight salt of her fingers and layered with her beautiful scent. They tasted everything, Yvette moaning over each bite. And he grew harder with the sexy sounds she made.

Finally, she put a hand to her stomach. "Oh my God, I'm stuffed." She laughed, sipped her champagne, then asked, "Are you ready for a swim now?"

He shook his head. "No. I don't want to swim."

She took a long swallow of champagne, then set the glass on the table amid the detritus of their meal. Standing, she took his glass, too, putting it on the table beside hers. Then she pushed him back on the lounge chair and climbed on top of him. "Good," she whispered. "I don't want to swim either." And she leaned down to kiss him.

It was a kiss like no other. Sweet with the taste of champagne, open-mouthed, her tongue swirling against his, her hair falling around them, her scent rising to fog his mind. He was no longer thinking when he shoved his hands under her dress to cup her bottom.

Shocked, but oh so pleased, he pulled back. "You're not wearing a bathing suit."

Her sultry smile turned his knees so weak he would have fallen if he wasn't already lying down.

"No," she murmured, her lips so close. "I'm not. And no panties either. I felt like doing a little skinny-dipping." She pecked his mouth, then added, "But later. Much later."

His heartbeat pounded against his eardrums when she reached down to palm him. And she smiled like a siren. "It doesn't feel like you want to go swimming either." Then she squeezed him.

He felt as if the top of his head might blow right off. Both of them.

"We need to take care of this," she whispered, tantalizing him with her words, her touch.

He couldn't say she'd ever been the aggressor. She loved everything they did, and she demanded the taste of him in her mouth. But somehow this was different. This was new.

This was everything he'd ever wanted.

Her hands disappeared beneath her skirt and pushed down his board shorts enough to free him. But she didn't get up, she didn't shove them off, she just let him nestle at the sweet spot between her thighs, shifting slightly, making him crazy.

Then she took him in her hand.

"I won't last long with you doing that." The words came on a rasp as she damn near stole his voice.

"Then maybe I need to do this instead." She rose over him, stroking him. Then she slid down, slowly, taking him in centimeter by centimeter.

He groaned, pushed back against the lounger, slipping deeper inside her. Closing his eyes, he focused on the feel of her body, warm, wet, surrounding him, engulfing him. He went mindless almost immediately.

But her whisper made it through his fog of pleasure. "Touch me."

With his thumb on the tight nub between her legs, he circled her, found himself seduced by how wet she was. Then he had to open his eyes to watch her. She was so damn beautiful, her head back thrown, rocking on him, increasing the pressure of his touch with every downstroke.

The ruby necklace sparkled around her throat as if it were his mark on her.

And she whispered, "Oh my God, oh my God, oh my God."

They entered that mindless state together, where there was nothing but them, nothing but sensation. She rocked and writhed, her body squeezing him, driving him closer to the edge while his fingers pushed her higher. Mewling sounds bubbled up from her throat, ratcheting up his desire, turning him harder inside her, pulling him deeper, faster.

He felt it start, her climax coming in the tightening of her body around him, the squeeze, the pulse. Then he felt the detonation, and she went as tight as a fist around him.

He knew her so well, knew what she needed, and he grabbed her bottom, pulled her down hard, rising to meet her, slamming inside her while she pummeled him. First the slow ride, then the fast pounding. She was still coming, still crying out, when he throbbed hard inside her, when he filled her with his essence, with everything in him. And everything he needed to give her.

BROCK TOUCHED THE NECKLACE AT HER THROAT. *His* necklace. "Did you wear that for me?"

"Yes. And I'm going to keep wearing it so everyone can see." Her body still trembling with the pleasure they'd shared, Yvette whispered, "Marry me." The words felt good, they felt right. Even if they were scary too.

He held her tightly against him, his arms a balm against the world. "Hell, yes, I'll marry you. As soon as we can arrange it. And I'll never let you go again."

She couldn't help bringing up the damper on the whole thing. "Adeline will go ballistic."

He put his hands to her face, cupping her cheeks, holding her away. "I'm not Pierce. I'll never let her come between us. If she tries pulling any of her crap, we're outta there."

A shudder ran through her, and it wasn't just the last throes of her climax. "I'm not living in that house again."

He pulled her down for a kiss, open-mouthed and sweet. "We're buying a flat in the city. I wouldn't subject you to her. I told you, I'm not Pierce."

Trailing a thumb over his lips, she met his beautiful blue gaze. "I know you're nothing like him. I'm not sure he truly wanted to marry me. I think Harris made him because I was pregnant."

Brock shook his head. "He loved you. He told me that."

"When? Before we were married?"

He nodded. "Then. And later too. He just couldn't live up to that love. Or marriage. But he did love you."

Her heart contracted. Maybe she needed to hear that Pierce felt something too. But he'd been a weak man. She thought her love could change him. It hadn't. "He was never the strong man you are. He couldn't stand up to her. Neither of us could."

He stroked her hair back from her face. "He was my brother, and I loved him. But I had no illusions about him. He was an alcoholic. He was a gambler. And yes, he was a cheater too. But it was never because he didn't love you. It was because of who he was. I sometimes wonder if he was born that way. He was always the wild child. Always getting into trouble."

"He was so different from you."

How many times had she wished that Pierce could be like his older brother? It had been a horrible thing to think, and she'd never said it aloud. Maybe that was the beginning of her falling for Brock, all those comparisons. "I still gave him the best I could. I tried to support him. I tried to help him."

He pulled her down into his arms, held her tight and murmured against her hair, "I know you did. I think that was our father's goal all along. That you would bring some sort of sense to Pierce. That he would change for love. But he never did."

"No. He never did." It had broken her heart long, long ago. But Brock had healed her with his love.

"Why did you change your mind?" he asked softly into her hair.

"About marrying you?"

He nodded against her. "Was it because the secret was out?"

"No," she said. "It was Adeline. She summoned me to her room."

Brock chuckled. "Summoned. That's so like her. And she demanded you stop our foolish affair immediately."

"I didn't give her the chance to demand anything." She kissed the tip of his nose. "I ripped the rug right out from under her and told her I wouldn't stop seeing you or loving you." Another kiss, sweet and hot. "Or sharing your bed."

This time, hands on her cheeks, he held her still for a passionate kiss that filled her soul. "I love you," he whispered.

She knew he was saying thank you for finally standing up for him. She should have done it so long ago. "And I love you."

With his body still buried deep inside her, she sat up. "I don't want to talk about Adeline or Pierce anymore. There's just us now. I love you. I want you. And I'm going to marry you no matter what anyone else says."

He drew his hands slowly down her breasts, over her abdomen, stroked her thighs. "Jodi and Kacey are good with us being together?"

She nodded. Then smiled. "We have their blessing. What about your sons? Have you talked to them?"

Hands once again on her breasts, he caressed her nipples with the center of his palms. And smiled. "Garth said he likes you a lot."

She puffed out a sound that might have been a laugh or a scoff. "That's all he said?"

Brock laughed. "He's a man of few words. Like me."

Leaning down for a quick kiss, she muttered against his mouth, "You are not a man of few words. I love the way you talk to me while we make love."

"And I love the sounds you make when I pleasure you."

She grew serious again. "What about Ethan and Malcolm?"

"They like you too."

Then he slipped his hand between them, touching her, exciting her all over again. And he whispered, "I don't care what anyone says. You're mine. You'll always be mine. I'm not letting you go. And I'm not letting anyone come between us again."

It wasn't just a promise. It was a vow. She recited it back to him. "I'll never let you go. And no one will ever come between us."

She made love to him again with all her heart and soul.

THEY SPENT THE DAY SWIMMING, EATING, AND LOVING. It was dark when they returned, the big house ablaze with light.

As they stepped inside, their children blew on paper whistles and threw confetti at them. *Happy New Year* banners, garlands, and streamers decorated the large living room.

Yvette put a hand over her mouth. "With everything going on, I forgot it was New Year's Eve."

Brock hadn't been touching her, but now he took her hand in his, looked at her with stars in his eyes, then at their family spread throughout the large room. "Since we're celebrating, it's a perfect time to tell you all that Yvette and I are getting married."

Yvette counted the silent seconds off in her head, one, two, three. By the time she'd reached five, Jodi launched herself across the room to throw her arms around Yvette in a tight hug. Then she hugged Brock too. Yvette's heart turned over. The hugs were everything she'd waited for, as if Jodi sanctioned their love.

For a long moment, Kacey stood back, looking at her sister. Then, much more slowly, she walked to Yvette and finally let her mother take her in her arms, whispering, "He makes you happy. And I'm glad about that."

Turning to Brock, she went up on her toes to wrap him in a hug, murmuring something Yvette couldn't hear.

Then the boys came, Garth hugging her almost as tightly as Jodi had. "You're good for him." Ethan, then Malcolm, pulled her close. They gave their father hardy handclasps, until finally Brock grabbed Garth's hand and reeled him in for a man hug.

It was obvious the two girls, Francine and Iris, didn't know what to do. Except to smile and clap.

Trevor came to Yvette then, enfolding her in his arms. "You two should have done this a long time ago." Reaching out, he pulled Lorna into the circle, then he man-hugged his brother and said loudly, "It's about time, right?"

Then the room erupted with party poppers and horns and whistles. More than for New Year's Eve, it was for them. It was the family's acceptance, and their good wishes.

Finally, Yvette asked, "Where did you get all the streamers and banners for New Year's?"

Jodi gasped and clapped her hands. "Olive thinks of everything. She's got an enormous closet next to the pantry where she stores decorations for every season and every holiday."

Yvette couldn't help smiling. "Well, thank you, Olive," she said even though the woman wasn't there.

Then Adeline strolled down the stairs, slowly, regally, as if she were the queen coming down to mingle with her minions. Yvette couldn't help the shiver that ran along her spine. But she'd vowed to Brock that no one would ever tear them apart. Certainly not Adeline.

And she said the words in her mind like a mantra, *I am not afraid of you.*

Stopping at the bottom of stairs, Adeline said, "I hear congratulations are in order." Her voice dripped icicles.

Brock didn't let her tone stop him. "Thank you, Adeline," he said, his voice just as icy.

They both knew Adeline didn't mean a word of it. Although she hadn't congratulated them either.

"And when are these nuptials to take place?" she asked coolly, her nose tipped in the air as if she smelled something bad.

"As soon as we get back home." Brock took Yvette's hand, his skin warm against the cold climbing up her arms. Being around Adeline was like feeling the cold of an evil spirit in the room. "Neither of us wants to wait." Turning from Adeline, he said to the room at large, "Of course you're all coming, right?"

Adeline didn't let anyone answer, her gaze piercing Yvette all the way across the room. "You shouldn't be so hasty, my dear." The word came out almost as a sneer. "There's something we all need to talk about first."

Yvette felt every ounce of happiness inside her die a terrible death.

Adeline wasn't done with her yet.

And Yvette's mantra seemed to have deserted her.

## 30

---

### ADELINE

I'd debated whether to do this with the entire family present or to take my dear son and his pathetic fiancé to my room for a one-on-one.

It might blow up in my face. After all, I didn't miss the way Jodi called me Adeline the other day. And the grandchildren might turn their anger on me instead of where it belongs: on their parents.

But at the same time, no one can deny anything if it's public knowledge. And so I've made my decision. "You should all sit down." I flourish a hand toward the living room sofas and chairs. Naturally, they all obey. All except Brock and that gold digger.

It wasn't enough that she stole Pierce. Now she's snared Brock in her web too.

Well, she doesn't have a prayer in heaven, not when I'm done with her.

Brock puts an arm around her. It makes my skin crawl.

"I'd hoped never to have to tell this story," I begin. Unbeknownst to them, I've held it in my back pocket for just such an occasion. Although truly, I never thought the occasion would arise. I never believed Brock could be so gullible. Or so stupid.

Brock's tone is one of bored tolerance. "What story are you making up now, Adeline?"

What's the best way, a long, drawn-out tale? Or the unvarnished truth hurled at them?

I like the unvarnished version. "Unfortunately—" And really, I don't smile. Even though inwardly I'm bursting with it. "I need you to know that Yvette is your father's by-blow."

One of those insipid girls running around with my grandsons asks, "What's a by-blow?"

Truly, Ethan can't want to marry this imbecile. But I have to answer. "It means that your father cheated on me, and Yvette is his daughter." I don't need to state the obvious, that it means Brock is her half-brother.

"You're lying, Adeline." Brock's voice is suddenly like a Brillo pad across my skin. But I expected that.

I give a long-suffering sigh. "Honestly, I couldn't lie about a thing like this." I put a hand to my chest. "It's just too painful."

"And how do you know this?" he barks at me. It's possible I have him running scared now, but one can never tell with Brock.

"Because Harris told me himself," I say, watching his face harden and his eyes turn... Could that be fear? I can only hope.

Actually, Harris said no such thing. He denied it when I threw the accusation at him. But I never believed him. I knew. I saw the way he looked at that chauffeur's daughter. It was so pathetic, like something out of that silly Audrey Hepburn movie, *Sabrina*.

Then the gold digger speaks up. I hoped she'd simply fall to the floor in a dead faint. But she doesn't. "If that were true, why would Harris have let Pierce marry me?"

Jodi, that traitorous granddaughter who was far too smart for her own good, or mine, says, "She's got you there, Adeline." Perhaps I've been too hasty in appreciating that she's like me. Because that is definitely a derisive tone in her voice.

I'll have to deal with that kind of disrespect later. But now, I must handle that all-important question. "Harris allowed it," I say distinctly, "because Pierce was not his son."

That takes the wind out of their sails. Not one word comes out of any of them. Until Trevor—when has he become so ungrateful?—says, "Isn't this just a little too convenient, Adeline? That would mean you had to tell Father you'd committed adultery."

I laugh. Bitterly. Because I am still bitter. Even more than fifty years later. "Of course I told him. I only slept with another man to pay him back for what he'd done." I straighten my spine. I'd like to hold on to the banister, but that might seem a sign of weakness. "Perhaps it was childish and immature, but I was young then, and yes, I threw that fact in his face."

"Who was Pierce's father?" Trevor wants to know.

I flap my hand at him. "Nobody of importance," I tell him. All these years later, I can't even remember the man's name. And now I make the salient point. "So you see, Pierce and Yvette were not brother and sister." I turn my gaze on the never-will-be-happy-again couple. "But you and Yvette are."

Brock swallows. Then his eyes widen, their depths turning a fierce blue. "You're making this up. You don't want us to be together, and you're trying to ruin our lives with your lies."

I look at him oh-so sadly. "I know you would like it to be untrue. But it's not. Just to be sure, I had DNA tests done."

That shuts him up. The gold digger shrinks just the way I

want her to. She will not have my oldest son, not after she ruined my favorite boy.

Brock, however, isn't down and out yet. "I suppose this DNA test is conveniently back at home."

I want to smile. Because I have him, and he's asked for it. But of course, I can't smile, not for the rest of my audience. "If you wait just a moment, I'll go upstairs and get it."

My dear traitorous Jodi just has to say, "You mean you carry it around with you? So you've known Mom and Uncle Brock were in love this whole time and you've just been waiting to throw down your trump card?"

Such a perfect question. "I knew nothing about their—" I curl my lip. "—relationship. I thought my son had more respect for his dear departed brother's memory. The document is something I carry with me always. Just as I carry my daily diary."

Then I turn on my heel and march up the stairs. Even if it makes my knees ache. Even if coming down again is worse.

But I hand the folder to Brock. He snatches it away, opens it, stares.

And I draw blood. "You better read both documents, one for you, one for Yvette. And don't forget the conclusion page."

The papers shuffle. Trevor puts a hand on his brother's shoulder.

Yvette stands stock still, staring at me. She used to wear an annoying if-looks-could-kill stare. But I've finally wiped that look off her face. I've won.

And she is utterly devastated.

"This can't be real," Brock says, his usual cocksure tone suddenly not so cocksure anymore.

I say, so calmly, "It's quite authentic." It had better be. I'd paid handsomely to make sure the two certificates looked as authentic as possible. No one could ever tell the difference.

"How did you get our DNA?" he asks.

This time I allow myself a laugh, but I make it sad, too, hiding the glee I feel inside. "Oh my dear boy, how many times have you eaten at my dinner table?" I look at Yvette, who is shrinking inch by inch, until she seems shorter than I am. "And so has Yvette. It was quite easy to secure a bit of DNA."

"So you've known for years," Trevor says. He points at the date. At least I assume that's where he points. "But you only did this five years ago?"

"I had it done as a safeguard after my poor Pierce passed away."

It is now that Yvette puts a hand over her mouth, and her pathetic cry is music to my ears. "Oh my God," she cries. Then she runs. Something she should have done years ago. It would never have come to this if she had. I would not have had to reveal my secret.

And I know she believes every word I've said.

Ah, at last, the chaos I crave.

My oldest son suddenly towers over me, his features strained, his voice rasping. "I won't let you do this."

I feel the slightest urge to quake at the ruthlessness of his tone. But I have never quaked for anyone. "It's too late. I've already done it."

He drops my folder of evidence to the floor, the papers scattering, and runs after his pathetic paramour. In the end, he will see I've done the right thing.

Now I feel the others' stares, like malevolent spirits swirling around me. My least favorite son, his pregnant wife, all my grandchildren. Then Trevor says softly, and with a menace I've never heard in his voice, "Why are you so cruel?"

"The truth can't be cruel. It's simply the truth." I sound smug even to my own ears. Then, with his wife's hand in his, he walks out the front door, my papers crumpling beneath his shoes.

It doesn't matter. He, too, will eventually understand that I've done what I had to do. They will all understand. It had to be done. I should have done this when she first stole Pierce. But Harris had been alive then. He would never have allowed it.

Finally, the silence in the room scrapes like talons along my skin.

I can't help myself, and I say, "It's a party. It's New Year's Eve. Please, enjoy yourselves."

And I tell myself this will all blow over in time.

My youngest granddaughter picks up a champagne bottle, then a platter of some ridiculously fatty appetizer Olive has made. Passing me, her eyes midnight blue pools of anger, Jodi says softly, venomously, "Why do you have to ruin everything?"

And as she marches to the front door, the DNA results mash beneath her shoes.

Without saying a word, the others gather glasses and champagne and platters and follow her out the door.

Until finally I am alone in the oppressive silence. And all my proof lays torn to shreds on the floor.

Yvette ran across the sand until finally she fell to her knees and heaved up everything she and Brock had enjoyed in their private cove.

Her eyes watered, her guts ached. And her heart bled.

With nothing left, she rose and kicked sand over everything Adeline had ripped from her. And she ran again.

She ran until there was no beach left, just rocks and pounding surf. She sat then, pulled her knees to her chest, curling her arms around them until she became a tightly wrapped, impenetrable ball.

She felt Brock sit beside her, but he didn't touch her. "It makes a perfect kind of sense," she said. Her heart, having lost all its blood, was nothing more than a withered, dying husk. "This is why she's always hated me. Because she believed your father got my mother pregnant. I thought Harris was visiting my grandfather. Because they were friends. And that's why he was always so kind to me. Even after my grandfather died, he made sure my mother and I were okay. When my mother got sick, he was there to help us. He gave me the job."

Finally, he spoke, "It isn't true."

But she knew the truth. "I can see now that he was in love with my mother."

"Adeline is lying," he insisted. "We have to fight her. Don't you remember the promise we made to each other in the cove? That we'd never let anything or anyone break us apart?"

"I remember," she whispered. "But Adeline wasn't there. She didn't hear us. And she didn't care what we promised."

He took her hand, pulling it to his chest until she could feel the beating of his heart. "She lied. Those test results are false."

"She'll never stop."

He pressed her hand to his heart. "I don't care what she does. We belong together."

Finally, she looked at him. "Pierce was always so different from you and Trevor. I thought it was because he was a middle child. But I realize now it was because he wasn't your father's son."

Brock closed his eyes, swallowed, then finally exhaled in a long sigh. "Oh yeah, I believe that part. My mother slept with another man and got herself pregnant to spite my father because she believed he'd cheated on her."

She curled her fingers around his. "No." She shook her head. "Because she knew your father didn't love her. That he loved someone else. That he would *never* love her."

Brock opened his eyes to look at her. "*My* father?" he stressed.

And she whispered, "*Your* father." Then she softly added, "*My* father died when I was very young. I don't remember him. But I know my mother loved him. Maybe Harris loved her. And maybe in the end she loved him too. But she always loved *my* father."

She placed her fingers over his. They'd made that vow to

each other in the cove. Nothing would keep them apart. Especially not Adeline.

And she whispered her mantra, "I'm not afraid of her." She wouldn't allow Adeline to win. "When we have our own DNA tests done," she said, "without your mother's influence, it will show the truth." She had to believe it. She *would* believe it. "My mother loved my father. And your father was just my grandfather's friend."

THERE SEEMED NO POINT IN STAYING ON THE ISLAND. After Darryl's misdeeds and Adeline's treachery, a pall hung over the family. The next morning, New Year's Day, Brock made arrangements to leave. He didn't go to Yvette's cottage. And she didn't come to his. What should have been a day of relaxation and celebration was more like a day of mourning.

With every fiber of his being, Brock knew Adeline had lied. He would allow nothing else. She'd manufactured those test results. It didn't matter how. It didn't even matter why.

But finally, after all these years, he understood why she'd always hated Yvette. Adeline had truly believed his father loved Yvette's mother, and she'd let that belief fester in her heart for over fifty years. Through births and divorces and deaths. And adultery. It was hard to truly imagine that she'd been so angry, she'd borne a child by another man. That Pierce had been his half brother.

There were so many unanswered questions that he would never ask his mother. He would never know if he was getting the truth or another lie.

Once again, Adeline sat in the plane's front row as they flew home. No one sat with her or spoke to her. Yvette had taken a seat facing her daughters.

Brock sat a few rows back, Garth next to him. His son asked, "What are you going to do, Dad?"

Mildly, Brock said, "About what?" Though he knew what his son wanted to know. And without further prompting from Garth, he added, "We'll get our own DNA tests." Then he looked at his son. "I never asked you outright if you're okay with this. Me and your aunt getting married."

"Aunt Yvette is a wonderful woman." Garth smiled. "She's always been good to me and Ethan and Malcolm. And they feel the same way I do. You both deserve to be together."

He wasn't asking for his son's blessing. He wasn't even asking permission. He was simply tired of fighting for his and Yvette's happiness. And Garth's words meant everything to him.

"I love you, son." His words were heartfelt. "I love all of you."

THEY WERE ON THEIR WAY HOME, THE TRIP CUT SHORT. But no one seemed to mind. The last few days had stripped away all the fun. Adeline was up front, facing the bulkhead, and the next three rows behind her were empty. No one wanted to get close.

Adeline had made her bed. And now she'd have to lie in it alone.

Seated across from her daughters, Yvette had her back to the woman. From here, she could see Brock, and her heart beat faster when their gazes locked. This would work out. It *had* to work out.

*I am not afraid of Adeline.*

She leaned on the table between her and the girls, the sound of the engines covering anything she might say from Adeline's prying ears. "I've decided to move out of the gatehouse." She paused, waiting for a reaction. But neither Jodi nor Kacey said anything. "I'd planned to stay until you were both done with college and in your own apartments. The gatehouse was your childhood home, but I can no longer live on the same property as Adeline."

"We understand, Mom," Jodi said, as if she and her sister had talked about it.

Kacey stared at the tabletop and the three glasses of champagne the flight attendant had poured for them. Her lips thinned, and she filled her lungs with a deep breath before she finally said, "Once we get home, I'm going straight back to school. I know it's not the end of the break, but I'm tired."

Yvette wondered if she wanted to patch things up with Darryl.

As if she sensed her thoughts, Kacey said, "But I'm never going back to Darryl."

Yvette reached across the table to take her hand and squeezed. Then she held Jodi's hand, and they formed a circle.

"I'm going back too," Jodi said.

If not for the disastrous events of this holiday, Yvette would have been devastated. As if they were leaving her. But she understood now. They all needed to distance themselves from Adeline, as well as from the vacation and all that had happened. "That's okay. I'm glad you'll be together."

The two girls looked at each other, and as if they'd rehearsed this, deciding who would say what, Kacey started with, "About you and Uncle Brock."

Jodi added, "What are you going to do?"

As their mother, she'd always wanted to keep secrets about the part of her life that didn't revolve around them. Her life with Pierce, his drinking, his gambling, his cheating. Her life with Adeline, her cruelty, her lies, her scheming. And finally, her affair with Brock. As if she were protecting them. But she had to wonder if she'd only been protecting herself.

Now, after everything that had happened, her protecting days were over. The truth was the real protection. "We're getting our own DNA tests. And then we'll make our decision."

Jodi's jaw tensed, and if they weren't in a plane with roaring engines, Yvette was sure she would hear her teeth grinding. Then her daughter said, "You know she's lying."

Jodi had always been so deferential to her grandmother. But now there was something in her tone, anger, maybe disgust. It certainly wasn't deference.

"I don't think she's telling the truth either," Yvette admitted. But since it was her life, hers and Brock's, she couldn't help the ripple of fear that Adeline might win.

*I am not afraid of Adeline.* She'd repeated the mantra so many times in the past two days that she didn't even have to truly think it; it was just there.

"We all talked about it," Kacey said. "After we left the party that was no party at all."

"And none of it makes sense," Jodi went on.

Kacey swirled her index finger in the champagne's condensation on the table. "I mean, they supposedly both cheat on each other, they have children with other people, and then they just go on like nothing happened?" She raised her hands as if she were mystified.

"Then they even have Uncle Trevor after that?" Jodi finished for her.

"And really." Kacey wagged her head. "If Grandfather knew Adeline was so angry with him for cheating that she paid him back by cheating on him and having a baby that wasn't his—" The sentence was almost too complicated to understand. But then, that was typical of Adeline's stories. "—why would he ever bring you into the company?"

"Yeah," Jodi said, getting into the argument as if they'd been over and over it. "Why would he subject you to Adeline's wrath?"

Adeline's wrath. Her daughter had hit the nail on the head, to use an old but very appropriate cliché. Why would Harris do that?

"Right," Kacey said, earnestness dancing in her eyes.

"You two must have talked about this last night."

"We did. And that's what Garth thinks. Grandfather never would have done that." Jodi looked over her shoulder at Garth, seated with his father.

"Maybe they forgave each other," Yvette suggested. Even if she'd never believe it.

Jodi barked out a laugh. "She never forgets. And she never forgives." So true.

"That's why we think she made it all up," Kacey said, as if they'd debated the whole thing and that was their conclusion.

Yvette looked at the bubbles still rising to the top of her champagne glass. And her heart was suddenly full. No matter what happened, her daughters' love filled her up. "Thank you." Then she admitted the truth. Because sometimes a mother just had to talk about her fears. "I was so afraid that you might never forgive me. I thought you might walk away from me forever." She couldn't help the tremble in her voice.

Both her beautiful daughters squeezed her fingers.

"I love you, Mom," Jodi said. Her voice wobbled too.

Kacey folded both hands around Yvette's. "I love you. I'm sorry I was so horrible to you. I only said all that terrible stuff because I was so upset about Darryl. But that's no excuse."

Yvette cut her off. "It must have been awful to walk in on us when you were already so scared."

Kacey left out a tiny laugh, not much more than a puff of air, but still a laugh. "You never want to think about what your parents are doing behind closed doors." She shuddered dramatically.

Yvette had to laugh with her. "Just like you never want to think about what your grown daughters are doing behind closed doors."

They giggled together, softly, but with a hint of joy.

Then Jodi's eyes turned serious. "I see the way you and Uncle Brock look at each other. I see the love. And I know you were meant to be together."

"We all see it," Kacey agreed.

Jodi added, "We've never seen you as happy as you were those first few days on the island."

"Before everything happened," Kacey finished as if they were speaking from one mind.

"It was because you were together." Jodi squeezed her hand. "We all knew that."

"At least we know it in hindsight. When I think back," Kacey said.

Yvette couldn't help the single tear that slid from her eye. "We are happy. And I'm so glad you're happy for us."

"You shouldn't have to give him up," Jodi declared.

"Just because Grandmother lied," Kacey finished.

Oh yes, they had talked this out, because Jodi added, "I think Adeline has been telling us a lot of lies for a lot of years."

Maybe it was a terrible thing for a mother to think, but she was glad that Adeline had finally shown her true colors without Yvette needing to say a thing. She wanted to get up right then, walk back to Brock's seat, and throw her arms around him.

Instead, she clasped her daughters' hands tightly. "I love you both with all my heart. And I always will, no matter what happens."

## ✺ 3 2 ✺

---

## ADELINE

We're finally home, but the flight has exhausted me. The seat didn't even lie flat, so I couldn't sleep. What was Brock thinking when he chartered that plane? Also, I had no one to talk to because they all refused to sit with me. But they'll get over it eventually. Especially when they think about my will. After all, I can leave everything to charity, especially this house.

They'll be back. So will Brock. Without the gold digger because I won't have her in my house again. Her daughters have left her, too, returning to school even before their Christmas break is over, and making their disapproval obvious.

Now what on earth is all that commotion downstairs?

A quick brush of the curtains reveals the boys packing up their cars. But at Berkeley, they have almost two weeks before the break is over. Why are they leaving now?

By the time I arrive outside, they're gone, them and their girlfriends. Well, good riddance to those two girls. Neither of them is good enough for my grandsons. But the boys didn't even say goodbye to their grandmother.

## CHAPTER 32

At least Trevor's car still sits in the driveway.

As I stand on the front porch, I hear another great clattering inside the house behind me. Trevor and my butler Nolan carry three massive suitcases down the stairs, Lorna trailing them.

My heart races. I'm sure it's glee. "You're taking over the gatehouse?" I ask as they pass me, marching down the front steps to the car.

Yvette is gone. Of course she is after that atrocious incident on the island. And after I revealed her unsavory origins.

But then Brock is gone too.

But he'll be back. He'll see I did what was necessary. Eventually he will.

On his way back, while Nolan helps Lorna into the car, Trevor, my least favorite son, says, "We're not moving into the gatehouse." I don't like the way he says that, with a drawl of sarcasm in his tone. "It's time Lorna and I find our own place. We might look for a house in Hillsborough or Atherton." I know the two are affluent bedroom communities on the Peninsula. "Lorna would like to do some gardening."

I'm not stupid. Gardening isn't the reason. Lorna will be too busy with the baby to do any gardening. No, Trevor is angry like the rest of them. Well, I've always been one to take the bull by the horns. "I only did what had to be done."

He doesn't glare at me. Instead, he resembles a sad puppy. He has never been the strongest of my sons. And yet his voice rings out powerfully. "Is that why you cheated on my father and had Pierce?" Before I can answer, he adds, "Am I even my father's son? Or am I another of your by-blows?"

I don't like the way he mocks me, and I feel the need to defend myself. "I only did what your father had already done. He deserved it. But you are his son. And you were never anything like Pierce."

He smiles then, humorless, his gaze flat and that mirthless

smile never reaching his eyes. "I'm glad I'm nothing like Pierce."

Before he can say what he thinks Pierce was, I preempt him. "None of you knew Pierce the way I did. None of you knew what he'd been through. None of you ever understood him. No one but me. And if it wasn't for your father's meddling, bringing that girl here, Pierce would still be alive. So you can blame her for that."

Trevor shakes his head, that cheerless smile still on his lips and never touching his eyes. "Pierce acted the way he did because you let him get away with all his bad behavior. And now we all know why, don't we? Because he was yours alone. Because he was your payback. That part of your story, I believe."

"I don't like your tone," I snap.

"No worries, Adeline. You won't have to listen to it again." He salutes me, then skirts around where I stand on the porch and jogs into the house, his steps almost jaunty. As if suddenly he is free.

Well, good riddance. He can't even have the decency to impregnate his wife with a boy. So really, what use is he? It's Brock who had the boys I required.

After hauling down another two bags, Trevor jumps into his overpriced luxury sedan. He doesn't say goodbye or even wave.

Nolan climbs the steps, stopping beside me. "Would you like tea, ma'am?"

"Yes, Nolan. I'll take it in the study."

But inside, after the front door closes behind me, the house is far too quiet.

They'll be back. I know they will. After all, I'm head of the family, the matriarch of the Donnelly dynasty.

## ❦ 33 ❧

**T**hey'd returned from the Bahamas two weeks ago. And now Brock took Yvette's hand. "Are you ready?"

They came to Adeline's mansion on the hill in a caravan of vehicles, two moving vans, Trevor in his car, and she and Brock in hers.

Trevor had rented a flat in the city while he and Lorna looked for the perfect home down on the Peninsula. Yvette and Brock had taken a flat in the same building while they searched for something permanent, somewhere close to the office but with a view of the bay. And today, they were here to collect what each of them couldn't live without, along with the girls' things. The rest could stay behind.

But first, there was Adeline. The woman could not be ignored forever.

Nolan opened the door before either of them could knock. "Sir. It's good to see you again. Your mother awaits you in the morning room." Then he stood back for them to pass through.

As they entered the big house, Brock raised Yvette's hand

to brush his lips across her knuckles. Then he kissed her, softly, sweetly. Their first kiss ever in this house.

Yvette wasn't sad that it would be the last in this place.

They climbed the stairs, while Trevor arranged with the workers driving the vans.

At the home's front on the second floor, the morning room afforded a magnificent view of the bridges, the water, and the city as the sun rose over it.

Seated by the window, Adeline looked at their linked hands. And her lips flattened. "To what do I owe," she said, then paused, dropping her voice a note, "this pleasure?" Her tone said it wasn't a pleasure at all.

Brock pulled out the sheaf of papers he'd stowed in his jacket pocket. Unfolding them, he crossed to Adeline's chair, Yvette there with him, hand still in his, forever in his, and laid the papers down on the tea table. Tapping two fingers on top of them, he said, "Did you think we wouldn't have our own tests done? Or that they wouldn't expose your lies?"

But Adeline was never cowed. And she would never admit when she was wrong. She put an arthritically gnarled hand on her bony chest. "I didn't lie. The tests lied. I know exactly what your father did. And if you've got a test saying she's not his daughter, then they hoodwinked you. Because that test is a lie."

A harsh laugh burst out of Yvette. She couldn't have stopped if she'd tried. And she didn't want to. "You just don't know when to stop, do you." It wasn't a question. It was the truth.

Adeline turned her hard gaze on Yvette. "All I've ever done is protect this family from women like you. Like your mother. I made Harris fire your whole family. But he just wouldn't stop wanting that girl." She looked at Brock once more. "If you leave with her now, never come back. I'll cut you out of my will. You'll never get this house."

He huffed out a breath that might have been a laugh. "I don't want this house. Or anything that comes with it."

"And I will make sure the board takes the company away from you as well."

Yvette felt Brock still beside her. And for just a moment, his fingers tightened around hers. Then he said in a voice harsh enough for a boardroom battle, "Go ahead and try, Adeline. You'll find you don't have the support you think you do."

As he left his mother's morning room, Brock's tension drained away. The noise from his former suite at the far end of the house signaled the movers packing up Trevor and Lorna's belongings.

Brock stopped Yvette at the top of the stairs, turning to face her. "There's not one damn thing I want out of this house. She can do whatever she wants with what's left in my rooms."

Reaching up, she cupped his face. "We'll make a fresh start. I only want to take the girls' things and the furniture they wanted." Kacey was already planning her own apartment when she graduated in the spring. "And the photo albums, the memories. Just that." Then she asked, worry in her voice, "She can't get the board to oust you, can she?"

He picked her up, whirled her around, feeling more free than he ever had in his life. "I've got more clout than she does. And even if she could do something," he said as he set her back on her feet, "I don't give a damn. Because I have you."

And he had his sons. He felt as if he had everything he'd ever needed or wanted. He loved the company, loved his work. But more than that, he loved his kids. And most especially, he loved Yvette. If it came right down to it, he didn't need anything else.

His mother, on the other hand, had fought all her life for some make-believe dynasty. She'd cheated, she'd lied, she'd schemed. But in the end, none of it had worked. The DNA tests had proven the one thing she hadn't lied about, that Pierce was only his half-brother. He and Yvette were no relation at all. The girls happily handed over their DNA, and Jodi and Kacey had DNA no one else in the family had, obviously coming from Pierce's father, whoever that man was. Trevor was Brock's full brother. Maybe their father had cheated, maybe he hadn't. But Yvette's mother had never given him a child.

Adeline's life was full of the lies she'd told herself.

Holding Yvette's hand in his, he said the only thing that mattered. "I love you. Now we're getting out of here. And we're never coming back."

BROCK AND YVETTE WERE MARRIED THREE MONTHS LATER in the garden of Trevor and Lorna's new Atherton home. On a sunny mid-April afternoon, flowers bloomed and the sun's warmth blessed them.

It wasn't a large affair, just the family. Yvette wore a cream wool suit over a coral blouse, Brock's ruby necklace at her throat, while Brock dressed in a dark suit, white shirt, and one of the silk ties she'd bought him for Christmas. They held a small reception afterward, catered with an elegant high-tea buffet. Tea sandwiches, sausage rolls, stuffed mushroom caps, a curried shrimp savory, bite-size Welsh rarebits, and all the sweets, from scones to cookies to single-serve flan. And the most delicious champagne that reminded Yvette of their island cove.

Garth made the first toast. "To the couple who deserves this day more than anyone I know."

Standing next to him, Jodi raised her glass. "To the happily ever after you both deserve."

Setting her glass down, she wiped tears from her eyes and hugged her mother. Then she threw her arms around her uncle, also her new stepfather, laughing and crying with joy that seemed as big as the joy Yvette felt.

Then Yvette folded her oldest daughter in her arms, and Kacey whispered, "I'm so happy for you."

Kacey had not gone back to Darryl. Instead, she'd applied to study a year abroad. "I've never been to Rome," Yvette had said, and Kacey had replied, "So now you and Uncle Brock will have a reason to visit." In that moment, Yvette had known Kacey fully accepted Brock.

"I love you, Mom," she said, still holding on to Yvette. "I'm sorry about all the grief I caused at Christmas. I was just in such a bad place."

Yvette cupped her daughter's cheeks. "Don't be silly. You don't need to apologize again. You were going through some hard stuff. So please stop worrying about it. I love you."

"Truly, I'm happy for you, Mom. You two are so good together." They held each other for a long moment, then Kacey turned to Brock. She gave him a hug that brought tears to Yvette's eyes. Finally, everything in her life was perfect.

She hugged each of her nephews. Or was she supposed to call them stepsons now? But they would always be her nephews, no matter what Adeline had done all those years ago, no matter how she tried to punish Harris for something he hadn't done.

Trevor hugged her then. "I want to welcome you to the family all over again."

She stepped back with her hands on his shoulders. "And you are the best dad ever."

"Hey," Brock butted in. "That's supposed to be me. And I've got the mug to prove it."

Lorna smiled, holding baby Freya, who'd come into the world six weeks ago. Lorna was radiant in her new home. "Let's not fight about it, gentlemen. You're both wonderful fathers."

"And I'm a great uncle too." Brock held out his arms. "May I hold my adorable little niece?"

He was just as adorable, cooing at the tiny baby in his arms. God, how she loved this man. Between them, they had five amazing children. They had a loving family.

And they had a future that seemed brighter than any star in a night sky.

## 34

---

### ADELINE

I look at Harris, the distinguished lines of his portrait face. He'd been such a handsome man. Too bad he was so faithless.

"They were married yesterday," I tell him.

He didn't answer, just stared down at me.

"I did everything I could to keep them apart. Together, they are an abomination."

I sit in my desk chair and sip my whiskey. "The house is too quiet," I say softly, as if now I have to be quiet too. In my own home, for God's sake, I have to be quiet.

And still, Harris is as silent as the house. But is that a smile growing on his lips? Or my imagination?

Maybe it's the whiskey.

I swirl the amber liquid in my glass and say to him, "They're all gone, you know. Trevor has his new home, his new baby, his wife. They haven't even come by for me to meet the baby. I wouldn't even know her name if it weren't for the online birth announcement. Well, good riddance. He didn't even have the decency to have a boy. You know, it's the man's sperm that has all the control." And yet, despite my words, my heart feels oddly heavy as I continue talking to my dead husband. "I walked through their suite, and there's nothing left of him. There's nothing left of Brock or the boys either."

I brood silently for a moment. True, they only came home on school breaks. But they always came *here*. Now they don't come home anymore. And the gatehouse is empty too. Good riddance to *her*, but I'll miss the girls.

The whiskey burns going down. And I look at Harris. "Don't you have *anything* to say?"

No one has called me in over three months. No one has come to the house. And they don't pick up when I call.

*Family.* I feel the sneer of that word and all it means in my mind. Then I tell Harris, "I'll disinherit the lot of them. Ingrates. And I will find a way to take the company from Brock."

"I made sure you couldn't do any of that," he finally says.

I laugh then. "The great man speaks at last."

"Except for the house, it's all in a trust." His lips seem to hiss on the word. "And Brock is the trustee. You can't touch it. He's even in charge of your allowance."

I hate my husband for setting things up that way. Wresting all the control away from me. Except the house. That's still mine. I might burn it to the ground so none of them can have it when I'm gone. "There has to be a way around it," I say to him. "Perhaps if I buy up all the extra shares floating around out there."

"You've already tried getting rid of him. It didn't work. And it won't work the next time, Adeline."

His words beat at me, drumming against the walls of this room, which seem to get closer all the time. I'd tried as soon as we got home from the Bahamas. But no one on the board would support me.

"You left me with no way to punish them for all the things they've done to me."

## CHAPTER 34

"I left you with no way to destroy them." He laughs. It's a humorless laugh, an angry laugh. A triumphant laugh. "And yet you still tried to find a way with your manufactured documents full of lies. You tried to beat them down with it."

"I did what I had to do," I shout at him.

"That's what you said when you accused me of fathering another woman's child, even though I told you it wasn't true. And you paid me back by telling me that Pierce, my second born, wasn't my child at all."

"What difference does it make now?" I hurl the question at him. "You got another child. You got Trevor."

"Yes. And you could never twist him and destroy him the way you did with Pierce."

I gaze at Harris's portrait, that handsome face, which now seems distorted by a sneer. And I murmur, "All you ever had to do was love me."

His words whisper back at me. "No one can love somebody who is completely unlovable."

I grab the bell pull, yank it so hard it rips away. And I say to Harris, "I'll show you."

When Nolan opens the door, saying, "Yes, ma'am?" I almost scream at him. Then I point at Harris. "Take down that portrait."

"Yes, ma'am." He doesn't bat an eyelash, and there's not even a quiver of his lips.

And looking straight at Harris, I order, "Take it down and burn it. And burn the one in the living room too."

Nolan has to call the gardener to help him, but together they take Harris off the wall. And long minutes later, I smell the bonfire as Harris goes up in smoke.

And then, I'm truly alone.

# EPILOGUE

**B**rock had found a lovely villa on the Caribbean Sea for their honeymoon.

Twenty-four hours after they were married, he lay with Yvette on the lounge chairs in their special private cove on that tiny Caribbean island where so much had happened.

He held Yvette's beautiful naked body against his. The weather was much hotter now than it had been at Christmas, and good lovemaking bathed their bodies in perspiration. Correct that, fantastic lovemaking. The best he'd ever known, the way it always was with the love of his life.

"Let's just stay here and never go home," Yvette whispered against his chest, her warm breath turning him liquid inside.

"Where do you want to go? The world is our oyster," he quipped. "We can do whatever we want."

She tipped her head back to look at him. "Don't tell me you'll give up the company after you fought so hard to make sure Adeline didn't take it from you."

Adeline had done her best—or perhaps it was her worst—but in the end, the board had sided with Brock. Adeline didn't have a stock share big enough to fight everyone. Brock would remain as CEO of Donnelly Shipping until *he* decided to step down. But the battle had delayed the wedding, just as it had delayed the search for their new flat.

But all the delays were over now.

Brock stroked his foot up and down her calf. "I've got a few more years left in me. At least until Trevor, Garth, and Jodi are ready to take over."

Jodi would join the company when she graduated in two years, and she would do summer internships until then. But free from their grandmother's influence, Ethan and Malcolm had now embarked on different paths. Malcolm wanted to go to medical school. And Ethan, even so close to graduation, had surprisingly chosen the life of a history professor. "Someday I'll write historical novels," he'd claimed. "Great sagas like Bernard Cornwell or Ken Follett write."

Yvette played with Brock's chest hair. "And I'll stay at the company with you." She laughed, that husky sound that excited him deep in his core. "I love locking the office door after everyone's gone and having my wicked way with you right there on your massive—" She pinched his nipple, making him groan. "—desk."

Laughing, loving her, he held her tight against him, wanting her all over again. He would always want her. And he would love her with his last breath.

"But then," she said, "when you give Garth his chance, I want to travel the world. An around-the-world cruise. I want to see Antarctica. And Iceland. The Great Wall of China and Angkor Wat. The pyramids at Giza and Antoni Gaudí's cathedral, Sagrada Familia, in Barcelona."

He kissed her. "I never knew you wanted to travel."

She widened her eyes. "I never knew I did either. But that's what I want."

They had never been a traveling family, despite being

shipbuilders. There'd been business travel, of course, but he'd never found the time to enjoy the sights. Beachcombing in the Bahamas for Christmas had been an anomaly. But now they would make it a habit.

"There's nothing stopping us from traveling," he said. "Starting with Rome when Kacey is over there." He laughed, joy rippling up from deep within him. "I'm CEO. I can take a vacation whenever I want." He kissed her, long and lingering. "But once a year," he said, before he let things go further, "on our anniversary, I want to come here. Back to our special cove."

So much has happened in this place. Some of it so painful it still wrenched his heart, but so much that was good had come out of it.

"I love you," he whispered, his lips against hers, his body ready to give her everything. "I think I've always loved you, even if I couldn't let myself admit it. I always will love you. And I'll go anywhere you want whenever you want."

As she looked at him, he saw the tears in her eyes. "Wherever we go, from now on," she said like she was making a vow, "we go together."

There would never be anything he wanted more.

"Now," she said, "about that puppy you said you wanted to get when we were married."

He laughed, hugged her tightly. "God, I love you. You never forget anything."

"And I love you. I'd also love a puppy. And to learn how to ride a horse."

"Oh baby, it's no different than learning how to ride me."

She tweaked his nipple. "Then you better get busy teaching me."

The *Once Again* series, where love always gets a second chance.

*Book 12* **Love Affair in London**
Can you really fall in love in three days? A sizzling mature romance!

*Dreaming of Provence* | *Wishing in Rome*
*Dancing in Ireland* | *Under the Northern Lights*
*Stargazing on the Orient Express* | *Memories of Santorini*
*Siesta in Spain* | *Top Down to California*
*Cruising the Danube* | *Margaritas in Mexico*
*Beachcombing in the Bahamas*
*Holiday in Paradise, Boxed Set Books 1 - 3*
*Love on Vacation, Boxed Set Books 4 - 6*
*Escape to Romance - Once Again Series, Books 7-9*

# ABOUT THE AUTHOR

NY Times and USA Today bestselling author Jennifer Skully is a lover of contemporary romance, bringing you poignant tales peopled with characters that will make you laugh and make you cry. Look for *The Maverick Billionaires* written with Bella Andre, starting with *Breathless in Love*, along with Jennifer's new later-in-life holiday romance series, *Once Again*, where readers can travel with her to fabulous faraway locales. Up first is a trip to Provence in *Dreaming of Provence*. Writing as Jasmine Haynes, Jennifer authors classy, sensual romance tales about real issues such as growing older, facing divorce, starting over. Her books have passion and heart and humor and happy endings, even if they aren't always traditional. She also writes gritty, paranormal mysteries in the Max Starr series. Having penned stories since the moment she learned to write, Jennifer now lives in the Redwoods of Northern California with her husband and their adorable nuisance of a cat who totally runs the household.

Learn more about Jennifer/Jasmine and join her newsletter for free books, exclusive contests and excerpts, plus updates on sales and new releases at **http://bit.ly/SkullyNews**

*She's Gotta Be Mine | Fool's Gold | Can't Forget You*
*Return to Love: 3-Book Bundle*

### Love After Hours

*Desire Actually | Love Affair To Remember*
*Pretty In Pink Slip*

### Stand-alone

*Baby, I'll Find You | Twisted by Love*
*Be My Other Valentine*

Books by *Jasmine Haynes*

### Naughty After Hours

*Revenge | Submitting to the Boss*
*The Boss's Daughter*
*The Only One for Her | Pleasing Mr. Sutton*
*Any Way She Wants It*
*More than a Night*
*A Very Naughty Christmas*
*Show Me How to Leave You*
*Show Me How to Love You*
*Show Me How to Tempt You*

### The Max Starr Series

*Dead to the Max | Evil to the Max*
*Desperate to the Max*
*Power to the Max | Vengeance to the Max*

### Courtesans Tales

*The Girlfriend Experience | Payback*

*Triple Play | Three's a Crowd | The Stand In*
*Surrender to Me | The Only Way Out*
*The Wrong Kind of Man | No Second Chances*
*Courtesans Tales, Boxed Set Books 1 - 3*
*Courtesans Tales, Boxed Set Books 4 - 6*
*Courtesans Tales, Boxed Set Books 7 - 9*

### The Jackson Brothers

*Somebody's Lover | Somebody's Ex*
*Somebody's Wife*
*The Jackson Brothers: 3-Book Bundle*

### Castle Inc

*The Fortune Hunter | Show and Tell*
*Fair Game*

### Open Invitation

*Invitation to Seduction | Invitation to Pleasure*
*Invitation to Passion*
*Open Invitation: 3-Book Bundle*

### Wives & Neighbors

*Wives & Neighbors: The Complete Story*

### Prescott Twins

*Double the Pleasure | Skin Deep*
*Prescott Twins Complete Set*

### Lessons After Hours

*Past Midnight | What Happens After Dark*
*The Principal's Office | The Naughty Corner*

*The Lesson Plan*

### ***Stand-alone***

Printed in Dunstable, United Kingdom